Breakwater

a novel

Breakwater

by VIVIAN WILDERBRIDGE

SONGBORNE & SEABOUND PRESS

SEATTLE, WA

FIRST EDITION

Published by Songborne & Seabound Press
Seattle, Washington, USA
www.sbsbpress.com
sbsbpress@gmail.com

Book design by Swivel Studio
Cover art and illustrations by Molly Pearce
Edited by Kyra Freestar

ISBN 979-8-9923759-0-9 *(paperback)*
ISBN 979-8-9923759-1-6 *(ebook)*

Library of Congress Control Number: 2025910884

Keywords: pregnancy; motherhood; climate change; near future; Florida; found family; book club fiction; resilience

For my family.

CHAPTER 1

Before the sinking of South Florida, Carey Marilla lived with her mom in a small cinder block house in West Miami. The neighborhood was technically named Westchester, but no one called it that. It wasn't important enough to be called anything by itself, just "near Kendall" or "west of the Gables." Like a woman known as Mrs. Somebody, or Grandma So-and-So, or That Kid's Mom, Near Kendall existed only in relation, only in between.

Near Kendall was composed, for the most part, of flat cinder block houses lounging between clusters of tame palms and wild ficus trees. An anemic system of artificial canals and lakes, some choked with weeds, some with trash, connected backyards to the Everglades, and eventually, if you tried long and hard enough and didn't mind sliding, snake-like, through a few storm drains and climbing over at least one rusted dam, to the wide turquoise waters of the Gulf of Mexico. The houses lay in neat rows, except for where the grid broke and bled for a lake. Most homes were beige, some were white, and a few, like the one Carey and her mother inhabited, were Pepto-Bismol pink.

Bird Road and Miller Drive, the main drags nearby, offered a variety of fast food chains, churches, auto shops, and strip malls of varying quality. Most places in this part of Miami were cheap, and that was lucky, because Carey didn't make altogether impressive wages as a music teacher at Panther Middle School. She had enough income to get by and had dutifully saved as much as she could along the way, but there wasn't much left for indulgences. That was fine, really, because Carey wasn't much of a shopper, preferring thrift stores and consignment shops to online fashion hubs and Dadeland Mall.

Panther Middle School was the same school she'd attended as a child, and where her mother had once worked as the school's secretary, when schools still had secretaries. Carey was grateful to hold a job at all in an economy that had continued to falter and sputter ever since the election of '32. Unemployment was high nationwide, but particularly in South Florida, where investors had been wary since the last major hurricane and the First Surge of water had caused economic collapse along the shoreline. And it was more than just a job. Carey appreciated that the kids at Panther Middle were earnest, the administration only vaguely oppressive, and her co-workers friendly enough.

Carey spent her free time caring for her mother and their house, noodling on guitar, and trying to keep things alive in the veggie garden she'd built one summer in the backyard. She sometimes trailered a small aluminum boat behind her mom's Volvo into the Everglades. There, she and Etta fished for shellcrackers and blue crabs, ate peanut butter and honey sandwiches, and chugged orange soda. Sometimes, during school breaks and cold snaps, they camped out among the cypress hammocks, blissfully trading city noise for the orchestrations of frog, bird, and bug. That made for a good weekend, the kind of weekend that kept both Carey and Etta deeply in love with South Florida. On a bad weekend, they went to the Miccosukee casino, where Etta fussed about losing money instead of the usual fussing about her health or feet.

Carey was thirty-four, which plenty of folks would consider young, though she didn't see it that way. She felt old. Very old. Spinster-like. Her colleagues, even the youngest ones, were nearly all married. The few who weren't were dirty old men or women of violent religion. The parents of the children she taught tended to be around her age, which she took to mean she was well behind life's curve. Sometimes she felt she would never catch up. Then again, she wasn't sure she wanted to.

This matters because when Carey found out she was pregnant, she did consider abortion, but not for very long. She was in no way opposed to abortion, despite having grown up surrounded by Catholic and fundamentalist families. It was just that politics didn't matter in that moment. What mattered was the vague feeling that somehow this might be her only shot at motherhood. She'd often been curious about pregnancy, but more than that, she knew that her mom wanted nothing so much as she longed for grandbabies.

The thought of parenting terrified Carey, as it rightly should. Not the pregnancy so much as the baby. The having-a-child part. As she looked down at the blue bar on the pregnancy test, Carey's first thought was: Change. Her second thought was, Fuck. Her third thought wasn't lingual but more like a heaving sob of relief and despair and terror and joy all at once.

She was alone in the bathroom, at home, on a Saturday afternoon. Etta was in the kitchen banging pots around to make her part-gringa version of bistec de palomilla for dinner. Pungent garlic and lime sweetened the air. Normally these would be welcome smells, but on that afternoon, Carey gagged and forced open a tiny window in the shower to try and clear the smell from the turquoise-tiled room. She stepped out of the tub and looked again at the blue line on the test that perched on the edge of the sink.

"How the fuck did this happen?" she said aloud and looked at herself in the mirror. She knew the answer.

Mario Santos was a seventh-grade math teacher. He was slim and handsome, and they weren't friends, exactly, but he'd helped her set up the risers for the winter concert last year, and ever since then, they'd occasionally shared a table for grading in the teacher's lounge or sat together amidst the mayhem of the cafeteria for lunch. Only once had they gone out for drinks. Exactly four weeks ago. Carey had worn her special shiny vinyl skirt and bright coral lipstick. The date had been okay, even fun, and when he drove her back to his apartment, they landed on his couch. That night, Carey thought for an hour or two that maybe there was something between them. But there wasn't.

She didn't see him for the next few weeks, mostly because she avoided the cafeteria and the teacher's lounge. He didn't text. He didn't call. Mario was kind, for all she knew of him, and handsome, and there was no reason whatsoever for her to avoid him except that she hadn't really known what to say or how to act, and he hadn't been the first to reach out. She wasn't sure she cared. She hadn't done a lot of dating since breaking up with Javi.

As Carey gazed once again at her future in the form of a blue line on a pee-soaked stick, she felt something like what she'd felt when she once hooked a large tarpon. She remembered the fish leaping out of the water, flashing its great silver body and shaking its massive head to be free. It was a joyful, terrifying battle. Eventually the fish won, splashing back into the wild water and sending Carey stumbling backward with her line and tackle still intact. That was the feeling she knew now: a thrilling disappointment.

Maybe she would miscarry. The thought rose in her throat like water in a clogged drain. Sarah, her childhood friend, had miscarried three times, and Sarah was actively trying to have a baby with her husband. It was horribly real how Sarah cried and mourned each and every time. Carey had never seen anything like it. But Sarah was in a different headspace. Sarah was happily married. Sort of.

Carey gagged again and spit into the scalloped sink. There was no way she'd be able to eat tonight. No way in hell.

She wrapped the pregnancy test in toilet paper and carefully hid it behind the Q-tip box in a drawer under the sink. She needed time to think. She needed to wait.

This is important because Florida, as a whole, was about to run out of time. At the very moment that Carey hid her pregnancy test, Etta turned on the ancient TV they kept at the unused end of the dining room table. The weather lady, Julia Santos (no relation to Mario), began to explain, in cheerful but no uncertain terms, that several low-lying areas along the coast were beginning to experience some moisture rising through the ground. This wasn't exactly news. Flooding on South Florida's coast, and plenty of other low-lying areas on the globe, had become business as usual for at least two decades. Annual tropical storms and five Category 4 hurricanes in one decade had hastened troubles for Miami, sure, but politicians, particularly those with crooked ties to construction firms, insisted they had it all under control. They promised that South Florida would emerge unscathed and that climate change predictions were still unreasonably pessimistic. Meanwhile, the Megaquake on the West Coast had gobbled up most of the national headlines and resources for the past five years. The Megaquake and the scattered seasonal wildfires that continued to blaze everywhere west of Oklahoma. Etta shook her head as she flipped the steaks, the sharp tang of her marinade wafting upward.

The news people were always so pleased with themselves when they delivered terrible headlines. Suffering was their livelihood, and Etta didn't particularly think less of them for it. They were young, and they thought themselves disciples of information and freedom of speech and other lofty, self-satisfying ideals. That was the thing about people that Etta both respected and pitied: most of them worked hard to achieve some ideal or another, to reach some kind of finish line. Etta knew better. She knew ideals were leprechaun gold. Life was mostly difficult, and if you were lucky enough to kid yourself for a while about that, then okay, but you'd wake up to the harsh light of day in time. You'd find the finish line missing, or cursed, or too expensive. Everyone did. Even the ones who seemed most happy. Maybe them especially.

No, for Etta, at her age, it was better to just accept reality. She pushed one piece of skirt steak around in the pan with a fork. It was browning now on the edges and sizzling in a satisfying way. Life had batted her around plenty, and she watched the news with no shock, no expectations, no particular passion other than a need for company. She flipped another piece of meat with the same casual vacancy with which Carey flipped the drain stopper in the tub.

Carey had the water going but hadn't adjusted the temp yet. She was staring at herself in the mirror, at how her breasts were already fuller, her nipples darker. Her boobs had never been all that interesting to her, but now she wondered with vague disgust if they'd start spurting milk or something and what the hell she would do if they did. No such thing happened, but as she leaned over the pink plastic of the tub to crank the hot water, her eyes landed on small black blobs swirling in the turbulence. She thought they were globs of mold or mud or something at first. She turned off the water and waited for the turbulence to calm.

She wadded up some toilet paper to try and fish the stuff out, but when she knelt down, she noticed their tails. Six black tadpoles were swimming in her goddamned tub. They were young, no sign of legs. Just squirmy black babies. Probably in no small part due to her condition, they reminded her of giant alien sperm. Gross, but true.

"Mom!" she shouted. Normally tadpoles wouldn't freak Carey out. She'd grown up playing with them, and plenty of other small nasty things, but at that moment she thought she might puke at the sight of them.

"MOM!"

Etta came. God love her, she'd been answering that call or something like it for thirty-four years, and once again, she came. Carey had no idea yet what a pain in the ass, and unholy terror, it is for a mother to hear her kid screaming, so she showed no particular gratitude.

Etta opened the door just as Carey grabbed a tattered old towel and wrapped it around her torso. Etta stuck her curly head in, the silver roots of her hair in stark contrast to the dark red she'd dyed it months ago.

"What's wrong with you?"

"There are tadpoles in my bath."

"What?"

"There are fucking tadpoles in my bath."

"Bullshit."

Etta peered into the tub and cackled. Her voice climbed an octave. "Well, look at those cuties!"

"They aren't cute, they're vile."

"I'll get a bowl."

Etta left, and Carey watched in disgust as the tadpoles swam about, happily exploring the length of the tub and bumping their noses against its walls. Etta returned with a plastic soup bowl and shoved it at her daughter.

"Mom," Carey whined.

"What the hell's gotten into you? They're frogs. *Baby* frogs. Not gators."

Carey whimpered.

"Christ almighty," Etta moaned, and kneeled down, her significant rump stretching out the white pants she wore over red striped underwear.

As Carey watched her mother fish out the intruders, she momentarily wondered what her life might be like without the older woman's grit. For as long as Carey could remember, her mom had modeled the fine art of getting shit done, even horribly sad and disturbing shit. For example, she had up and left Carey's alcoholic father when Carey was five.

Carey didn't remember it, but Etta said at the time he'd been gone for three straight nights and returned only to raid the cupboards and holler about money. When he passed out on the back porch, a pile of filthy denim and flesh, she'd packed up and driven straight through from the Panhandle to Miami in ten hours, stopping only for bathroom breaks, coffee, and french fries. Carey remembered the french fries.

Etta got an apartment the following day in South Miami by sheer force of personality, and then a crappy job shoveling seafood at tourists. She'd waitressed and babysat and scrounged for years to make ends meet. When she'd finally landed a job as a school secretary, she'd been able to save up and take out a mortgage on the little pink house. They never received a dime of child support; but then, they never expected to.

The grease-stained realities of her life had not raised Etta to the status of some sacrificial saint. She bitched plenty. She didn't hold with happy-go-lucky. Nah, she'd grown up in a world in which happy-go-lucky was strictly televised. If she or her kid needed something, she figured it out. She shopped at garage sales. She puzzled out how South Florida functioned and she survived. She made sure Carey survived. It was hard work.

As all mothers do, Etta sometimes imagined the different life she might have had if Carey hadn't been born. But she swore left and right that Carey's existence had saved her from a man she might never have left otherwise. Carey wasn't sure she bought that story, but ultimately she respected her mother's ability to bite down and persist. Even during Carey's teenage years, when she'd hated her mother with a seething passion, Carey still couldn't shake the deep-down feeling that her mother was actually the best person she'd ever know.

So, Etta fished out the tadpoles and stood back up, knees popping, face hibiscus red, and waddled out. Carey closed the door behind her.

Carey drained the tub and filled it again. No tadpoles this time. She lay down in the pink basin and watched her knees float up like lobster buoys. Her belly had never been particularly flat, but now she eyed the gentle slope of her middle with suspicion. She wondered what exactly was going on in there and why exactly it was happening to her. But these were pointless questions. She'd gone off birth control after Javi left town and hadn't stopped things to ask Mario about condoms because she was so desperate for a lay. She'd been afraid to lose the mood, the momentum. To be fair, it had been a long, long time since she'd had full sex.

The warmth of the water soothed and calmed her wild nerves. It would work out. It would have to. She could handle a baby. Probably.

Despite her natural curiosity, Carey didn't know much about the miracle of life. She'd never studied it, though she'd listened hard when Sarah talked about the treachery of her multiple pregnancies and miscarriages. Carey had just never imagined herself going through childbirth, or any part of domestic life, really. That didn't mean it wasn't interesting, in an HBO drama sort of way, but she'd imagined her life more as an indie film or documentary. Rough cuts of touring the world, hanging out in dives and hostels, working her way onto stage with her guitar. In the end, it hadn't happened like that. Instead, she'd spent eight years with Javi, playing the occasional tourist bar or beach party, and then became a middle school music teacher. Javi had never been the kind of dude who talked about babies. Not seriously. They'd sometimes laughed about how fucked up their kids would be if they had any.

When Carey hit thirty, she'd stopped joking about babies and their future, but Javi hadn't noticed. He noticed less and less in general, until they broke up, the band dissolved, and he left town. She stayed. She had a steady job, and she could live with Etta again to save money. Her mom's health wasn't great, and it felt like the wrong time to wander off.

A frantic knock on the bathroom door startled her alert.

"What?"

Etta opened the door but didn't enter. "You better get out, honey," she said. "We've got a project."

Etta's "projects" were never the fun kind. Never the cut-and-paste or crochet type.

Carey flipped the drain open. It gargled and guzzled, and she remembered the tadpoles. Her skin prickled with disgust. She stood up and grabbed a towel.

"What happened?" she asked, stepping out.

"It's the backyard," Etta answered. "They got it wrong; the water's already here."

The Water. Such old news, but inconvenient and therefore largely ignored. Last summer's rainy season, following Hurricane Pedro in October 2039, had made sure that much of the area south of Miami was permanently sunken and unlivable. The Lower Keys had been boarded up for a decade, but the Upper Keys had begun to fail recently. No one seemed to care much about these losses, as the bulk of Florida tourism had already shifted north. It wasn't until parts of Key Biscayne and Coconut Grove, among the wealthier areas in Miami, had begun to disappear that anyone in power became alarmed. Now there were dams being built, and pipes being laid, and grand plans in process to somehow hold back the sea. Government officials promised, routinely, to ensure the safety and security of Miami's citizens in ample time, and mostly people believed them. It didn't feel like delusion; it felt like optimism. Any other option was impossibly grim. Still, there was the matter of the incredibly high levels of the residential lakes. And the canals that sometimes spilled over the roads.

Carey met Etta at the open back door. Etta gazed pointedly down at the cement slab of their carport. Worms lined the edges, and two neighborhood cats napped, curled together on the hood of the black Volvo that Carey drove to and from work. None of this would normally faze the two women, but it wasn't raining. Not a drop. It hadn't rained at all in a few days. Sun shone down through crystal-clear February skies. The temperature, if they'd had a thermometer to check it, would have read eighty-two degrees Fahrenheit.

The cats, for what it's worth, weren't at all alarmed. They, like most of their kind, are adept at anticipating and accepting nature's turns of temper. They rarely or never say to themselves, "I swear winters never used to look like this," or "Damn global warming." These cats, in particular, were aged and battered and accustomed to the harsh realities of South Florida's weather. They didn't startle at thunder. They knew how to lie still in the shade during a heat wave. And now, as the waters rose around them, they'd resolved to make the most of any newly homeless rodents and simply nap on higher ground. No big deal. It would, they noted, probably be more complicated for those fussy humans.

"What do we do?" Carey asked.

Etta shrugged. "Buy more sandbags."

"I'll get dressed."

Back in her childhood room, Carey closed the door and took a deep breath. Posters of Beyoncé, Phoebe Bridgers, and Joni Mitchell greeted her with their usual faded, aloof ecstasy. They paid no attention to her naked body as she pulled on underwear, jeans, and a T-shirt and threw her hair into a damp brown ponytail. Despite their lack of interest in her own life, Carey had always favored the oldies. These three had stood a distracted guard over most of her adolescence, though few of her friends recognized all of them. But her adolescence was nearly twenty years ago now. It was 2041, and while Bridgers still played venues from time to time, and Beyoncé could still command arenas of fans at age sixty, Mitchell was long gone. Carey's younger self had cultivated her musical interests along somewhat old-fashioned lines, believing that the only way to become a successful musician was to study performers who had perfected their styles and stood the test of time. Her older self now found the faces of these vintage virtuosos more comforting than inspiring. She didn't want to be Joni Mitchell anymore, but she still wanted to have coffee with her. She wished she could hug Bridgers. She wished, maybe more than the other two, that she could just sit and listen to Beyoncé talk about what she'd learned and what she regretted. She wanted all these things, but she also, overwhelmingly, wanted to feel less nauseated. She grabbed her bag, a fringed leather thing, and met Etta at the Toyota.

Etta was already in her seat, buckled in, and sweating profusely. She hated Carey's truck. It was hard for her to climb in and out, but since she also didn't like to ride in her own temperamental Volvo (it stalled at least once a week), she didn't grumble. Etta would never say it out loud, but she loved having Carey drive. After so many years of being the sole driver, the sole navigator, and the sole adult responsible for their well-being, it was a deep comfort to have Carey at the wheel. Plus, Carey was a good driver, and Etta felt sincere pride in this.

They pulled out, and Carey drove them to the closest Home Depot, located just up Kendall Drive. It was slammed. The parking lot alone was a nightmare, and people had begun parking on the medians.

"Jesus," Etta said. "We're screwed."

Carey pulled out again and turned toward the freeway.

"Where're you going?"

"North," she said. "We'll hit one that's less popular."

Etta smiled and patted her daughter's knee.

"Atta girl."

GPS took them to a Lowe's in Miami Shores, about forty-five minutes north. It was busy, but nothing like the other place.

Carey got a flat cart and asked where the sandbags were. Etta agreed to wait near the exit since her knees would probably complain about wandering on the concrete floor. She occupied herself with the seed packet display, never out of season in Florida.

After Carey loaded about six of the sandbags on the cart, cursing viciously the entire time, an older man approached her.

"How many you gonna need?" he asked.

"I don't know. A lot."

He squinted.

"Probably twenty-five or something," she said.

"Your car ain't gonna carry that weight."

"I drive a truck."

He squinted again.

"Pull up over here." He pointed to a side exit.

"Okay."

She didn't thank him. She was too nauseous and sore and annoyed that he assumed she drove a goddamn hatchback or something. The reality was that she'd likely already blown out the muscles in her neck and lower back, so she swallowed her pride.

Etta greeted her at the exit with two paper bags stuffed with seed packets.

"What's all that?"

"Seeds."

"Why?"

"To grow vegetables."

"The backyard's a lake."

Etta cocked her head in defiance. "Not forever."

"So they say."

"I just wanted them."

"Fair enough."

Carey pulled the truck around as two younger dudes, one wearing extremely thick industrial glasses, loaded twenty-five sandbags in the truck bed while Carey paid for them at an outdoor register. The older man who had approached her inside punched in the numbers with thick, tobacco-stained fingers.

"You dealing with water too?" he asked.

"Yep."

"How you gonna unload all this?"

"I'll manage."

"If you ask me, you'd be better off hightailing it to Georgia before the traffic gets bad. Another few weeks and it's gonna be nuts around here."

"Maybe."

"No maybe about it. My wife's already packing. There's just no point."

Carey looked into the yellow whites of the man's eyes. She was used to older men sharing their opinions with her, unprompted and unwelcome; she was also in a mood foul enough to punch him in the mouth. "Gee, mister, thanks so much for your unsolicited advice. Whatever would I do without you?"

The man's eyebrows lifted momentarily, but he'd worked in customer service for forty years. This sassy little thing couldn't faze him. Truth be told, something about her reminded him of his girl, Annie. The creases around his mouth deepened. "Alright then, missy, take it easy." He handed her some change with a wry smile.

If Carey had been eleven years old, she might have kicked him in the shins and run. As it was, she shrugged and walked away.

"Good luck, sweetheart," he added as she yanked open the truck's cab door.

Carey gritted her teeth and huffed into her seat.

"Bet they're cleaned out in a week," said Etta.

"Probably." Carey slammed the door.

They drove home down I-95. Carey's temper cooled, slowly. As telephone poles and light posts whipped by, she felt a pang of shame about how angry she'd been at that old guy. So much of her life as a teacher was about keeping emotional control and checking her rage. Keeping order. Life with Javi, an emotionally unstable musician, had demanded and cultivated similar skills. The result was that she routinely lost her shit on random people in the service industry instead of people who she'd have to see again. It wasn't something she was proud of. At all.

Carey's gaze skimmed over the concrete boxes of office parks, the tiled roofs of housing developments, the plastic alphabet of shopping mall signs. Palm trees and small human-made lakes lay trapped inside the curve of each exit ramp. She exhaled sharply as her imagination pushed ahead in time. Those meager bodies of water were likely to rise and escape their confines soon enough.

It seemed to Carey that the traffic headed north was more dense than usual. Maybe the Lowe's guy hadn't been entirely wrong, and people really were on the run, though the cars they passed weren't obviously packed with material possessions. She didn't count an abnormal number of trailers. Probably she was overthinking it. Damn the power of suggestion. Probably most folks would stay and sandbag up, as usual, and it would all be over in a month or two.

Back in Near Kendall, the cats were now both splayed on the Volvo's roof. A quarter inch of water covered the carport slab. Common enough, when there'd been a long dump of rain, but increasingly strange and swift under the cloudless afternoon sky. Which, as if in response to the rising water, had now begun to rust at the edges. It was getting late, and Carey noticed, with some enthusiasm, that her nausea had abated and her appetite had improved. She backed the pickup in and killed the engine.

"I can't unload this on my own," she said.

"I'll call Jim after dinner."

Jim Schoenbart was their neighborhood yardman. No one was sure of his age or his address. Likely, he lived in the dingy van he drove around. He parked in a pub parking lot most weekends. To look at him, you'd think Jim was on death's door. His sun-damaged skin hung slack off his bones, veins snaking beneath. The shock of white hair on the top of his head only slightly distracted from the stark emaciation of his face and the four yellow teeth that remained in his smile. He usually wore a clean undershirt with a pair of filthy cargo shorts and well-beaten plastic chancletas. He reeked of tobacco and sweat and gasoline. He carried a thermos of cold coffee and never had less than two packs of Winstons on his person. It was hard to look at the man without worrying he might not live the day through, but he'd been around as long as Carey could remember and never showed signs of any new deterioration.

Jim kept himself alive with constant yard and handy work. Unlike most people in his field, he was entirely disinterested in efficiency. Instead, he prided himself on propriety. Jim's mowing was lackluster, his edging was questionable, his pruning looked more like machete work than organic sculpture (to be fair, it was machete work), but damn it when he knocked at the door, his hands were neatly folded, his head was bowed, and he said please and thank you. If Etta was in any way put out, he refused payment and offered to help. He unclogged drains for free, insisting that no lady should ever be denied the basic right of functional plumbing. He swept the Marilla porch when he did their neighbor's yard, just because. He left cut flowers and fallen coconuts in neat collections by the back door.

The only thing he routinely asked, at the end of a good week, was that his favorite customers, Carey and Etta among them, come marvel at the small cooler he kept on the passenger seat of his van. There, he showcased his steaks. He'd slide the cooler's lid back to reveal a New York strip and show it off the way another man might flash a photo of his boat, or a giant fish he'd caught, or a new baby grandchild. Carey always congratulated him enthusiastically on whatever cut of beef he'd procured that week from the Winn-Dixie. Jim's yellow smile made her feel ashamed that they never invited him in for dinner, but then, he probably wouldn't accept anyway, arguing it wasn't proper or some such.

Later that evening, Etta sat in her chair in the sunken den off the living room, her swollen feet propped high on pillows she'd piled on the foot of the recliner. She yammered on the phone with Jim for a while before getting to the point.

"Yup. Already rising. Tomorrow mornin's great. Whatcha gonna do, Jim? You got a dry place? Uh-huh. Alright. That's fine. See you then."

Etta stared too long at her phone before she pushed the End Call button. Carey waited. Etta set her phone down and looked at her daughter, who was standing there with her hands on her hips, waiting for the report. Carey looked awful tired, but still young. Still the child of her heart.

"He'll be here at eight," said Etta. "Says he's already had seven calls today. People are panicking. It's ridiculous."

"Is it?" asked Carey. "How long you think we have before we'll have to move?"

"This is just life," said Etta. "There's always something. We'll be fine."

Carey was old enough to know that her mother's opinions were faulty, but young enough to feel comforted anyway.

Etta leaned back, adjusting her feet and rubbing them against one another. The air-conditioning unit in the room kicked off. Quiet circled and settled close to the two women like the old dog they didn't have.

CHAPTER 2

Jim knocked at 8:00 a.m. on the button. Etta opened the back door and invited him in. He wore his usual white T-shirt, now with cargo pants instead of shorts. His pant legs ballooned comically over the tops of high black rubber boots and reminded Etta of some kind of old-fashioned Soviet soldier she'd seen in a documentary about World War II a few weeks back.

"Those seem like a good idea," she said, pointing at the boots.

"Oh sure," said Jim, stretching his smile wide. "I've had 'em forever, but they're in mint condition. They don't make 'em like this anymore."

"I'll bet," said Etta. "Makes me think we should get us something before they run out. Did you hear about the Home Depot yesterday?"

"Sure did," said Jim. "Totally slammed. Same as Publix. Might be like that for a while."

"You think?"

"I know. Remember Cleo?"

Hurricane Cleo had battered South Florida in 2036 with even more violence than Hurricane Pedro in 2039. Cleo's reign of terror had been brief but brutal. In one twenty-four-hour period, vast swaths of development south of Miami had been torn away like useless sheets of scribble in some vast geographic notebook. The Florida Keys had never recovered. Etta, true to the character that would later define their lives, insisted they continue trailering the boat down to Key Largo or Big Pine twice a year, even after weaker hurricanes picked off what was left of the low-lying real estate. She'd never been interested in the bars and T-shirt shops anyway. Her heart belonged to the creeks winding through mangroves, the white sand shoals, the shining schools of mackerel and snapper. She'd raised her daughter to love the Keys too, just as she'd raised her to love the Everglades, where they sometimes camped in winter, and the urban waterways and lakes that offered the last true wilderness inside the sprawling city limits.

And anyway, ever since the storms, there were fewer people and less traffic, so she'd reasoned there would also be more fish to catch. She wasn't wrong. Backcountry fishing was better than it had been pre-Cleo, but the nostalgia once for sale in the Keys was now replaced with pink plastic warning signs waving brokenly in the sea breeze. Hotel buildings sagged and gaped where they'd once beck-oned or boasted "No Vacancy." Somehow there were still a few stalwart innkeepers who operated in cash only. This, Etta insisted, was how the Keys should have always been.

"Fair point," said Etta to Jim. "I'll have Carey make a big run later today, just in case."

"It's time," said Jim. "You should get enough for a long haul."

Etta frowned. "Come on now, no need to scare people."

Jim persisted. "I'm just sayin'. I've been stashing supplies for the last six months, and I'm still at it."

"That so?"

"True as your life."

Etta laughed. "You want some coffee?"

"No, ma'am, I'm fine, thank you. What do you ladies need done today?"

Carey had been standing in the hallway, scrolling through her phone, half listening, half battling a wave of nausea, when she heard this cue.

"Mornin', Jim," she said as she entered the kitchen and found her mug, the one printed with bars from Ode to Joy. Then she remembered Sarah complaining about how she couldn't have caffeine during pregnancy. Carey frowned and set the mug down. "We've got those sandbags in the truck, that's all. Plus, anything else you think we should do."

Jim nodded.

"You don't want coffee?" Etta asked her daughter.

"I don't know. I ... maybe ... don't feel like it."

"Well, Jim, guess that settles it: The end is nigh! The day my daughter refuses coffee is the end of us all." Etta cackled.

Carey frowned.

Jim noticed. He'd have nothing to do with upsetting Carey. If he knew anything, it was that takin' sides with somebody's mama was sure to get you in big trouble. "Right then, I'll take a look around," he said. "I'd say you should dig a trench or two, but you've got a lotta limestone here. I'd need a machine."

"I'm not digging up the yard," said Etta. "No way."

"Message received," said Jim. "I'll be off then, ma'am."

The old man bowed his thanks and exited by backing out the door as if leaving a throne room.

"He might need some help," said Etta once he'd closed the door.

"I know." Carey surveyed the fridge and then the pantry. Nothing looked good. Maybe cereal, but not with milk. The thought of milk made the back of her throat clench. She poured Chex in a bowl and scooped it out with a spoon, crunching angrily at the table.

"What's with you?" asked Etta.

"Nothing."

"Bullshit. I've never seen you eat dry cereal in your life."

"I feel sick."

"Should I make you an appointment?"

"No."

"If you're sick, you should see a doc."

"Mom ..."

"No point in waiting. There's a new clinic at Fountainview that's open twenty-four seven."

"Mom ..."

"Yolanda says it's a cheap one. Course your insurance is great, so ..."

"Ma! I'm okay. I'm fine."

Etta stood, leaning heavily on the table. She placed the back of her hand on her daughter's forehead. "No fever."

"I'm not twelve," grumbled Carey. "Anyway, I heard you want me to go shopping." She took another bite of dry, nearly tasteless cereal.

"Well, yeah. Wouldn't hurt to stock up. My prescription's ready too."

In an hour or so, both women were ready to go. Carey noticed, with some affection, that her mother had applied bright pink lipstick. This was Etta's sole effort at makeup, which she broke out only for grocery stores and casinos. Carey, by contrast, used an old tackle box to hold her collection of thick eyeliners, vibrant eye shadows, and rainbow lip stains. Now that the band was broken up, she didn't use any of it all that much. Though, she had worn makeup that night with Mario.

They hit the A&E Sports Store first. Purchases included two dozen freeze-dried meals (mostly chicken or beef stew), two water purification systems with extra filters, five boxes of hooks, three spools of monofilament, a case of bug dope, a case of sunblock, two large tarps, a thick spool of half-inch nylon rope, a pack of storm-proof matches, a large crab net (their old one had gone overboard during the last Keys trip), a handsaw, a camp hatchet, two large flash-lights, and extra batteries.

At checkout, the cashier gave them a knowing look.

"Están listas," she said.

"Sí, gracias," said Carey.

"Pero, no se preocupe. El gobierno dice que es un problema pequeño."

Carey shrugged. "Maybe." Could be a year from now they'd need to take a giant camping trip upstate to justify today's purchases.

A year from now. A year from now. The other side of nine months. Carey gripped the counter and closed her eyes as the room tilted. The cashier frowned, her mouth stretching like a grouper's.

Etta placed a hand on Carey's shoulder. "Hey now," she said gently, "easy there. Breathe, honey."

Carey breathed, and opened her eyes again. The room righted itself slowly. The cashier's grouper frown retracted to more normal dimensions.

"¿Enferma?" she asked.

"No sé," said Etta.

"I'm fine," said Carey. "I'm not sick."

"Jesus Christ, you're full of it," said Etta. "Come on, let's get you home."

"I just need to eat. It's a blood sugar thing or something. I'm starving."

Etta turned Carey's body gently toward her and looked into her daughter's eyes, the brown forest pools flecked with gold and green that she cherished. They were the part of her daughter's face most like that summer boy, soaked in cheap whiskey, the once keeper of a smile that lit the world. "Okay," she said gently. "What sounds good?"

"Tierra del Mar."

"I'll drive."

The restaurant was empty, having just opened for lunch when they arrived. Carey ordered fried snapper and Etta, the seafood chowder. Mother and daughter didn't speak for a while but lounged in the red vinyl booth, vaguely watching the news streaming on the screens over the bar. Images of trucks and pumps at work, water gushing into canals and Florida Bay. Smiling men in hard hats pointing at buildings and piles of sandbags.

"We should get back soon so I can help Jim," said Carey.

"Maybe you shouldn't, honey."

"Mom—"

"Okay," Etta cut her off.

"I think I'm pregnant."

Etta drew a long breath. She nodded. "You're pregnant," she repeated.

"Sorry."

"Sorry?"

"I don't know. I don't know what to say."

"You sure as hell don't need to say sorry." Etta reached over the table for Carey's hand and gripped it. "What are you thinking?"

"I don't know. I think I'll keep it?"

"Okay." Etta still held her breath.

"I mean, I don't know. What do you think?"

"Doesn't matter."

"Yes, it does."

"Nope." Etta breathed out. "You make this call. You want to raise a kid? It's hard as hell."

"Thanks, Mom."

"I mean it. I've never lied to you. Not about what matters. Children gobble up your freedom like it's free."

"Okay ..."

"But they're fun. Being a mother is ... it'll make you feel alive."

"I've gotta think."

"Course you do."

Carey reached for her ice water, and her hand shook. She felt her mother's grip on her other hand tighten and then release. Etta's lip trembled.

"Oh, Ma."

"Not sad. Not happy. Just overwhelmed. I'm allowed."

"Sure. Okay."

Their food came and they ate. They didn't talk about the pregnancy, and Etta didn't ask about the father. It burned her up not to ask, but she knew her daughter well enough to wait. If Carey hadn't told her yet, there was a reason. Her girl would say something when the time was right.

In fact, Carey said something that afternoon. Not because the time was right, but because they ran into her baby's father in the freezer aisle at the grocery store.

Carey was about to reach for a bag of frozen peas when she saw Mario Santos two freezers down. Her first impulse was to run. Her second impulse was to hide. She leaned toward the peas. There wasn't enough room for her in the damn freezer. She considered walking briskly down the aisle in the opposite direction, but her mother, who was examining a box of sugar-free popsicles on the far side of him, would probably call out. Carey's hand closed on a bag of carrots, not peas.

"Carey?" His voice came from behind.

She turned. There he was in the fluorescent light of Winn-Dixie. Mario Santos, wearing a rumpled pale blue polo shirt and khaki shorts with chancletas. She'd never noticed before that his hair was thinning a bit on top.

"Oh, hey, Mario. How's it going?" She closed the freezer and casually tossed the bag of frozen carrots in her cart. Mario and Carey leaned toward each other. Their cheeks touched briefly for a standard Miami kiss hello. He hadn't shaved that morning.

"Good, great. How are you?"

"I'm okay. You know, shopping with my mom."

Etta arrived on cue, dumping three boxes of popsicles in the cart.

"Hello," said Mario, turning to Etta. He offered his hand and Etta gripped it momentarily.

"Hello."

"Mom, this is Mario. He teaches math at Panther. Mario, my mom."

"Etta."

"Good to meet you, Etta."

Etta turned to her daughter. "I'll grab a number at the deli."

"Be right there." Normally, Carey would be relieved by her mother's disinterest, but this time she wondered at Etta's lack of intuition. It was silly, but it seemed like Etta should somehow sense the blood ties already at work.

"I haven't seen you at school much," he said.

"Yeah, I know. I've been hardcore busy."

"Sure. Yeah."

"I have," she said, defensively.

"No, I know. I didn't mean to sound like ..."

"Oh, I thought you didn't believe me or something."

"No, I just. I know it's busy. It's crazy."

"Yeah."

"I hope ..." He looked at the freezer handle near him. "I hope you don't think I was, like ... I just wasn't sure, you know, if I should text or whatever, cause ..."

"No, I didn't think that. We should hang out," said Carey.

"Yeah, okay." He brightened. "Sounds good."

"Great, I'll text you."

"Great."

"Okay, I better go help my mom."

"Okay."

She leaned in again and pecked him on the cheek. Something she would have done even if they hadn't been intimate, even if she weren't pregnant with his child.

"This is you on the weekends, eh? Still in a polo shirt?" she added playfully.

"Yeah," he said and smiled. It was a kind smile. "You're ... more relaxed."

Carey wore cutoffs and an oversized black T-shirt from a local concert. Neon pink flip-flops. Her weekend uniform. "Well, more of a slob maybe," she said.

"Nah."

"See ya." She pushed the cart down the aisle.

"See ya."

Etta stood at the deli counter while a young woman in a hairnet sliced ham.

"That was him," said Carey.

"Who?" asked Etta.

Carey lowered her voice. "That was him." She threw her thumb toward the freezers.

"Oh!" Etta's mouth opened. "No shit?"

"Yeah."

"Does he know yet?"

"No. I know I've gotta tell him."

"You better—"

"Mom, don't ..."

"Fine. I know."

Carey asked a few excessive questions at the deli counter, stalling for time. Why is that prosciutto so much more expensive? What do they put in the brine to make the turkey taste like that? How long do they actually smoke those hams anyway? This proved unnecessary, as she didn't see Mario again, not during checkout, not when she loaded bags into the back of the Volvo. She looked for his black Mazda in the parking lot, but it wasn't there.

Back at the house, Jim had made significant progress. Sandbags lined the carport and barricaded the front door and the back door off the TV room. They'd done similar bagging before, but never this high. The side door that led to the carport was still clear, and that was the only one they used anyway. It was a step higher than the cement slab of the carport. Carey questioned him about a line of cinder blocks in the yard.

"Truth is, you should probably prop up your appliances or unplug 'em," said Jim. "The water's not gonna slow down real soon. The way I see it, the biggest problem we've got at the moment is electricity. Soon as that blows, folks are gonna lose their minds."

"You think?"

"I do. You want me to help with that?"

"That would be great, Jim. Thank you."

"You got a jack in your truck?"

"Yep."

"You grab it and I'll get mine. They'll save our backs."

"Right on."

They did the fridge first, pulling it out to get at the backside. Luckily, there were no cabinets above it, so Jim used some old bricks, one side at a time. He stacked the blocks as they went.

"Jim, how'd you know how to do this?" asked Carey.

"Lived on the Mississippi in my thirties," he said. "You've never seen water 'til you've seen that girl shuck her bridle."

Jim's past lives were varied. He'd worked as a lumberjack in Maine, on a shrimp boat in New Orleans, and he'd even taught woodshop at a high school in Mobile, Alabama. He'd been in the Navy at some point. He had the tattoos to prove it.

"What were you doing on the Mississippi?" asked Carey.

"Well." Jim stopped jacking and pulled a yellowed rag from his back pocket. Gripping the wall for support, he stood and wiped the sweat from around and under his eyes, smoothing the tight grid of wrinkles on his cheekbones momentarily. He pushed the rag back in his pocket. "Believe it or not, I was chasing a sweetheart."

"No kidding? I bet that's a good story."

"Not really. She married somebody else, feller with a bunch of money."

"Aw, Jim."

"It's true. I didn't have a dime. Story for the ages. She was a smart one."

"Did you ever marry anybody else? Did you have kids?" Carey felt some embarrassment that she'd never asked before and guessed correctly why she had the urge now.

He rubbed the back of his left hand with his right, lingering there. "Well, that's another story, there. Don't think I'm drunk enough to tell it." He grinned and his attention moved to Carey's hand, resting at her side. He liked Carey. He liked how she was direct about things. He liked how she took care of her mother. He could talk about the past with Carey, maybe, but he hadn't given those days much thought in a long while. Probably no point. Lots of sadness that way. "You let me buy you a beer one day and maybe I'll spill it."

"Fair enough. I don't mean to pry."

"Oh, I know. Just takes work to tell it right, that's all."

"I understand."

Jim breathed out. "One more round here, and I think the cinder blocks'll fit."

"Sure thing."

"Jim," Carey caught him before he turned. She didn't know why, but she wanted him to know. "I think I'm pregnant."

The old man's face softened, then stretched into a wide grin. "That sure is a blessing," he said.

"Thanks," said Carey, unsure if she agreed.

"All the more reason to get you set up right."

"Guess so."

They did the stove next and then the washer. There weren't enough blocks for the dryer, so they unplugged it.

Carey told Jim about the tadpoles in the bath. He checked the outdoor valve and pipes but couldn't see a problem. He left just before dinner, taking only $300 for a full day of physical labor. He grumbled about it, insisting it was too much. Carey knew well enough not to press hard. Jim could be easily insulted.

Another week came and went. And then another. Well into February, the little pink house remained dry as a bone, though the front yard and backyard fell to swamp. Permanent puddles formed at the base of the sloped driveway that led to 47th Terrace. Mosquitoes darkened the air at dusk and dawn. Etta regularly complained about the height of the stove, and Carey wondered if Jim hadn't been a bit too aggressive with the cinder blocks.

Carey's nausea bloomed so wild she cut coffee, then dairy, then green vegetables from her diet. Mushrooms utterly repulsed her. So did sweets. Steak and eggs helped, but not before two in the afternoon.

Against her own judgment, she avoided Mario. She told herself it took all her effort to get through the workday without puking in front of her students. Then there was the emotional upheaval resulting from her situation. She had little energy in reserve, and the thought of working through things with him exhausted her. Anyway, she sure as hell couldn't eat cafeteria food, and the cafeteria is where they usually ran into each other. But cafeteria odor triggered her gag reflex. On his side, Mario didn't seek her out either, despite their moment in Winn-Dixie. Carey noticed this and oscillated between disappointment and gratitude. The dizzying emotional results contributed to her unrest and discomfort. Maybe it was better he didn't seem all that interested. She tried to believe this. It kept things simple. Straightforward as a blue crab's commute.

After the fifth pregnancy test hacked away at her disbelief, she called and made an appointment with an OB-GYN. Dr. Paulsen's office would not see her before the eighth week of her alleged pregnancy, and she was only at week six, so Carey resolved she would wait and tell Mario after that appointment. This, she argued with herself, was entirely fair. Let a doctor confirm things. Let a doctor make it official. No need to upset anyone prematurely.

Meanwhile, she watched the children in her classes with new fear and fascination. To her, they'd always been small people who were generally undervalued and misunderstood by adults, and capable of far more than even their parents, or admirers, expected. She'd fancied herself their ally, their advocate. Not their peer. That was going too far. But someone who understood they were more than just the hope of what they'd become.

Now they seemed something else entirely. Creatures who'd been grown in a woman's womb, then birthed, then fed, then kept from harm for so long they were now walking and talking and misshapen by puberty and circumstance. Some of them had visible scars. Some of them were sick. Some of them were miserable and angry. Others were sweet and energetic and kind. All of them were between infancy and adulthood and related somehow to what grew inside her.

Carey searched the risers of the music room for signs of how her child might look or behave. Most of her students bore no resemblance to Mario or to her, but there were a few she favorited in the secret way that even excellent, fair-minded teachers do. Miguel Peraza qualified. A scrawny boy of twelve who excelled at the trumpet, he wasn't popular or reviled. He had too much acne for anyone his age to pay him much mind. He slumped at the perimeter of every social scene, and yet whenever Carey had the class play a new song, or if she complimented his pitch, he glowed like a new candle. He clearly had the music bug, and Carey adored him for it.

Today, Miguel cleaned his trumpet while kids around him talked trash and failed at flirting. Carey considered: It wouldn't be so bad if she had a kid like Miguel. Miguel was all right.

He looked up, but not in her direction. Someone repeated his name.

Pablo Gonzales, a towering and aggressive boy who played, or attempted to play, the saxophone gestured as if polishing his own anatomical trumpet. A group of kids around Pablo burst into hysterics. Gigi, a kind, freckle-faced girl, noticed Carey's attention and shushed them. Miguel grinned awkwardly and went back to his work. That was the thing about Miguel, he never bit whatever bait some kid threw at him. It was like he'd been hardwired to avoid trouble.

Pablo Gonzales, by contrast, was a huge pain in the ass. And even he wasn't the hardest kid in the class, cause he made some effort. The hardest kid, or to be fair, the kid that most haunted Carey, was Yessica Larges. Yessica sat in the back row with a hood pulled over her face, arms crossed, and a will of steel. She did not participate. Except for entering and exiting the classroom, she did not move. Carey had approached Yessica a few dozen times, in a variety of ways, but Yessica never responded. She wouldn't remove her hood. She wouldn't go outside. She wouldn't go to the office. When Carey called home, it went straight to voicemail. The school counselor said Yessica lived with her father and uncles and that "the poor man has no idea what to do for his daughter."

Yessica's father claimed not to know what was wrong. Two months ago, the Language Arts teacher down the hall had snapped and called the office on Yessica. The girl had been suspended for three days, but she returned the following week and took up her usual place and posture in the back row of Carey's class, unfazed and unchanged.

Carey had attempted to back off Yessica's case ever since. The girl clearly had enough problems without a music teacher harassing her. She would flunk music, of course, but at least she was sitting in a classroom and not doing something more dangerous or destructive.

Today, Yessica was asleep or nearly there, using her black backpack as a pillow on the edge of an adjacent empty chair. Carey imagined picking up a trumpet and cheerfully blasting a reveille in her direction. That would get everyone's attention.

"Miss?" A high-pitched voice entered Carey's consciousness. "Miss Marilla, when are you gonna start class?" Gloria Fuentes, flute player, sat in the front row. If Yessica Larges needed to care more, then sweet, cloying Gloria Fuentes needed to care less.

"Right now. Thank you, Gloria."

"You were, like, spacing out."

"I was."

"What were you thinking about?" Gloria leaned forward with the hope that her teacher might confide. She licked her lips, tasting the raspberry lip gloss she applied liberally between every class, watching Carey with the intensity of a heron on the hunt. In Gloria's mind, school was an exhilarating arena in which to test her brilliance, her charisma, and her devotion. Teachers served one purpose, and that was to validate her efforts. Or sometimes, rarely, to challenge her to new heights. On occasion, Gloria met a teacher like Miss Marilla, who seemed less than impressed by her efforts. Unfortunately (for the teacher), this only fanned the flames of Gloria's ambition and brought out an almost rabid desire to succeed and win over a reluctant heart.

Carey grimaced. "Not much."

"We're your favorite class, right, Miss?"

"Usually," said Carey. She pinched the bridge of her nose.

Gloria beamed.

Carey attempted to hide a grimace. If Miguel's glow was like a new candle, Gloria's was a fluorescent bulb in a windowless room.

"Good morning, Panthers," said Carey in her teacher voice. "Please settle down and take out your instruments and music. We'll begin in ten, nine, eight ..."

Counting backward had an almost mystical effect on the preadolescent crowd. Everyone, excepting Yessica, scrambled to attention, and though there was no known consequence for reaching zero without compliance, they were all, except for Yessica, ready at two and proud of themselves for it. From there, they launched a loud and earnest rehearsal of "La Bamba." Miguel Peraza didn't know it yet, but he'd get to be a featured soloist in this song. That is, if they ever learned enough of it to get to that point.

That afternoon, a tired and irritable Carey used the grungy staff bathroom on her way out of the building. The fog of routine cleared quickly when she found traces of blood in her underwear. At first sight, her impulse was to flip through a mental calendar and determine how she'd missed the approach of this period. Then, she remembered she was pregnant. Then, she realized this could mean miscarriage. The stall she occupied was small and sturdy, which was good, because even though she was sitting on a toilet, Carey had to reach out to both walls of the stall to hold herself upright. Her bowels churned and her head ached. She examined her underwear.

There wasn't much blood, but it was definitely there. She wadded up some toilet paper and wiped. Definitely blood. Definitely from her crotch. Not much though.

Usually, when her period began, it began this way. Slow and steady, followed by an unceremonious two days of red deluge that sucked all patience and energy from her being. She steadied herself against the stall's partitions again. Breathe, she told herself. This was a way out, maybe. It could be the moment she regained her freedom and future. It didn't feel like freedom, though; it felt like crisis. Carey reached for her phone. She listened to make sure no one else was in the bathroom. Silence.

It wasn't her mother she called, or a doctor; it was Sarah.

"What's up?" Sarah answered.

"Can you talk for a minute?" Carey's voice sounded alien to herself, low and fragile.

"Yeah, hold on. I'll step away from my desk." Sarah worked as a programmer at a web design firm. They handled websites for big

South Beach hotels and a variety of local seafood and tourist chains. She made not a moderate amount of money and had near total flexibility with her schedule. It was a good life, except when it wasn't. Sarah was an expert on miscarriages.

Carey waited.

"Okay, what's wrong?"

"I'm kinda freaking out, and I don't know who to call, and, but, you're the only person I know who knows about this, and I don't have a doctor yet, so ..."

Sarah waited.

Carey continued, "I thought I was pregnant, but now I'm bleeding."

"You were pregnant?"

"Yeah, I think so. Maybe I'm just, like, three weeks late? Maybe I just skipped a period."

"Slow down. Go back."

"Remember that dude, Mario, from work?"

"I think so."

"We got together, and then I did some pregnancy tests, and yeah. Oh my God, Sarah, I was pregnant." Carey's voice broke like a child's dam of mud and sticks, giving way to grief and fear. She cried. "I'm sorry I didn't tell you. I was afraid."

"That's okay, sweetie. That's fine. I wondered where you went. Listen, I'm gonna ask you what the nurses ask, okay?"

"Okay."

"How much blood is there? A teaspoon, or more?"

"No, less, I think. So far. Just some staining when I wipe and in my underwear."

"That's just spotting."

"Okay, just spotting."

"Do you have any cramping?"

"No. I don't think so."

"Do you feel abnormal? Do you feel sick?"

"I mean, I puke all the time, so yeah, but not especially today."

"Any other symptoms or pains? Have you taken any medication or had any drugs or alcohol in the past forty-eight hours?"

"No ... no."

Sarah took a deep breath. "Then you're probably okay. Some light spotting is normal in early pregnancy. You should see your doctor though, just to be sure."

"It's normal?"

"Yeah. Some spotting isn't a big deal. A miscarriage is ... different."

"Jesus, Sarah. I'm sorry."

"You don't need to be sorry. This is fucked up though. I mean, I'm not mad—it's just fucked up, you know?" Now Sarah's voice strained with an ache Carey could only imagine.

"It's absolutely fucked up."

"Go see a doctor and then call me, okay?"

"Okay. Sarah—"

"I know. Just call me later."

"Okay."

Carey wiped again, terrified. She tried to imagine what a teaspoon of blood might look like spread in a thin layer on tissue or fabric. But there was no more blood. She dressed and stood and washed her hands. Out, damned spot.

CHAPTER 3

The following day, after no further spotting and some time on the phone with a nurse, Carey ordered a book on pregnancy. This, the nurse had said, would help her understand what was happening to her body. Carey wasn't sure that was a desirable outcome, but she did what she was told. There were still two weeks until her first doctor's appointment, but Time, it seemed, had already begun to slow, and gain weight, and lumber forward with increasing sloth.

Florida grew heavy, too, and saturated. Signs showed in the corners of the Marilla living room, where the beige carpets grew damp and then wet. Etta started wearing thick flip-flops, then advanced to wading boots. Carey reluctantly joined her. They kept laundry off the floor and tied power cords up and out of the way. They stopped trying to mop up the moisture with extra towels. There would be no mopping up. The house began to smell like wet dog, and then of mildew, neither of which helped Carey's incessant nausea.

Jim, without prompting, returned in the next week with more cinder blocks and sandbags and further barricaded the little pink house. He even offered to put their beds up on cinder blocks.

"You really think we're in for it that bad?" Carey asked as he slid the door of his van open.

"Look at this," said Jim. He stood in at least an inch of water in the carport. "Course I do."

"Dammit," said Carey. "What the hell are they even doing? They said they'd have it under control by now."

"They always *say* plenty."

"I can't believe it's this high already."

"Might be a gift," said Jim. "Otherwise, they'd spend seven fortunes trying to stop it before they realized they can't win."

"So you really think we're sunk."

"Now, I didn't say that, but we're in for it." Jim's mischievous, nearly toothless smile reminded Carey of a seven-year-old Huck Finn. Magical, how it landed so easily on the face of a grizzled seventy-something-year-old man.

"What's the difference?"

"Well, we're not gonna drown or nothin'. We'll get through. Just gotta work harder."

Carey watched a grackle perch on the far side of the backyard fence. There were at least four or five grackles who visited their property frequently. She loved those scrappy birds. They weren't particularly beautiful or anything, but she aspired to their confidence. They gave hell to a clan of local blue jays, fought glorious aerial and ground battles with each other, and when they weren't brawling or bitching, they raised racket for no apparent reason other than sheer love of clamor. It must be nice to so purely know your purpose, thought Carey.

This grackle was newly bathed. She shook and puffed her green-black feathers to dry. She then commenced shouting about it.

"Okay," said Carey. "Guess our beds are going up."

They raised the beds together, and Carey had to admit it was comforting to see her blankets and pillows so well out of the way.

"You need any help with your stuff, Jim?" Carey asked.

"Thank you, but I'm all set."

"I bet you are." Carey smiled. "How's your stockpile coming?"

"Oh, it's a beautiful thing." Jim grinned, but then winced. "Had some security issues recently, so I had to shuffle things. All's well now."

As far as Carey knew, Jim's stash could be nothing more than a garbage sack of toilet paper and cigarettes hung up in a tree somewhere. It didn't matter. Good for him for preparing himself. She shook her head in wonder as Jim's van rolled away. Inch-deep water on 47th Terrace fanned out behind him. The old man had the confidence and independence of those grackles. She resolved to get her own shit in order. She could handle herself. And a baby. And her mother. Sure she could.

<center>~~~~~~~</center>

Her first order of business was work-related. She drove to Best Buy and purchased a small electronic device and headphones.

Back home, atop her stilted bed, Carey loaded well over a thousand songs on the device, selecting albums and tunes that had reached her in one way or another. It took several hours over the next few days, moving alphabetically through her digital collection, but when she finally loaded Yo-Yo Ma and Yo La Tengo, she was done.

On Monday, in third period, she slipped Yessica Larges a paper bag with a note stapled to it. The note read:

"Yessica, I don't know what's troubling you, if anything, but when I'm sick of life, music is the only thing that matters. Please don't tell the other students about this gift, because I can't provide it for everyone. And please don't use this in other classes, because another teacher might take it away. You don't need internet to use it.

With concern,
Ms. Marilla"

Yessica didn't open the bag that period, but she took it with her, and the next day, she wore the headphones during class.

Pablo Gonzales, always interested in a reason to stall class, noticed the subtle change in Yessica's behavior and complained. "How come she gets to listen to music, and we don't?"

"Because you're making music," answered Carey.

"Yeah, but not good music. I don't want to play this crap if I can listen to my stuff instead."

Carey called him up to speak with her in private. Pablo was the kind of student who would not back down if he had an audience. One-on-one, he wasn't so tough.

"What?" he asked, avoiding Carey's eye.

Carey lowered her voice. "Pablo, I need your help. Yessica's unhappy, and I think she needs to listen to music and be alone. You know what I mean? If everyone listens to music by themselves, I can't do my job. You guys won't learn anything. So, I need this one exception to be okay with you and not a big deal. I'm trying to do the right thing for her and for you. Can you help me with that?"

Pablo bowed his head. The trick to managing him was simple. He had a heart. He didn't like to show it, but it was certainly there, and Carey knew it. He mumbled his reply. "Okay, Miss. I got you."

"Thanks," she said. "I appreciate it. I'm hoping she'll be okay."

"Me too, Miss."

"I know."

Pablo's mouth twisted in a sly smile. He rubbed the back of his neck, letting his mind wander off to some things that Miss Marilla didn't know. For example, Yessica had been a good friend back in first grade. He remembered eating watermelon with Yessi in the summer on his front porch and trying to spit seeds in a paper cup. He remembered swimming with her at the community pool, diving in the deep end and watching her hair fan out and billow around her. He also remembered that Yessi hadn't told anybody when he'd pissed his pants that one time they'd been chased by his neighbor's doberman. Pablo was still kind of afraid of dogs, but Yessi hadn't made fun of him or anything like that. She just told him she was afraid of things too, but she wouldn't say what. Anyway, he figured he owed her at least a little slack, even if Miss Marilla was being totally unfair.

He nodded his agreement and then tromped back to his seat, knocking off another boy's hat as he went. Carey said nothing, but rolled her eyes in solidarity with Pablo's victim. She led the class in warm-up scales.

From that day forward, Yessica wore her headphones every day in music. Carey noticed, with relief, that Yessica took them out of her bag at the start of the period and returned them to her bag at the end of class. These actions meant that Yessica was likely not wearing them in every period and between classes. It also meant that she cared about the music enough that she didn't want it confiscated. Carey had been teaching long enough to know that one gift couldn't grant a kid the sudden urge to succeed in school, but she watched Yessica carefully, and with new hope for the girl's well-being. A small, strong part of Carey's psyche was now free to attend to other worries.

On the day of her first OB-GYN appointment, Carey washed and trimmed more carefully than usual. She wasn't sure what would be involved in this appointment, but she guessed that some uncommon attention would be given to her nether regions. Plus, she'd ordered a substitute for her morning classes and worked extra hours on sub plans and materials so, by God, she was going to try and enjoy a slow morning.

Etta had breakfast waiting when Carey arrived in the dining room dressed and combed. Etta was also gussied up. She wore her finest tracksuit and gold hoop earrings. Her snazzy fit was somewhat lessened by her rain boots.

Carey poked at her eggs. "You remember how they do this?"

"What?"

"The doctors. When you're pregnant. What happens at these appointments?"

"No idea. I must've blocked it out."

They drove Carey's truck down Sunset Drive to one of the squat office buildings that housed a myriad of medical practices. Carey noticed that the building, like most these days, was barricaded with sandbags. A pump ran out of a low window in an adjacent building and sprayed water into what looked like a giant steel truck bed parked outside. Traffic cones and barricades prevented anyone from entering the area, but a few had already drifted from their posts.

Carey's OB-GYN's office was next door to a skin cancer clinic. Etta pointed this out as they walked in. "Jesus, honey, did we pick the wrong gig or what? I bet those guys are rolling in it."

"Mom, not so loud."

"Sorry."

Etta sat on a taupe couch while Carey checked in with the receptionist. This person loved makeup and Carey, in return, felt immediate affection for them. Anyone wearing such a distracting shade of orange lipstick had to be cool.

"Is this your first visit with Dr. Paulsen?" they asked.

"Yes."

"Name."

"Carey Marilla."

"Age?"

"Thirty-four."

"Are you pregnant?"

"Yeah, I think so." It felt strange to tell someone other than her mother or Sarah.

"Congratulations." Their orange lips smiled sweetly. Carey wondered how often patients were not happy to be pregnant. Congratulations assumed a lot.

"Thanks."

"What was the date of your last period?"

"Um, hold on." Carey took out her phone and scrolled through her calendar. "Okay, December. The twentieth."

The receptionist took out a dial and spun it. "You're almost ten weeks pregnant?"

"No, I don't think so. I'm eight weeks, I think."

"We count from your period."

"I wasn't pregnant when I had my period."

"That's how we count."

"But ..."

"It's just how we count."

"Okay ..."

"Please fill out this information, and we'll call you shortly."

They handed Carey a tablet and Carey sat. The questionnaire was long and elaborate, asking details about her health, habits, and history. Carey was pleasantly surprised to see that some of her medical information had successfully transferred from her primary care doc's records. She reviewed, checked boxes, and then came to a section about family history. It was in this moment, and not before, that Carey fully realized that Mario Santos was more than the guy who had knocked her up; he was The Father. A man she barely knew. He could be riddled with health concerns or be the healthiest man on the planet. She had no idea. She didn't even know his age.

There were now three other people in the waiting room. One woman was extremely pregnant, ready to pop. Her partner, a man, read a magazine while she rested her head on the wall behind her chair. The other young woman was buried in her phone.

"Mom."

"What?"

"I've got to ask you some questions about my dad."

Etta inhaled and pulled herself up a bit in her chair. "Okay. Right."

"Any health problems in his family's history? Genetic disorders? Heart conditions? Cancer? There's a giant list here."

"Jesus. Lemme think."

"You wanna see it?"

"Sure."

Etta dug into her handbag and pulled out her reading glasses. Carey watched as her mother scrolled through the questions and checked boxes. No heart conditions. Some cancer. One genetic condition, on her mother's side, not her father's. Hydrocephalus.

"What's that?" asked Carey.

"Your great-aunt Betsy had it. It's when there's too much fluid around the brain, so the head swells. Caused all kinds of problems for her."

"Did she die from it?"

"No. She died of glorious old age somewhere out in California. She was a singer, you know."

"No shit."

"Never got famous or nothing, but you woulda loved her. Anyway, that's all I've got."

"Okay."

"That baby's gonna be healthy as a horse."

Carey didn't know how to respond to such an entirely unfounded declaration. "Okay," she said again.

Etta didn't ask questions about Mario, for which Carey was grateful.

When they called Carey in, Etta offered to come, but Carey patted her on the hand. "You can come if they do an ultrasound, okay?"

"Damn right I can."

"I'll be right back."

Etta grabbed her daughter's hand before she could get away. "Hey. I love you."

"Love you too, Mom."

Dr. Paulsen was a trim woman in her fifties with short hair and hip, thick-framed glasses. She wore a surgical mask for the entirety of the exam. She asked a series of questions and recorded answers on the computer. She requested that Carey provide blood and urine samples. She measured Carey's uterus. After the full exam, she removed her gloves, washed her hands, and took off her glasses to clean them. She placed them back on her face.

"Everything looks good to me, Carey. You're in good shape, you're young, and there are no signs of trouble with your pregnancy.

The only bad news is, and I'm sorry to tell you this, but you'll need to find another doctor for delivery. Our practice will be closing in three months."

"You're closing?"

"We're closing. We can't operate safely in the conditions that are likely coming, and our building insurance company has declared they won't cover us if everything floods. I'm happy to see you until that time, but you're probably better off finding another practice."

Carey ground her teeth. This felt oddly like being dumped after the first date. "Which doctors are staying?"

"To be honest, I doubt many will. It's going to be a liability nightmare."

"Then what am I supposed to do?"

"If I were you, I'd probably consider moving too."

"Leave Miami." It was a question, a consideration, a recommendation, but to Carey it felt more like a sentencing.

"Unless you want to raise your baby in a swamp."

Carey saw, for a split moment, the world to come. A vast stretch of water and river grass, a child sitting astride the branches of a mangrove tree, the slick back of a nurse shark snaking away. In the distance, purple clouds billowed and lit with erratic lightning. It wasn't a peaceful image, but it didn't instill any terror. Not for Carey. Most people might have negative associations with the word "swamp," but for her, the word offered a wilderness that in no way repelled her.

"I apologize—that was blunt," continued the doctor. "You're capable of making your own decisions. Just please consider your options carefully. It's my opinion that this water isn't going away."

That was Carey's opinion too, but until that point, she hadn't exactly mapped one future onto the other. Now she did. Florida was sinking. She was having a baby. The two were happening simultaneously. It felt like the work of whatever sloppy dark magic produced rain during movie break-ups and fog in graveyards. What was the term? A pathetic fallacy. A Hollywood scenario she must now live out. This must be what people meant when they said that having children changed everything. The complexity of possibilities and consequences of any future multiplied by an astronomical number inside Carey's mind. Simple and straightforward had never been the defining characteristics of Carey's life, but now both felt unattainable. Carey's breath came quick. It was time to leave the office. Dr. Paulsen was still talking, but Carey wasn't listening.

"Okay, I get it. I need to go now," said Carey.

"Right. We'll email your other test results within forty-eight hours. We'll call if there's something urgent. Feel free to contact us if you have any questions."

Carey reached for her jeans. The doctor was still typing something into her console. She turned back to Carey. "Just in case you decide to stick this out, Baptist Hospital will likely stay open until the bitter end. They have world-class facilities and plenty of money."

"Right. Thanks."

Etta looked up from her gossip magazine in the lobby. When she saw Carey approaching, she stood. "How'd it go, sweetheart?"

"Fine. Everyone's healthy."

"When's your due date?"

"September 26."

"Oh Jesus, a Libra baby." Etta's face spread in a Cheshire cat grin.

"Mom."

"That little one's gonna have opinions."

"Ma."

"I'm kidding."

Carey didn't smile. "So, this office is gonna close because of the flood. I have to find another OB."

"What? That's bullshit. What a pain in the ass."

Carey drove over the speed limit on the way home, sending wide wings of water up onto the parking strips and traffic medians of West Miami. Disappointment began nesting in her consciousness, pacing and turning around in tight circles to make its bed, pawing and kneading the ground with razor-sharp claws.

Like most people, a younger Carey had once imagined a future unburdened by the stresses and loneliness of her childhood. Adventure, wealth, freedom. Travel abroad and sexy affairs and bass lines pumping under pulsing lights. These were common, middle-class hopes. Something entirely uncommon stirred in her blood now. Something defiant and bitter. Something like the hide of an alligator or the beady eyes of a buzzard. If she couldn't live a glamorous life of privilege and adventure, she'd make her own adventure. She'd scavenge. She'd throw a life together with whatever scraps she could find. If she had to be pregnant while the water came up, then so be it. Fuck doctors. Fuck newscasters. Fuck government dicks. She'd make her own nest. Maybe curl right up with her disappointment and get cozy. Those bastards could shake their heads at her all they wanted. Her whole life she'd been taught—by Etta, by heartbreak, by the constant grind of life—to take no shit and give no slack.

The next day, back at work, Carey marched into the cafeteria and tapped Mario on the shoulder. He looked up at her from his tray of undercooked tater tots and overcooked chicken strips.

"Can we talk?" she asked.

"Yeah, sure. Of course. Sit down."

"Not here."

"Oh, right. Sure." He stood up, leaving his food. Carey grabbed his arm and lowered her voice.

"Bring your lunch. This will take a bit."

"Right. Sure."

He followed her back to the music room and set down his lunch tray on the only table, at the base of the risers. He pulled a chair over and sat.

Carey couldn't feel much. Something in her chest flopped around like a fish in the bottom of a boat. She pulled another chair to the table and sat.

"So," she said, "I'm pregnant. That's why I've been avoiding you."

Mario set down his plastic fork and swallowed the food he hadn't yet entirely chewed. "Wow, congratulations, Carey. That's great."

He didn't get it. He didn't get it.

"Mario, you're the dad."

Now he got it. He flushed and shook his head. "What? How? What do you, what do you mean?"

"You know how, and you know what I mean."

"Oh my God."

"Yeah."

"Oh my God."

"Yeah."

"Oh my God. So ... now ... ?"

She had to give him credit. He could've been angry or defensive.

He could have launched into panic or self-centered concerns. But he didn't. He just waited for her answer and looked vaguely ill.

"Well, I'm going to have a baby." She nodded. "I'm okay with it. Mostly. I'm due in September, and I know there's a lot of bullshit going on with this flood, but for now, I think, I'm planning to stay here and raise the baby with my mom. I don't want you to think I'm trying to trap you or anything. And I'm not trying to push you away. It's your decision. But just so you know, I think it would be fine if you wanted to help out and get involved or whatever." She paused. "My dad wasn't involved, and that's never been great." She paused again, unsure if she'd said enough. Probably too much too fast. "You can think about it, of course. I just wanted you to know."

A silence stretched between them. He was processing. She was scrutinizing his expression for some sign of reaction. There wasn't much there, just a kind of stunned concern, the mouth slightly open, the brows knit. Her former attraction to him had now transformed into a kind of desperate curiosity. Who was this man, anyway? What stuff was he made of? What kind of a father would he be?

Mario nodded. "I'm glad you told me. I'm ... I guess I should apologize."

"It takes two to tango."

"Yeah, but I wasn't—"

"I know. I didn't stop us."

"I hope we can work this out," he said, weakly. He stared at his tray. "I need some time to think, but yeah, I don't want to be an asshole."

"Okay."

"What am I even supposed to say right now?"

"Well, I had my first OB appointment, and so far, everyone is healthy."

"Sure. That's good. Sure." He nodded robotically, still processing. A light sweat had broken out on his forehead. "Is it, like, do you know if ..." He made eye contact. His eyebrows, Carey noticed again, had a nice shape, even though they were still scrunched in disbelief.

"Oh, I don't know the sex yet. That comes later, or so says the pregnancy book."

He turned back to his tray. "This is unreal."

"Yeah, except, you know, turns out it happens every day, and has for millions of years."

He showed no sign of amusement. "You're definitely gonna keep it?"

"Yeah. I'm sure."

"But, why? You know, like, why *now*?"

His question hit sharp, like stepping on the sudden edge of an oyster shell when expecting only the soft squish of mud. Carey drew a breath.

"I know it's not convenient," she said, slowing her speech down, "but I don't have a strong reason to not have it. I'm healthy, I have a loving home, I have enough money. I'm thirty-four. And I'm not, you know, I'm not a bad person. And you're not a bad person. Probably."

"Thanks."

"No, I mean, maybe I don't know you that well, but yeah. And I feel like life isn't what I thought it would be anyway, you know?"

"Yeah ..." He didn't look up from his tray. Would he ever fucking look up from his tray again?

"When I found out," Carey continued, "I didn't want to end it. I was freaked out, but I didn't need it to stop, so, I'm still pregnant."

"You're keeping it by default?"

Carey's jaw clenched. "Okay, I think we're done here."

He looked up from the tray, alarmed. "No, sorry, it's just, I'm trying to understand."

"Okay, fine. It's not by default."

"You want a baby. You want one now."

"There are plenty of rational and irrational reasons to keep a baby, but the main reason I can offer is it happened, and I didn't need it to unhappen. My instincts say it's fine. I don't have to actively want the baby, but I'm okay with having one."

Mario rubbed his face. He rubbed his eyes. He hadn't eaten a bite since the start of their conversation, but he drank something from his thermos now. She imagined it was coffee, black, and probably lukewarm. "Right," he said after a long break. "Yeah, I need to think."

"I understand."

"Parents, huh?" He raised those well-shaped eyebrows in a comic kind of disbelief, the first moment of humor in the situation he'd acknowledged.

Carey nodded gently. "Yeah. I mean, listen, like I said, I'm not trying to trap you. I hope you can be involved, I think that would be good, but I'm not, like, trying to drag you down and give you no choices of your own. You know?"

"Yeah."

"Sorry about this."

"Nah, you said it. Takes two to tango."

"And procreate." Carey smiled, but Mario had turned to look at the clock.

"Should we set a time to talk again?" he asked.

"You can just text me when you're ready."

"Yeah. Thanks."

"Sure."

He gave her a peck on the cheek and left the room. There were still ten minutes left in the lunch period. Carey wondered that they hadn't had more to say to one another, but then, he was in shock. She'd had weeks. He'd had minutes.

She wiped down the table where he'd been sitting, even though there was no mess there, and tried to remember which class she was teaching next and who was in it and how she'd ended up becoming a teacher in the first place and then pregnant and then telling the father during her lunch break.

Outside, high in the atmosphere, where such forces move that humans struggle to predict, moisture gathered and spread in a pattern that meant Florida would soon be dealing with more than soggy carpets. Hurricane season was still three months away, but Rain had other plans.

Rain would come when she wanted, and oh, she wanted. She wanted more than she ever had wanted before. Perhaps she felt the call of the vast waters already rising from the Florida springs and bays, a longing for kinship and connection with her distant relations. Or maybe she only wanted to help beat back those waters with her own misguided, childish efforts. Maybe she just needed to throw a magnificent tantrum. Whatever the case, Rain was about to come, and stay, and wreak havoc on South Florida and the millions of already anxious people living there.

CHAPTER 4

It was unlucky that Miamians started to pile up their spoiled possessions on curbs at the same time that Rain made her grand entrance. The city rapidly became awash in floating debris. Broken furniture, half-submerged plastic bags of God-knows-what, and bottles of all shapes and sizes sailed through front yards, bobbed merrily along the streets, and spilled willy-nilly into driveways and parking lots. Garbage trucks still ran, but trash cans no longer stayed put. They bobbed and tipped and floated free. Only the most densely packed receptacles remained at their appointed place and time for pickup. Once emptied, they too made a break for it. It was a stinky, nasty time—the perfect supplement for Carey's nausea.

Carey's first trimester, and the worst of her morning sickness, came to an end just as this problem grew significant enough for the government to send out people wearing thick gloves and masks to battle the trash tide. Locals were asked to please carefully contain and restrain their trash until the garbage trucks were due, and then to meet them at the curb. If work hours prevented this, as they would for almost everyone, people were instructed to take their garbage to public waste facilities themselves. You might guess that this didn't go over so well, and you'd be right. Instead of complying, people started to drop off their garbage at government buildings. Post offices, libraries, and community centers became impromptu dumps. Schools were spared, but many were already closed. The global pandemic of twenty years earlier had left several digital and remote learning structures in place, and plenty of parents had opted for such digital classrooms. Others now belatedly and reluctantly began to switch their kids to the online life they remembered hating when they themselves were young.

Panther Middle was on slightly elevated ground, and so remained open despite the rain, though buses stopped running and attendance fluctuated. While plenty of students were already stuck at home, there were now new students from closed schools whose families needed the childcare. The district had allowed transfer on an emergency basis, but no one could seem to keep track of the details, and it was, in a nutshell, utter chaos. Carey showed up every day, despite the near-constant class list confusion, and did her best to fulfill her duties. Music and routine, she knew, were medicinal in times of crisis, for both her and her students.

Yessica, at least, was still attending. And sweet Miguel with his quiet attention and deep commitment to the trumpet. Carey couldn't deny that something about that boy's presence made her feel a glimmer of hope for them all. Unlike annoying Gloria Fuentes, who found new ways to offend someone every day.

"Miss," Gloria announced one day, "you're a lot nicer than you used to be."

Carey looked up from her desk, where she'd been searching for the copies she'd made that morning. Gloria stood disturbingly close, having come around the left side of Carey's desk. "I'm sorry, Gloria, what did you say?"

"You used to be kind of mean to us, but now you seem like you're, you know, easing up. It's a compliment."

"Okay. Thank you? I didn't realize you thought I was mean."

Miguel Peraza had come up to sharpen his pencil and must have overheard their conversation, because he turned directly to Gloria and stated, rather firmly, "Ms. Marilla isn't mean at all. She's one of the nicest teachers in the whole school."

For a moment Carey thought Gloria might descend into petty insults, but she simply stiffened and responded, "No one asked you."

Miguel shook his head and, making eye contact with Carey, shrugged his shoulders in solidarity before returning to his seat.

"Just like," Gloria continued, "you know, you were always snapping, and you seemed really tired." She leaned on Carey's desk in an overly familiar way that grated on Carey's nerves. "But now it's like you're finally trying to be a good teacher."

"That's …"

"I bet you're just kind of a moody person."

"That really isn't appropriate to say, Gloria."

"No, it's not bad, Miss. My abuela says that all ladies are moody, and all men are stupid."

Carey smiled despite herself. She found the handouts she'd been looking for and quickly sorted the papers into groups for the class. "Well, I might disagree."

"You think my abuela is wrong?"

"There are plenty of women who aren't particularly moody, and plenty of intelligent men. And anyway, it's not kind to call anyone stupid."

"So why were you so mean to us the last couple of months?"

"Gloria, please go sit down."

"Okay, okay, sorry, Miss. Don't get mean again."

"I'm not … just sit down."

"Oh my God, you're mean again."

"Gloria."

"Okay, okay. Sorry, Miss."

There was some truth to Gloria's observations. Carey hadn't felt cheerful in a long while, but now, as her second trimester began in late March, she noticed an uptick in her energy level. She felt slightly less wrecked by an average day, though she still required naps. While March's rain wasn't nearly as constant as April's rain would be, it still cast an adequate sleep spell in the afternoons. All South Floridians know that a good thunderstorm can lull any raging beast to sleep. Though she tried to resist, Carey routinely passed out in the small office attached to the music room during her fifth period prep. She also, more than a few times, took a fifteen-minute snooze in her car before driving home. In other, drier times, this delay might have meant that Carey would find herself battling rush hour traffic, but that too had changed.

The streets were emptier than ever. Then, in early April, they felt eerily dead. A slow and steady mass exodus from South Florida had begun in earnest. The only traffic to be found was on I-90 headed north. Thousands upon thousands of trucks and cars packed to the gills with people and household objects slowly sloshed their way to Georgia and Alabama. Houses and apartment buildings in South Florida were abandoned, some shut tight against the elements, some gaping open to stalwart graffiti artists who scrawled them with obscenities, prophecies of doom, or, among Carey's favorites, portraits of leaping fish and spouting whales.

Mario came to see Carey in her classroom on the last day before spring break. To be fair, he'd texted her several times over the past few weeks to see how she was feeling, to ask if she needed anything, and to report that he was still figuring things out. She had dutifully responded and tried hard not to grow increasingly annoyed with his indecision, but it had now been over a month since her announcement.

"Do you think we'll reopen after the break?" he asked, sitting high on the back of a wooden chair.

"I don't know. Probably? But I heard the office started flooding. I mean, I guess, if the rain stops and the water goes down ..."

"Doesn't seem likely," he said.

"You never know."

"Are you doing anything for spring break?"

"I might take my mother to the Keys."

"Yeah, right." Mario smiled and shook his head.

"No, I'm serious. There's nobody down there right now. It could be great."

"You know we're in a national emergency zone, right? You know that there are three inches of water almost everywhere? The Keys are completely under."

"They're not gone yet."

"Um, but like, they might have a month left at most."

"That's an exaggeration."

"Is it? Have you been down there lately?"

"No, not in a few months."

"Okay," he shrugged. "Just be careful."

"Okay ..."

Carey looked at the father of her child: blithely perched in her space, dispensing advice on her plans, and admonishing her for her choices.

"Is there something you want?" she asked. "I need to pack up some things in case we do close."

Mario frowned. "Right. Okay. So, I thought long and hard about your situation."

Carey noted his use of "your" and consciously refrained from wincing. "Uh-huh."

"I'm going to do everything I can to support you and the child, but I'm still not sure what that means for me."

She noted his use of "the" child. "So ..."

"So, what do you need?"

Carey looked at him and saw clearly, and for the first time, that Mario was not what she needed. She liked him. She knew her child might need him, but she didn't. Not right now. She needed something else entirely. She didn't have much to say to him, really. It was uncomfortable.

"I don't need anything right now. I'm fine." She picked up a chair to stack on another.

"You're mad?"

"No, I'm not mad. I'm good. I appreciate what you're trying to do, and I'll, you know, I'll let you know."

"What about money for the doctor bills?"

"All covered. Insurance."

"Do you need company at the appointments?"

"No, my mom comes with me."

He frowned, so she added, "But if you want to come, you can. It's your kid too."

"Right. Yeah. I mean, I guess I could come to one or something."

She noted his use of "one or something." He was trying, but the results were less than impressive.

"Can I, like, buy you something or get baby stuff?" he asked.

"No, thanks. I don't think so. I'll need baby gear eventually, but I can't think about that yet. I'm not ready."

"Do you, like, want to get married or anything?"

For the first time in the course of the conversation, Carey smiled, and then shook her head. In place of a laugh, she exhaled a short burst of air from her nose. This wasn't her first marriage proposal, but it was the least enthusiastic.

He blushed. "I know. It's old-fashioned."

"You don't need to worry about that."

"It's what dudes are supposed to say, right?"

"Yeah, so, fuck that." She shook her head again.

"Okay."

"Listen, like I said," continued Carey, "I'm ... appreciating your efforts here, but there's nothing I need right now. I mean, other than my house to dry out, and my classroom not to flood, and the fucking rain to stop falling."

"Yeah, for real. I hear that." Beads of sweat had broken out on Mario's forehead.

"I'll let you know when I have another appointment, and you can come or whatever."

"Okay, yeah. Thanks."

"No problem."

"See you soon, then," he said.

"Yeah."

He climbed down, ungraceful and leggy. His glum expression suggested he knew he'd missed the mark somehow. He pecked her on the cheek and left.

Carey sat down. There was nothing particularly wrong with Mario. At another time in her life, or maybe in another situation, she might have still found him charming and interesting. Today, he was neither. He was just some guy who didn't find her charming or interesting either. He didn't long to spend time with her. He didn't yearn to know about her history, her secrets, the things that made her afraid or alive. He didn't need to be close to her or hold her hand. And she couldn't blame him, really. She was already sharing her body with something, with someone, else.

She moved to the piano, sat on the bench, and ran her fingers lightly over the keys. Eventually, she messed around in E minor. Piano had never been an easy instrument for her—she was pureblood guitar—but she understood why people loved it. The resonant ring of the keys filled her body and the classroom. She wondered if the baby could hear it yet. Probably not, but maybe. Maybe. She should be reading her pregnancy book. At least once in a while. Where was the damn thing anyway? Could be in the car.

These were the thoughts that tumbled through Carey's consciousness as she let her fingers ramble through old songs and improvise new ones. Later, she would wonder if some instinct or prescience had guided her to play piano that day. In less than a week, that particular instrument would meet its demise, and then many years would pass before Carey touched a functioning piano again. Pianos, you see, are much harder to put up on cinder blocks, or to move up to the roof, or to perch among the new swamps that were coming. Pianos were one of the many luxuries that South Florida would sacrifice to Rain in the months ahead.

When she lost interest in playing, Carey loaded several of the school's best brass, percussion, and woodwind instruments that had not yet been distributed to students into her truck. She tucked the others up on high shelves, or at least on stacks of chairs, and shut down her office computer. She unplugged everything there was to unplug, as she'd been instructed to do by the administration, and locked the windows. It felt more like the beginning of summer than spring break, but Carey left without that sense of release and freedom that June usually gifts to teachers and students. No, there were no gifts today. There were just looming uncertainties, and there was rain, falling hard and consistent in the streets.

On the drive home, Carey passed a small duplex that had been abandoned and boarded up. Someone had painted a black Y on one side and a maniacal clown face on the other. The clown's toothy smile mocked Carey in her pickup. She shot him a bird.

The light at the next intersection was dark, shorted out, and Carey carefully navigated a left turn through a deeper area of water where the road dipped. A mullet leapt from the pool, its silver body flashing momentarily and then slapping down on the exposed edge of a median before flipping back into the water.

"Christ," Carey said aloud and stopped the truck. It wasn't a real appeal. She hadn't been to church since age five, and she'd never bought into all that God business anyway. It was just that seeing a fish leap out of the intersection of Miller and 124th stirred in her a genuine sense of awe, trimmed with panic.

Once home, she related this episode to Etta in the kitchen, neglecting entirely to share any of the conversation she'd had with Mario.

"No shit?" responded Etta, stirring a pot of chili. "That reminds me, there was a goddamn turtle on the front porch when I got the mail yesterday."

"You're joking."

"Yep, looked at me like I'd just walked into her living room, and what the hell did I want anyway?"

"Was she there today?"

"No, but she'll be back. This is her return to Eden."

"If Eden is a suburban trash swamp."

"Heh." Etta tapped her wooden spoon on the rim of the pot and set it aside.

"Ma ..." Carey hesitated.

"Yeah?" Using a dish towel to protect her hands, Etta moved the pot of chili to the table and set it on a metal trivet shaped like a crab. Bowls were already out. She went back for spoons.

"Nothing."

Etta returned and sat at the table. She pulled off her boots and rested her swollen feet on an empty chair. "I know it looks bad, but we're okay for now."

Carey nodded and served them. "You still wanna go down to the Keys for a few days?"

"If we can get there."

"My phone says the roads are closed, but I bet there's local access."

Etta nodded. "Maybe. It's fine if we don't make it. This rain ain't letting up, so I don't think we'd get much fishing done."

"We can wait a couple days and see."

Etta nodded and they set to eating.

Jim showed up the next day for what would have been his weekly yard service. He knocked on the back door as thunder struck. Carey let him in. The old man now wore a thick rubber parka and a wide-brimmed rain hat that made his wrinkled face appear disproportionately small. He stood dripping on the already soggy carpet.

"Mornin' Jim! What are we gonna do about all this water, eh?" asked Etta. She was propped up again at the dining room table with a cup of coffee and her tablet.

"Damned if I know, pardon my French." Jim took off his hat and held it in front of him.

Carey passed him a cup of coffee, black.

"Thank you."

"Sure thing."

"'Fraid I can't do much about your yard. Mower won't run in all this. You want me to prune something?"

"Nah, not worth the trouble," said Carey. She sat opposite her mother and slurped a coffee of mostly milk and sugar. She'd read that one cup a day or so was okay during pregnancy.

Jim's brow crinkled. "You need any cinder blocks or sandbags?"

Carey shook her head. "Don't think so, thanks. I think you've got us pretty well sorted out. I don't see how any more blocks would help at this point."

Jim gazed into his coffee cup. He hadn't drunk any yet, which was strange for him. "Guess I'll be going, then."

Carey slurped and nodded.

Etta kicked her under the table. "Don't go just yet, Jim," said Etta. "I'm sure we've got some work for you around here somewhere."

That was that thing about Etta Marilla. She was no-nonsense, all-business, get-whatever-done-at-any-cost, until she saw someone's feelings plummet. Then it was stop-everything-and-make-it-right or back-up-and-listen until it helped. Etta was hard-skinned but soft-hearted. Truth be told, Etta wished, often, that Carey had inherited a bit less of that soft heart. Maybe then her daughter wouldn't have wasted so many years with that asshole Javi.

Carey sat right up. "Oh, sure, yeah. Actually, I need to figure out how to store a bunch of instruments up out of the way, but we don't have the space in here. I don't know what to do about it."

"No problem at all," said Jim, now smiling so that his wrinkles spread in wide arcs from ear to ear. "You mind if I nail a few boards up in the carport?"

"Go right ahead," answered Etta. "You do your thing, Jim."

"Sure will. Thank you, ladies." Jim downed his coffee in three long chugs, placed his mug on the table, bowed awkwardly in his classic way, and backed out the door from whence he'd come.

"That man's a sweetheart," said Etta. "I bet he's coming on hard times with no lawns to mow." She looked thoughtfully out the window.

"I'd think people would need plenty of help right now," said Carey.

"Sure, but they might not think of Jim. He's more of a yard guy than a handyman." Etta's thumb traced the smooth rim of her mug and her face slackened as she remembered, momentarily, how her father had once taught her how to hammer properly and how to use a table saw. Papi had been a quiet, skilled woodworker and an inspired guitarist. She'd heard once that his own father, her grandfather, had been semi-famous in Puerto Rico for the guitars he made by hand. But Etta had never met her Puerto Rican grandparents. They must have been kind, though, cause Papi was one of the good ones. He'd died in a car accident the year after Carey was born. Etta shook her head as she arrived back in the dining room. She slurped at her coffee, going cool now but still delicious. "The Kents are gone, you know," she concluded.

The Kents lived catty-corner from the little pink house and had three daughters, all of whom were slim and long and looked frightened all the time. "Cathy stopped by before they left and asked me to watch the house. They're going to her aunt's home in South Carolina or something. Must be a big place. She babbled about how her aunt did well in finance. Blah. Blah. I don't know. I zoned out. That woman has always bored the pants off me. Point is, they were Jim's customers too. I bet he's lost more than a few."

"Well, I'm not sure what we can hire him for after this."

"We'll think of something."

Carey wobbled her mug to stir the remains of her coffee. She didn't wonder at her mother's loyalty to Jim; he was a fixture in their lives. He'd always been there for muscle jobs, ever since Carey was small, and if Etta thought of him like family and wanted to care for him, Carey didn't think much differently. She gulped the last of her coffee, delighting in that extra sugar at the bottom. It was just that she wouldn't have assumed Jim needed help. Not at the moment anyway. Carey saw Jim as an independent soul with bulletproof confidence. Certainly no charity case. But they were all in need at the moment. In need of the rain to stop falling and, dammit, in need of a plan.

Maybe to avoid thinking farther ahead, Carey packed for the Keys. She stuffed a duffel bag with T-shirts, shorts, bathing suits, and sunblock. She loaded their eighteen-foot aluminum boat with poles and tackle. She packed a cooler with ice and drinks and loaded that too. She tied down the top of the boat and hitched the trailer to the truck. All of this she did over the next few days in light rain. The forecast called for more of the same, but Carey, in a mood something to do with denial and something to do with mental exhaustion, ignored it.

Jim worked near her, hammering boards up under the carport for crude shelves. They didn't speak to each other until noonish a few days later, when Carey invited Jim in for a cool drink. They were both drenched in sweat and rain, shivering in the AC.

"Where you headed?" asked Jim, mopping his face with a dish towel.

"The Keys," said Carey. She searched the fridge for leftovers. "Mom, you need anything?"

Etta was ensconced in her usual chair at the dining room table with her feet up and her show on. "No, thank you, baby. I just ate. There's chicken on the bottom shelf, right side."

Jim frowned. "The roads down there might be closed. Have you checked?"

Carey shrugged. "None of the maps are right these days. We'll just see what we see."

"Pardon me for saying it," said Jim, "but I don't much like the idea of you two heading toward the water."

"I get it," said Carey, "but look around. We're already in it." She found the chicken and set it on the counter. "You want something to eat, Jim?"

"No, but that's kind of you to offer. Just seems, and forgive me if I'm overstepping, it might be better if you two headed north to drier ground."

"Now look, Jim," said Etta, annoyed as much with the interruption to her show as with his interference, "we have the same rights as you to stick around. I don't see you packing up and going north, so why is that?"

Jim cackled. "You know full well."

"No, I don't."

"I'm all set up." He grinned like a toad in his hole. "That's why. I don't need to go anywhere. Got myself a proper shelter now and all."

"Oh, where's that?"

"Bit north, mostly west."

"A swamp fort, huh?"

"Yessiree."

"Ha! The bugs'll eat you alive if the gators don't getcha first."

Jim cackled again. "The bugs don't like me, my blood's too sour, but I'll tell you what: this rain ain't gonna let up. You'd be smart to get out."

Carey swallowed her bite of cold chicken as her temper rose. "We can handle our own business." Her voice, she realized too late, was sharp and bitter.

Jim bowed his head. "Beg your pardon. I shouldn't have said ..."

"That's fine," said Carey with a wave of her hand. "Sorry. It's just, we're not leaving yet. It's our decision to make."

"It sure is."

"There's plenty of time."

Jim didn't answer. He nodded without raising his head all the way.

"We're gonna go try and catch a few fish. We'll be right back."

He nodded again.

Carey tried for a peace offering. "You sure you don't want something to eat? You can take it with you."

"No, ma'am. I'll finish up." He backed out again and closed the door.

Carey looked to her mom, but Etta had already returned to her program.

"You packed yet, Ma?"

"Uh-huh."

"You wanna leave after your show?"

"Sure."

CHAPTER 5

With no traffic, the drive from Near Kendall to Key Largo would be about an hour and a half. From there, the chain of islands stretched another two hours to Key West, though Carey and Etta never ventured that far. Too many tourists and noisy biker bars, though most of those places were long gone now. The Marilla women had been partial to the quieter Middle Keys, especially Sugarloaf or Long Key. In recent years, and since the First Surge, there wasn't much left of those places either, so they'd started to stay in the Upper Keys. There were more grocery stores and bait shops, more vacancies, and, perhaps most importantly for Etta, several still-open, well-air-conditioned waterfront motels with pools where she could soak her feet. They always stayed Gulfside, if possible. Their boat wasn't near big enough for the open ocean. Even the backcountry could be daunting if breezes bloomed into winds.

They loaded up about one o'clock. Etta pushed her seat back as far as it would go and propped her feet up on the dash. Carey set a thermos of iced mint tea in the cupholder.

"You got your stuff?" Carey asked.

"Yep. You got the tackle?"

"Sure as shit."

"Hit it."

They made their way to the turnpike, taking the most flooded streets slowly. Carey monitored the trailer in her rearview while Etta ran commentary on freshly boarded-up buildings and homes.

The rain let up. The turnpike itself was high and dry. Traffic north was steady, even normal, except for the preponderance of U-Haul trailers and trucks. Traffic south was nonexistent, a spooky condition even on a rainy day.

"What do you think, Ma?"

Etta rubbed her wide face. "Hell, I don't know. It's not like we're the last people here." Etta scanned the soaking neighborhoods, the Australian pines slouching in the rain. "Christ, is that a gator?"

It was. Less than fifty yards ahead, a massive body lay in the center of the highway, blocking the better part of two lanes.

"Is it dead?" Carey asked, slowing the truck to get a better look. There was nobody behind them, but she still flicked on her hazards.

"I can't tell."

"He will be if he stays there. He's gonna cause an accident."

"Nah. He's huge." Etta's voice rang with admiration. "You can't miss him."

"Depends how dark it gets or how drunk the driver."

"Fair point."

"What the hell is he doing here anyway?" Carey asked, although she knew the answer.

"Missed his exit."

"Hilarious, Ma."

"I try."

"I'm gonna scare him off."

"What?"

Carey pulled the truck over to the left and up about ten feet from the beast. They could see his left eye open and the creases in the hide around his massive throat. He watched them with complete disinterest. Not a muscle stirred, even when Carey backed up, jack-knifing the trailer, to get a better angle on him.

With another check in the rearview, Carey leaned on the horn.

In one violent movement, the gator stood up and opened his jaws in alarm. Carey pounded the horn again. The animal thrashed a complete 180-degree turn and took off toward the side of the road from which, apparently, he'd come. His thick body moved with lightning speed, and his wide tail disappeared in one furious swipe through the reeds that lined the ditch.

"Hoo! He coulda been nine feet," said Etta, delighted with her assessment.

Carey put the truck in gear and continued down the highway.

"Remember when we hooked that little one when you were a kid? You must've been seven or so. We were in the canoe."

Carey knew the story well. She nodded. Etta loved to tell it, and Carey liked to hear it.

"Sure. How'd it start?"

Etta slapped her knees. "I had a big ol' peacock bass on the line, and I was taking my time reeling him in, just enjoying the moment, when all of a sudden the line goes screaming out of my reel like I'd hooked Moby Dick himself, and sure enough, we saw this sweet little gator thrashing around in the shallows not far away. You didn't know what we were looking at, so you said, all cheerful and excited, 'Mama, you caught an alien!' and I said, 'No, honey, that's an alligator.' You started screaming like it was the end of days. Cracked me up. An alien was fine with you, but the thought of an alligator made you damn near lose your mind."

"They're spooky bastards."

"Says you."

"That thing was huge." Carey thumbed behind them. "You can't tell me you'd be happy to meet him on your front porch."

"He'd be more interesting than a turtle."

Carey didn't answer. Her mother's love of alligators was baffling.

They drove on in silence.

Meanwhile, the gator they'd left behind caught his breath. His blood slowed. He slipped quietly down into the ditch on the side of the highway that had grown into a canal. He smiled a slow, wise smile. The waters rose ever so slightly, but continually, around him. He could be patient. His ancient kind understood patience well. He knew, deep in his dank flesh, that his time would come again. Soon now. Ever closer. Ever deeper. The wild ways would open once more, as they had so many thousands of years ago. There would be no more hiding, no more waiting.

***

Carey and her mother made it to Key Largo and continued on, largely to see if they could, to Tavernier Key and then Plantation. As in Miami, many of the businesses and buildings were now closed and abandoned. The road, in both directions, was quiet.

Windley Key was the last island open to through traffic. Wide orange barricades blocked the bridge to Islamorada just past the famed entrance to Circus of the Sea, a tourist attraction from the last century specializing in close encounters with depressed dolphins and decrepit sea turtles. The barricades were unstaffed but thorough. A metal gate on one end showed signs of frequent use (the pavement had been scraped in a wide arc), but now the thing was locked tight with a thick padlock. A sign read "Local Traffic Only," another stated "Dead End," and a third offered a more thorough explanation:

"KEEP OUT. Highway closed until further notice. Flooding and emergency conditions. No further access to the Florida Keys. Unstable land and failing infrastructure ahead. HIGH RISK."

"So that's that," said Etta. "Looks like we'll hafta set up back in Key Largo after all."

They turned around, the trailer creaking in protest as it slowly swiveled and reoriented.

Carey checked her phone. "Map says there's a few places open near Ocean Drive. One's the Holiday Inn."

"Figures," said Etta, who hated the Holiday Inn with a fiery passion. Something about cockroach eggs in a pillowcase. Turned out she didn't get the opportunity to complain; the Holiday Inn was boarded up after all, and so was the Bayside Inn nearby. The Marriott Courtyard was also closed, which would have been too expensive anyway.

"I should've brought the tent," said Carey.

"We can probably get one if the General Store's open. Guess that's questionable at this point."

"Map says there's one more place."

The one more place was inappropriately named the Key West Inn, and it was open. Very open. Several handwritten signs posted on the door announced this. Elena, at the front desk, enthusiastically greeted them in a purple satin kaftan. "You're the only guests we've had for more than two weeks," she proclaimed, as if this were not bitterly sad. "I sensed you were coming, I swear I did. Stayed open just for you."

"That was kind," said Carey, eyeing Elena's pink hair and her collection of crystals and suncatchers clustered in the front and side windows of the shabby lobby.

"Mama told me, God rest her soul, to always listen hard for the signs, so you know I do. Hasn't failed me yet. My gut says you gals are gonna have a fabulous time down here all by yourselves. Tell you what, those fish are bitin'."

"That so?"

"Yes, ma'am. My boy Georgey caught a magnificent hog just two days ago, out oceanside. Hadn't seen one so fat in thirty years."

"Good for him! You sell any bait?" Carey ventured, catching a bit of Elena's glee.

"We sure do. Georgey comes by in the morning with whatever you need. You just say somethin' the night before."

Etta answered. "We need shrimp and chum. What are you charging?"

"Relax, honey. We won't mark you up. Ten dollars per dozen shrimp and fifteen for a block of chum." Elena smiled wide and shook the gold hoops in her ears. "You got nothing to worry about at the Key West."

Etta smiled. "In Key Largo."

Elena cackled. "You got that right."

Their room was on ground level. Etta settled them as Carey put the boat in at the public ramp down the street. The ramp was short and the docks low, so her job was easy enough. She didn't feel nearly sixteen weeks pregnant, but then, she didn't really know what sixteen weeks pregnant was supposed to feel like.

By nightfall they were on the porch drinking whiskey (Carey allowed herself a splash) and OJ on the rocks. They ate cold chicken they'd brought from home. Except for Elena, they hadn't seen a soul all day.

"Strange here, ain't it?" asked Etta, between bites.

"I don't mind being left alone," said Carey. "It's kinda nice."

"Sure, but I can't see how they all jumped ship so quick. You'd think the Conch Republic would be the last holdout. These people used to be famous for their grit and stubbornness."

"Maybe it's generational? Elena doesn't look like she's going anywhere."

"Maybe." Etta slurped her drink and smacked her lips. "You're young, and you're still around."

Carey stripped the last of the meat from a drumstick and picked at the bone. "Yeah. Course you raised me to love this place, and I do. More than most. I still don't get how people can live in Miami all their lives and never step foot in a boat, or catch a fish, or swim in a lake, never mind the ocean."

Etta nodded. "It's a mystery, that's for sure."

"Plus," Carey continued, "there's too much else that's changing. I'm all full up on change."

Etta sighed. "I get that too."

Carey nodded. She didn't get it much herself, but here they were. Their small boat bobbed cheerfully in the canal beside the inn. Normally, there'd be other boats—taller, grander boats, dwarfing their humble rig. Seemed like most of those boats were long gone. Others hung on the far side of the canal, shrouded in tarp and dangling from cranes above their ports. Carey watched their little boat wobble in its mooring and hoped, vaguely, that tomorrow might make more sense.

They pushed off at nine in the morning, late for fishing, but early enough for pregnant. It had taken a couple hours to prep, procure bait and ice, pack lunches and drinks, and suck down their coffees. Their spirits were high as they puttered out and southwest, making slow progress toward Tavernier Creek. The weather cooperated, so the ride was pleasant. More than pleasant.

They slid through the mangroves and out into the Gulf just as a small pod of dolphins broke through the surface of the creek's northern mouth. Shining fins slipped in and out of the water like phrases of a song almost remembered. Etta cooed, and Carey felt tears escape in the wind of the boat's movement. Dolphins were easy to love. They never stayed long, but it seemed to Carey they knew to show themselves when it most mattered.

And now the lead dolphin leapt, breaking the surface with more than her back, letting the entirety of her sleek body feel the sun, the bright air, and the gaze of her audience. Dolphin knowledge, shifting and watercolor, flashed in her consciousness and then through the shared spirit of her family. In a language of light and vibrant sensation, she felt, more than saw, that a distant relation, one who needed her, needed them, was near. This relation and her mother would remember, on occasion, in their human dreams, the ancient connection of their kinds.

Dolphins need no such dreams. They know, by the grace of salt depths and wild blood, the connection of all. So it was here, in this plane of sound and force, where the human vessel roared through their sacred queendom, the humans needed more than a brush with optimism, and the dolphins knew it. Their leader leapt again, and her family followed, each in turn, showing the gentle whites of their bellies and the sparks of their eyes. When the youngest had jumped a second time, exuberant and prone to showing off, the dolphin family slowed and fell back into the open water of the humans' wake.

Carey thanked them under her breath and turned the boat back northeast across the flats. Around them, Gulf waters spread smooth and silver as a promise.

They hadn't fished this far north in years, but there were still a few spots tagged on Carey's maps. She navigated to the closest one, a hole in the shallows, about ten or fifteen feet deep. It wasn't sunny, but the wind lay low. They could just make out the shadow at the edges of the hole as GPS announced their arrival. Carey pulled safely away, against the tide, and threw out the anchor.

Elena at the Key West Inn had spoken truth. There were no other boats as far as the eye could see. The only one they'd passed on their way over was a large yacht cruising slowly south.

"What d'you think, Ma? Ready to limit out?"

"Damn right. Gimme that pole."

Etta grunted and adjusted her rump on the vinyl boat cushion. She straightened her visor, rammed her sunglasses back in place, and dug her hand in the bait sack. She chose a medium-sized shrimp, but he kicked out of her hand. She cursed, stooped, ushered him onto her hook, and finally, with a contented sigh, cast her line out about twenty feet.

Water slapped the sides of the boat, and Carey guzzled some orange juice. It wouldn't be long now. It wouldn't be long.

"There he is!" Etta set the hook. Her line whizzed as the pole bent with the weight of some creature's doom.

"Whatcha got?" asked Carey.

"Feels like a snap."

"Ha!"

Etta reeled the fish in, a fifteen-inch mangrove snapper, pink and pissed as hell. They threw him in the box, celebrated with laughter and a high five, and settled to the serious business of catching his friends and family.

The next hour or so of fishing was better than typical. They caught six more legal snapper right away before a plague of shorts set in. A dozen fish later, they paused for snacking on Doritos and green olives. Etta made herself a Bloody Mary with V8, black pepper, Tabasco sauce, and a generous helping of Smirnoff.

Carey was the first to cast again and happily hooked a grunt. No limit on those. Her next catch was a small barracuda. "We might have cleaned out the big snaps," she said, carefully unhooking the small but vicious jaws of the barracuda. "You want him?" They sometimes kept small 'cudas if the day was slow.

"Nah. Let him go. We've still got plenty of bait. I might grab us a few pinfish in case there's anything massive down there."

Carey tossed back the snake-like fish and reached for a shrimp. "Good plan."

Etta switched poles to a dainty toy rig. She reeled in three or four tiny snapper before her first pinfish, bright silver and prickly as its name. She caught two more.

Carey quickly filleted one of the pinfish and baited their biggest pole, affectionately called Ol' Blue. It had once belonged to Etta's papi, Mauricio Marilla, who Etta rarely talked about. Carey knew he'd been fond of fishing, deeply proud of his Puerto Rican heritage, and maybe the only decent part of Etta's early life. That was it. Etta's mother, Janine, had been abusive and left them when Etta was ten. If Papi was a bit of a mystery, Janine was nothing but a shadow.

The clouds cleared, and the wind picked up ever so slightly. Carey sank her bait close to the center of the hole, risking a snag in hope of some greater catch. Etta rested. Carey waited. The wind turned the boat northward.

"Sweetheart?" Etta prompted.

"Yeah."

"You gonna tell me what you and Mario are thinking, or no?"

"'Bout what?"

"'Bout your family."

Carey flipped her bail and pulled up to check if her bait had hit bottom or found trouble. Nothing yet. "We're not a family."

"You will be."

"Well, Mario's sweet ... but I don't think I love him."

Etta nodded, so Carey continued, "I don't think he loves me either."

"As far as I know, love isn't an on or off switch. It's more like a dial."

"Sure."

"Could you love him eventually?"

"I'm not sure."

"Think you'd try, for the baby's sake?"

Carey watched the slope of her line, barely visible against the water. "I'm not convinced that's necessary. The baby will have plenty of love from me and you."

"Okay, but from where I sit, a father would be helpful."

Carey felt something knock at her bait. She lifted the rod tip just a bit and reeled in some slack.

"For the baby or for me?"

"Both."

Carey sighed. "Yeah. I know. I'm not trying to shut him out. It's just hard to gear up for some big effort when my mind and my body aren't up for it, you know? I'm already occupied. This," she gestured to her middle, "is plenty to think about."

Etta nodded. "None of my business." She paused, looking out at the islands. "It just wasn't easy for me. Single, I mean."

"I won't be on my own."

"God willing."

No one in that little boat was deeply religious, but they were, Carey knew, still at the mercy of more than her choices. Plenty could take them down and out. Although it felt possible, at that moment, in that place, with the sunlight and the fish in the box and the recent memory of dolphins, to imagine a way forward. Offshore maybe, but afloat. Buoyant.

Something massive struck her bait, and Carey stood to reel slowly down. She set her hook with a fierce, sharp pull to her right. Ol' Blue protested, and line screamed from the reel.

"Got 'im. Hoooooo Lord, I got 'im!" Carey spread her feet and leaned back to balance her weight against the strength of the fish. "Mom, get the net. Christ, is it a shark?" She reeled, pulling steadily at the rod and straining to see through the wind-ruffled surface of the water.

Etta stood to find the net. The small boat tipped dangerously.

"Careful!"

"I'm getting the goddamned net."

"Hurry up!" The fish was heavy, active in surges of downward pull rather than out or side to side. "It's a grouper," said Carey. "It's gotta be."

Etta sat, rocking the boat, net at the ready. She rubbed angrily at the elbow she'd just bashed on the cooler. "Get him up! Get him in the boat!"

"I am. I am." Carey grunted and adjusted the pole. Usually, she would anchor it on her belly, but a new awareness of the life inside made her tuck the pole on her hip. One of a thousand tiny adjustments pregnancy already demanded. Her hip helped, but it was far harder now to bear the weight of the fish; her arms were already getting tired.

"Mom, I don't know. It could be a shark."

"It's not a shark."

"Could be."

"It's not a shark."

"Get the knife in case it's a shark."

"Okay."

The fish rose at last, a large strawberry grouper, its mouth red and wide, its wild eyes glaring from beneath the surface of the water. In a choreography mother and daughter knew well, Etta leaned dangerously forward while Carey stepped back to counter her weight. The net plunged deep to the side of the fish, the fish gave one last great thrash, and Etta lifted the net up around the tail and past its head.

"Got him. Lifting *now*!" Etta directed. She pulled up and sat down as Carey stepped forward. The boat dipped and settled as the great pink fish flopped angrily on the bottom.

"Atta girl!" crowed Etta. They slapped a high five and beamed. Here was the high they chased. The trip's whole purpose. Worth all the money, the effort, the uncertainties. Here, in the bottom of the boat, was a fish that could feed them three meals, caught with their own hands, together, under the wide spring sky. And more than that, here was a memory, a story they'd tell for decades. Here was a reason to love Florida, to stay, to fight for the beauty and bounty of the damned place. It was the fattest, most beautiful grouper they'd ever caught.

While Carey worked to untangle the net, the fish calmed. Her body lay still while her gills pumped, flashing electric red. The warm, wet browns and deep scarlet of her speckled body shone in the sun, and Carey felt a familiar mix of victory and guilt. So much beauty at her mercy. Such a glorious life to feed her own. With quiet reverence, Carey lifted the fish by her bottom jaw out from the net, untangling each spine of dorsal fin from the nylon fibers and removing the hook without further damage to the soft brown flesh around the mouth. She laid out her catch for measurement, a full twenty-seven inches. This particular variety of grouper had no size limit in these waters, but both women cheered at the revelation of her length. Even if she'd been a gag grouper or the rarest black, she would have been legal. They laid her in the cooler, thanking her silently for all she'd given and had yet to give. They sat back.

"Should we head in already?" asked Etta. "The day's not gettin' better than that."

"Don't know. Maybe. You spent?"

"Not yet."

"We have plenty of meat. What a trip."

"For the record book."

Etta lifted her visor, folded the tangled mass of her hair up into it, and set it back down. She looked out past the helm at the blues and greens beyond. No denying she felt an itch to explore. "We could run the boat a while. See why the roads are blocked."

"Are we allowed to look around?"

"They can't control this much water. If it's posted, we'll turn back."

"Okay, but if we get stopped, this is your fault."

"Fair enough." Etta grinned and put her feet up on the box. Her lime green flip-flops were about as worn out as her feet and curled perfectly to the contour of her heels.

"Alright. I'm gonna tidy up the boat. You have another drink, then we'll hit it."

"Yes, Cap'n."

The glory of the morning gave way to a wicked heat. Carey slathered sunblock on her neck, arms, and the tops of her hands and feet. Etta wore a bright white stripe down her nose and a smear on each cheek. Most of the bait was already dead, so Carey twisted the bag closed and placed it in the cooler. Dead bait worked better than no bait. She laced up the rods and wiped off the sideboard where she'd filleted the pinfish. She stowed the tackle box and straightened her seat cushion. Eventually, when both women had newly wiped sunglasses and a mug of iced tea, Carey pulled up the anchor. Something about the chain and the hand-over-hand effort of this task satisfied her bones.

They motored southwest, following the thick line of islands and overseas highway that comprised the Upper Keys. Plantation and Windley flew by, then Islamorada, once a busy resort destination bristling with sailboats and oversized yachts, now empty and quiet. The green of Lower Matecumbe Key gave way to a dense housing development. The water grew rough as the islands became separated by larger expanses of water. Bridges leapt up and settled down again, running along the water like the low path of a wind-savvy seabird.

Carey pulled them closer to the shoreline and near the bridge past Long Key. No cars, no trucks, none of the usual fishing boats were present. Nothing but gulls wheeling skyward and pelicans standing sentry on pilings and posts. This was the first time they'd been close enough for Carey to notice a significant change in the shoreline. A small, brightly painted resort was not so much waterfront as water-in. Waves splashed gently against the boarded-up French doors of each unit. Palm trees that might have once bedecked a small beach now rose at odd angles directly from the water. Low-slung fish-cleaning docks and sunset-gazing piers were vanished, replaced with a few crowded camps of seabirds. A neon pink flag that read "Fish On" dragged in the sea.

"Mary, Mother of God," said Etta in summation. She stared at those French doors. There was something about them. A memory, slow and strong, surfaced in her mind like a sea turtle coming up for air. Decades ago, Papi had brought her to this exact resort for one of the few vacations he'd ever allowed himself. Twelve-year-old Etta had waded in those waters, hunting for shells and tracking parrotfish. She'd fished off those sunken docks. She'd sat with Papi in the evenings to watch the sun set in the Gulf while he smoked and hummed quiet songs. The memory of his voice spread like an ache in her chest, that rare kind of hurt she couldn't wish away.

Carey turned the boat toward the next island. After a few minutes, they approached. "Mom, what's that?" she asked.

"What?"

"Over there. Over there." Carey waved her hand at a black structure sticking up and out from the mangroves near another boarded-up building.

Studying it, Etta took off her sunglasses and squinted.

"I think it's a boat."

It was, or it had been. The carcass of a large yacht, burnt and hollow, rose menacingly from the shallows. The building near it, Carey saw, had also been partially burnt. Several pieces of plywood had been pried off windows and across a pair of French doors. Across one wall, a warning had been scrawled in red: "Looters will be shot."

As if on cue, a pickup truck skidded to a halt between two of the buildings, dust billowing behind it. A man stepped out and slammed the door.

"Time to buzz off," said Etta. Carey turned sharply to the left and steered them away under the bridge.

The next group of buildings was much the same, not so much neglected as ravaged. New nausea rippled through Carey, quite different from motion or morning sickness. They puttered past one last resort. Someone had constructed a rough wooden arch between the buildings. Long, ragged objects dangled from it on meat hooks. Carey's mind lurched. Were they bodies? No, not possible. Not human. They were sharks. A dozen or more, in various states of decay, hung baking in the sun and wind. A breeze suggested their stench. Another handmade sign posted above them read "Keep Out." Carey gagged.

"Turn back," Etta barked.

Carey didn't, or somehow couldn't, respond, her mind numb with the horrors revealing themselves. Their boat moved slowly but certainly in the direction of the bodies.

"Turn the boat, honey. TURN."

Carey came to and threw the motor in reverse. Water churned and bubbled around them. Gasoline fumes encompassed the vessel. Carey retched again but brought them round.

Not a moment too soon, as another boat, unnoticed until now, pulled out from behind a sheltered dock. It was a thirty-foot fishing vessel, in poor condition, and there were three figures on board.

"Honey," said Etta.

"I see them," said Carey. She pushed their boat forward, but did not accelerate dramatically, so as not to appear to be running. There was probably no reason for alarm. Except for those sharks.

The boat behind them accelerated. Carey cursed.

"We can't outrun them," said Etta. "They've got at least 300 horsepower."

Carey accelerated. Their 90 horsepower Yamaha was easily ten years old. The boat behind them was already gaining, making no pretense of other interests. It barreled straight toward them.

Carey thought quickly. If they were pirates, they might just take the fish and gear and leave. If they were worse, she and Etta had no means to defend themselves except maybe a flare or two. The only option would be to swim for it, and Etta wouldn't make it to shore.

Carey thought of the shore, of the hotel they'd puttered past on the previous island. There were flats out front of it. That was their best chance. She veered shoreward and pushed their motor to its maximum speed. It roared to life. "Hold on," she called to her mother.

The next key was Long Key and they were minutes away when the boat behind them met their wake. Carey glanced back. Three men stood behind the windscreen. She couldn't make out their faces, but she didn't want to.

She cut right and made for the closest bridge. The larger boat had a wider turning radius, but it made the turn and gained on them again. Carey threaded through a narrow place in the bridge's beams, but not narrow enough. The boat followed. She maneuvered a tight spin to the right and sped back directly through the same gap. The larger boat turned but was forced to pull more widely around and made it back through a gap farther west. Now there was shouting from the boat.

Carey sped forward, and before the boat regained their wake, the flats spread before them. Inches deep, there would be no safe way for the larger boat to navigate this water. It was still dangerous for Carey to take their much smaller, mostly flat-bottomed boat through, especially at high speed. One rock, one bit of wreckage, one sunken post could destroy their vessel. Carey'd choose that fate over whatever the fuck waited for them in the boat behind her.

Their little boat sped forward, directly inland, and then turned sharply left along the shore. Carey had no idea how far these flats stretched. If the men behind her had better knowledge of the area, and if that knowledge told them the flats were brief, there was no hope. They'd simply cut around to the far side and wait. But they seemed to know different. The boat fell back. More shouts lifted from inside the roar of the engine. No intelligible words made it through.

Carey watched the water ahead with the eyes of an osprey, scanning, scanning, but not for fish: for coral heads or snags or fans and sponges that might destroy the motor or rip the boat apart. Twice, she swerved wildly to avoid an indeterminate obstacle. Once to avoid a sea turtle lazing her way. Finally, after what felt like an age, she pulled the boat around the north point of the island and raced east, still on the flats but now out of sight of whoever, whatever had chased them.

She did not slow down, aware that there were plenty of other ways for their pursuers to cut east on the other side of the islands, maybe cut them off at the next bridge, or the one past that. Her mind leapt to other possibilities. They might radio to other boats. Maybe trouble would wait for them back at the motel.

None of this came to pass outside Carey's mind, but her imagination charged her panic. They sped back toward Key Largo, full throttle.

The flats ran out an island later, so Carey turned them a farther distance from shore. A tense silence spread beneath the roar of the outboard.

It was midafternoon when they pulled up to the Key West Inn. They had encountered no other boats. Carey climbed out of their vessel, her hands and knees weak. Luckily, it was easier than normal to disembark. The docks were bizarrely low, or rather, thought Carey, not bizarrely, considering the state of things.

They went about the business of unloading the boat and then sat in the air-conditioning of their room. The fish still needed cleaning, but both women were tired and heartsore.

"What can I getcha, baby? You want a V8? How 'bout an iced tea?" Etta asked.

"Just water, thanks." Carey's nerves were still alive.

"You okay?"

"I don't know. You okay?"

"Probably better than you. Not pregnant, thank God."

"Pregnant is only one part of the problem."

"Sure." Etta stood slowly and made her way to the kitchenette. She opened a cabinet for glasses and ran the tap. "The Lower Keys are further gone than I thought; that's a lot to take in. Course, they were always wild. You're probably too young to remember the old Keys, but legend says they weren't so different from what we just saw."

"Rotting fish and terrifying men?"

Etta rinsed and dumped the glasses. "No, I just mean Conch Heads are their own breed. Your papi told me the Keys used to be full of misfits and misanthropes. Libertarians. Then money rushed in, and everything turned posh. I can remember that part. When the water rose, my guess is the can-haves and the would-haves split real quick. Looks to me like the pirates are the only ones left."

"I guess."

Etta handed Carey her water, and Carey drank. Etta returned to the simple armchair next to her daughter.

Carey closed her eyes and leaned her head back. "It looks wrong to me," said Carey. "It looks like war."

"Probably is," said Etta.

"You'd think the government would do something."

"Popular thought these days."

The air conditioner groaned as it kicked to a higher gear.

"Mom."

"Yeah?"

"You think it'll get that bad in Miami?"

"I don't know. I don't think so. Mainlanders are different."

"Hmm. I wonder."

Etta put her bare feet up on the inn's glass coffee table. "I'll do whatever you want, but there's no running from trouble."

"Mom, I'm serious. If people start kicking up shit, we should go."

"I know. I said it before. I'll do what you want. It's your call."

Carey grimaced. "Thanks a lot."

"What now? I'm trying to be supportive."

"Nothing, it's just, I'd appreciate some help with major decision-making."

"Oh, honey, major decision-making is fifty percent of motherhood."

"What's the other fifty percent?"

"Minor decision-making." Etta chuckled.

Carey frowned and drained her glass. She moved to set it down. There was no side table, and the floor was too far to reach. She could sit up and stretch for the coffee table in front of them or stand up and put it in the sink. She should probably slip her shoes back on and go deal with the fish, get them cleaned and stored. But it was cool in here, and she was tired. And shaken. She tucked the glass between her side and the arm of the chair. Just another minute or two of rest, she thought, just a bit more of nothing.

CHAPTER 6

As Carey and Etta finished what would be their last Keys trip, sinkholes began to open throughout the Miami metropolitan area. The first hole opened downtown, on the corner of Flagler and Second Avenue. This event proved minimally disruptive, as there were few people still commuting to work. City workers barricaded the roughly five-foot-by-five-foot pit and closed the closest building, a bank. The only casualty of that particular sinkhole was a stuffed rabbit named Duli, recently dropped on the sidewalk by Martina Gomez, age four. The girl had walked the area moments earlier, hand in hand with her abuela, who worked at the bank. When the sinkhole claimed Duli's small, plush body, Martina had yet to miss her toy, but she would. She would cry for several nights, praying ardently for his return. Alas, Duli was gone forever, swallowed by the watery beast stirring and stretching beneath Florida's limestone.

The next sinkhole was actually three. They opened several yards wide along Kendall Drive and collapsed a large overpass of the Ronald Reagan Turnpike. Two people died in the disaster: a middle-aged truck driver who stalled under the bridge as it collapsed, and a young Target employee who'd been walking home after a double shift when he unknowingly stepped into oblivion.

A total of fourteen sinkholes opened that week, killing nine people and wreaking utter havoc on local traffic and anxiety. Newscasters and government officials discussed in earnest whether any of the sinkholes could possibly be attributed to terrorists. No one was sure.

They weren't much interested in drawing connections between these local calamities and those plaguing other nations and states. Entire islands had already vanished into the Pacific. Vast swaths of forest and suburban real estate out west of the Mississippi were now ember and ash. California was in ruins. But the official response to these matters went something like, "Yes. It Is Indeed a Grim Time to Be Alive."

Carey and Etta were driving slowly home from the Keys as a sinkhole claimed a power station in deep Homestead, knocking out power for approximately six square miles. The Marilla women saw the wave of darkness sweep by as they drove north on black and flooded streets. Carey chewed on her bottom lip.

Arriving home, she backed the boat and trailer into the swamp of the side yard, methodically unhooked it, propped it up, and locked it all down, then pulled the truck around to the driveway. The carport was now two inches underwater, a shallow swimming pool. Leaves and twigs and dirt and trash had floated in and collected in the corners and around the Volvo's tires. Carey's instruments were still high and dry in the makeshift rafters Jim had built.

They entered the house and found, aside from the thick smell of must and mildew, no new disasters. Carey opened several windows and turned on every fan. That night, despite the riotous choir of frogs who blasted the little pink house with their most fervent psalms, Carey slept like the dead. She woke the next morning, refreshed and bright-eyed, well before her alarm.

"You gonna be okay today, Ma?" she asked as she stabbed the last of her second fried egg with her fork. She hadn't cooked a third, but she was still hungry.

"Yep," Etta replied over the rim of her coffee mug. Truth was, she was worn out from the Keys trip and planned to do nothing but flop around the house that day.

"I don't even know if school's open," continued Carey. "I'm assuming yes, since I haven't heard a word."

"We'll see."

"If Jim comes by, can you ask him about putting our dressers up on blocks? Maybe ask him about that smell too. Do you think we should pull up the carpets? I've been thinking they're done for anyway."

"Sounds smart."

"Wish we could put the whole damn house up on blocks," Carey sighed.

"That'd be nice," said Etta, with no enthusiasm.

"You okay?"

"Sure."

"You're not saying much."

"Just tired."

Carey gave Etta's shoulders a quick rub and put on another pot of coffee. "I'm taking the truck."

"Be safe, honey."

"I will."

As Carey closed the back door, Etta tilted her head back and exhaled. She'd been tired in one way or another for decades, but this particular brand of tired was new. It was a tired born of boredom, without the will or energy to do anything about it. A thickness of mind. The Keys had staved it off for a bit, but she was home again.

Now there'd be TV, news, there'd be meals with Carey and chats with Jim, but not much else. Maybe she should be happier, more grateful for their relative security and peace, but it all felt flat. Not like the turbulent struggle of Carey's early years, and nothing like the wild ride of her adolescence. It was all easier now. And lesser.

The baby might change that, Etta told herself. A baby would demand new purpose, and heartbreak and terror and joy. With any luck, the baby might even wake her up, get her out of her chair, start those engines again.

<hr />

The school was open, but Principal Villanueva, a sour woman in square-toed shoes, called an emergency staff meeting at 8:00 a.m. It was, as usual, held in the music room, giving Carey zero time to prep for her first-period class. In all fairness, Carey probably should have given her lesson plans some thought over spring break, but she hadn't. Not in the slightest. There was too much else clamoring for attention. Dr. Villanueva started their meeting promptly at eight, even though it looked to Carey like half the staff had not yet arrived. The ones who had, including Mario, were silently nursing their mugs of coffee and avoiding eye contact so as to avoid conversation. Mario nodded hello to Carey but sat in the back row. Carey perched in her usual place, farthest right in the front row.

"Good morning, everyone," said Dr. Villanueva in a chipper, grating tone. "I trust you all had peaceful and restorative spring breaks. Coming back, we have a new set of challenges before us."

Carey found herself vaguely impressed with the formality of Dr. Villanueva's speech thus far. Normally it would have been annoying, but given the circumstances, some degree of profundity was welcome. "You can see that we are understaffed. We have been for several weeks now. The difference today is that we can no longer hire enough substitutes to fill even half of the vacant positions. Luckily, or unluckily, our student body is also significantly reduced. Even so, we have a duty to our children and to their families. We must provide the best education we can, for as long as we can, no matter the climate."

This was, Carey noted, a vast departure from the usual pattern of closing the school given any minor threat of tropical storm or high winds. Maybe school administrators in South Florida were finding a new passion for their calling, or maybe they simply saw an opportunity to rise in reputation and rank via the crisis. Or maybe it was just that Dr. Villanueva enjoyed being the martyred captain of a (literally) sinking ship. Whatever the case, Carey couldn't disagree that they should stay open if at all possible. The pandemic of her childhood had exiled students online for years, in some cases, and had taken a significant psychological toll on families and teachers alike. Everyone who remembered it remembered the difficulties of isolation and then the difficulties of coming back from isolation. And anyway, if every school closed, there could be no more pretending at normalcy. Blue-collar families, the increasingly few left, would have to quit work due to lack of childcare, or leave South Florida.

"In this spirit of survival," Dr. Villanueva expounded, "the superintendent has decided to consolidate our students and staff. We'll be joining forces with Canal Middle School next week. Their campus is compromised far more than ours, so students and staff who opt out of online learning will commute here. Dorothy and I are working on a new schedule for you all, but please be prepared to welcome Canal students into your classes and adapt your courses to facilitate these changes. They are, of course, temporary. As soon as we receive notice that Canal is reopened, and once our own staff and students return, we'll be back to normal. Possibly as soon as next month."

Dr. Villanueva continued to detail the district's transition plans, including the possibility of returning to the fully online learning models that frosted the hearts of most educators, especially those, like Carey, in the performing arts. But Carey's attention, and faith, had flown. If Dr. Villanueva believed that Miami could be back to normal in a month or two, she'd gone off tune. It would take far, far longer than that to get Miami schools functional again, though Carey couldn't quite let herself imagine a point of no return.

First and second periods were all but empty. Third period arrived, and Yessica Larges slumped in with her black backpack. Gloria Fuentes perched in the front row, flute at the ready. Sweet and studious Miguel Peraza arrived on time, of course he did, but Pablo the Loud arrived a few minutes late, clearly taking advantage of the school's general abnormality. Carey didn't bother lecturing him.

"Miss, how are we supposed to play ensemble pieces if we're missing so many instruments?" asked Gloria as Carey labored over her attendance.

"We'll manage," said Carey gently. "We'll need to get creative with what we have." She glanced up toward Yessica's row and was astonished to see that Yessica had not yet taken out her headphones. Maybe they'd been lost or stolen at last. Yessica made brief eye contact with her, but then slumped and disappeared behind her black hair.

"I practiced all the time over spring break, Miss," continued Gloria. "I can't wait to show you." Gloria crossed her legs and smoothed her skirt at the knee. She liked the fabric of this skirt; it was smooth and stiff and wouldn't catch on her leggings. She refolded a lazy pleat and pointed her toes. There was much more to her spring break story, if anyone asked. In truth, her interest in music was only partially sincere. She had practiced, for sure, but mostly because she wanted space away from her older brothers and younger sisters. She routinely locked herself in her abuela's room, making musical excuses, and though Gloria did play a few exercises on the flute, she spent most of that time alone, sneaking peeks into Abuela's jewelry box and playing with the porcelain manger scene that remained at the old woman's bedside year-round. Gloria pouted her lips, unconsciously mimicking the expression on Baby Jesus's face.

"Wonderful," said Carey, flatly.

Not content with this reply, Gloria pressed on. "I bet no one else practiced much. I bet everyone else is using the flood as an excuse."

"Possibly," said Carey, rapidly losing patience for Gloria's neediness.

"My mom says it's just sinful the way people are leaving and giving up. This is all God's punishment, and we're meant to endure it."

"Well, I don't know about—"

"No, it's true, Miss. It's been coming for a long time. There's so much sin in our world. If people run away now that God is showing himself, they'll have to pay double. We deserve this. We're *supposed* to suffer."

Carey allowed a new tenderness for the girl. Here was evidence of Gloria's burden to bear: Her mother must be a religious fanatic, or a masochist.

"Gloria, I'm not going to argue any religious ideas in class, but I want everyone to know that I understand if it's been difficult to practice lately. We're all distracted, to say the least. Maybe we should switch it up and try something new. What do you think?"

The kids nodded, as if in a daze. Even Gloria seemed game, surprised by this sudden softness, this change of tone from her teacher. Miguel's face held the usual light of his interest and curiosity. Yessica didn't move, but her stare, peeking from the curtains of her hair, fixed on Carey.

"Okay, let's do this: Find something to write with and a piece of paper." Carey stood and plugged in her phone to the class speakers. She browsed until she found the song she wanted and then turned back to the kids. "Let's listen to some music and have a discussion. Okay? We'll try different kinds of sounds and styles. You won't like everything you hear—we all have different tastes. But let's see if we can figure out whether we have any common responses to some of these sounds and why. Let's think about what the musicians might have been feeling or exploring when they created their sounds. Fold your paper in half, it doesn't matter which way, and on one side of the crease, write 'Response.' On the other side, write 'Why.'"

"Aw, Miss, you gonna make us write?" whined Pablo. "That's no fun."

"You don't have to write," said Carey, "but I'd like you to respond. You can write, or draw, or if you don't want to put anything on paper, then I'd like you to discuss it with us. It's up to you."

"I'm not writing," said Pablo with a triumphant fist pump.

"We'll look forward to hearing your thoughts then."

"Unless I draw."

"Unless you draw."

Carey hazarded a glimpse at Yessica. The girl hadn't moved to retrieve any paper or pen, but she also hadn't donned her headphones.

Gloria's hand shot up.

"Yes, Gloria?"

"How are you grading this? Do we need to fill the page? I'm not sure what you mean by response."

Carey pushed on. "We'll listen to a song all the way through. The first time through, just listen. You don't need to write anything. Then we'll listen to it again, and I want you to write down anything the song makes you feel, think, or imagine. Maybe you feel excited, or you think of puppies, or you want to dance. Whatever. Just write or draw your ideas, and then think about why you had those responses and theorize—that's make a guess—about why. For example: I thought about puppies because the horns reminded me of playful barking. There are no right answers. I'll grade you on participation this time. Okay?"

Gloria looked as if she'd swallowed a bug.

"This is gonna be fancy classical crap, ain't it, Miss?" groaned Pablo.

Carey smiled. "Probably." She cranked the volume and hit Play. Drums first, then the slinking confessions of a sultry female voice accompanied by growling guitar. "Only Happy When It Rains" by Garbage was an anthem of Carey's youth. The sound was simple enough: Euro-pop grunge from the late 1990s, a time well before Carey's adolescence, but one that called to her from the reaches of history. A pulsing dance hall beat, dirty guitars, and a rusty alto voice. Distant from "fancy classical crap," but still an oldie to this crew.

Most of the kids giggled and squirmed in response to the opening bars. Miguel closed his eyes in concentration, rocking slightly to the beat, intent on the assignment. Gloria diligently scribbled in a pink vinyl notebook while her eyebrows betrayed a genuine horror. Only Yessica remained still. Carey watched her. Inside the shadows of the girl's hoodie, a sly smile slid into place.

The song finished. Pablo protested the whole affair. Carey started it again. The class squirmed through the second playing. Pablo lay down across three empty seats and pretended to sleep.

"Right. That's it. I'd like to hear from everyone now. You can hand me something written, or you can add to the discussion. Who's first?"

Carey avoided looking in her direction, but Gloria's hand shot up once again. No one else moved.

"Yes, Gloria?"

"That song was angry."

"Okay, what makes you say that?"

"The music was, like, shouting at me."

"Interesting. That's one interpretation. Can we hear another?"

A voice came from the back row. "It wasn't angry. The singer was enjoying herself, but also, she was, like, trying to convince herself that she was enjoying it."

Yessica's posture hadn't changed. Her hood was still pulled up. The only indications she had spoken were the gaping mouths and arching eyebrows around her. Her peers were aghast. Carey forced herself not to comment on the rarity of the moment.

"What makes you say that?"

"The lyrics. She says she wants more misery cause, like, it makes her happy. But they're opposites. So, she's saying a riddle or something. And the music is kind of aggressive. Like she's forcing something. She's trying to work through it."

Miguel's hand rose.

"Yes, Miguel?"

"I agree with Yessica," said the sweet boy with earnest focus. He turned to look at his peer. "I think it's a riddle too. Or maybe she's just trying to be mysterious, you know? Like saying 'You don't know what it's like to be me, I'm a puzzle.'"

Carey shook her head in awe. Miguel was a kid she could always rely on to step up when someone needed support. He had a big heart, that kid.

Yessica didn't smile, exactly, but she nodded at Miguel, and he turned back to Carey, triumphant.

Emotion surprised Carey with gentle heat in her tear ducts. A new dryness seized her throat. She swallowed and nodded. "Yes, good, those are thoughtful responses. Thank you. The lyrics do seem to contradict themselves. Other ideas?"

A few hands went up, and the discussion continued. Yessica never spoke again, but at the end of the class, she handed in two paragraphs of looping cursive. At the bottom of the assignment, a note read,

"Ms. Marilla. Thanx for the music. —Yessi"

Carey sailed home in high spirits that afternoon. It was a rare day when teaching paid off, but when it did, the feeling was a sweet, sweet reward. As she rounded the last corner toward home, she saw Jim's van parked in front of the small beige house at the end of their block. Jim was up on the roof, constructing what looked like a second story of plywood and aluminum. A younger man, who Carey didn't recognize, was working with him. She'd have to ask Jim about that project. Seemed like an odd time for an extensive remodel.

At home, Etta was propped up in her chair in the living room, a large Diet Coke on one side and a bowl of pretzels on the other. Her rain boots leaned against the corner of the coffee table, ready should she decide to move, unlikely as it seemed.

"Hi, Mom." Carey dumped her purse and keys on the dining room table. Though that particular surface had always been multipurpose, it was unusually unkempt these days, littered with bills, rolls of duct tape, fishing lures, prenatal vitamins, Etta's various medications and ointments, and now, Carey found, as she shifted a few items, a board book of *Are You My Mother?* by P. D. Eastman.

"What's this?" she asked, holding up the book.

Etta didn't look away from her show. "What?"

"Mom. This. What's this?"

Etta glanced over. "Oh, I saw that at the drugstore and had to get it. Forgot to tell you. It used to be one of your favorites, remember? You were such a cutie."

Carey's good mood tightened, hardening slowly into a knot of anger. "When did you buy this?"

"A while ago. Must've been lost under the mail." Etta had not yet realized her transgression.

Carey looked down at the spindly cartoon bird on the cover of the book. Yes, it was a familiar book. Yes, it should be fine for her mother to buy things for the baby. Yes, their lives would soon be filled with baby books, and baby clothes, and baby toys. None of these facts kept her from wanting to rip the book to shreds, hurl it at her mother, and howl.

"You should have asked me." Carey spoke quietly.

Etta chuckled at something on the screen and slurped her soda. She rubbed her feet together and glanced again at her daughter. "How was your day, honey?"

Carey set the book down and covered it up again with mail. She took a breath, steadying herself, unsure if she'd be able to shake off her fury. Her phone buzzed.

"It's Sarah," she said. "I'll be in the back."

"Hey, stranger," said Sarah.

"Hi ..." Carey closed the door to her room and locked it, a petty but needed protest.

"How are you?"

"Okay," said Carey. "I mean, complicated. How are you?"

"Kind of a disaster, actually. Can I see you? Please?"

"Yeah, yeah. Of course. What's wrong?"

"It's just all this fucking water, you know? It's fucking horrible," said Sarah. "Our kitchen flooded last week, and no one will take care of it. Then Joe got laid off."

"Oh no. That sucks."

"I know. And I can sense the fucking axe at my work too. It's coming. I don't know what we're gonna do. Are you still working?"

"Yeah, but probably not for long."

"It's beyond. Like, the world is ending, right? Why isn't anyone saying that? We're fucking doomed, and everyone's like 'La la la, business as usual.' Can we please get a drink? Please? It's Joe's birthday this weekend, but next week there's nothing."

"Sure. I mean, I'm not drinking, but ..." Carey paused, but Sarah's acknowledgment didn't come. "But yeah, I'd love to see you. Whatever's cool."

They agreed to meet the next Friday at six o'clock at Sarah's house, since no one was sure what restaurants or bars were still open or would be by then. Carey hung up with a new heaviness. It used to be that time with Sarah was something to look forward to; now she wasn't so sure. She thought about calling one of her other girlfriends. Maria maybe, or Carolina. But talking to anyone she hadn't seen since her pregnancy news seemed too stressful. She group-messaged instead:

> long time no hear. u girls around?

True to form, Carolina replied promptly:

> at parents house in NC. u still in
> Miami? get out of there!

Carolina was Carey's best friend from high school. While they'd both had good grades, Carolina had proven far more industrious in college, eventually attending law school and rocketing straight into a corporate law gig. For the past few years, she'd been constantly busy, but also highly efficient and pragmatic.

Maria replied shortly thereafter:

> I'm here 2 but we r packing.
> What's up?

Maria had become Carey's friend during her days with Javi. They'd met at a punk show and hit it off right away. She'd been a fixture in Carey's social life for a good four years before she suddenly disappeared into an intense relationship with a software engineer. They married after less than a year together.

Carey texted them her pregnancy news. The next thirty minutes or so brought a veritable shower of baby emojis and congratulations, followed by another twenty minutes of warnings and worries and apologies that they couldn't be closer. To their credit, Carolina and Maria both expressed some understanding that things with Sarah must be difficult, but neither of them had any particular advice. They were both married, with children, and had never had any difficulty in the fertility department. The text chatter ended abruptly when Carolina had to go. Maria offered to come by for a hug before her departure on Sunday. Carey said sure. Maria's response was classic:

> But I'll b back soon anyway they
> best fix this.

That was the difference between Maria and Sarah. Sarah saw through the media's bullshit. Maria didn't.

The next few days were quiet. Carey finally remembered to ask about Jim's project down the street when he stopped by Wednesday night. She stood on the back step and greeted him as he unloaded a sump pump from his van.

"How are you, Jim?"

"Peachy, and yourself?" He set the pump down and stood up, rubbing at a twinge in his back. There was no sarcasm in Jim. He said what he meant. Despite the disaster unfolding around them, he'd had a fine run of work lately, and, what's more, he'd been able to take it. His trouble knee, the left one, had been awful sore last week, and though he wouldn't admit it to anyone, that had spooked him pretty bad. He needed things like knees and shoulders and back muscles to cooperate, especially now, but thank heaven he mainly felt well again. That was all Jim needed to proclaim himself peachy. He smiled at Carey fondly.

"I've been better," she admitted. "Getting more worried about all this."

"Well, I don't blame you for that. Seems it's gonna get worse." Jim didn't like to sound negative, but Carey was bright, and most folks weren't taking this situation serious enough.

Carey nodded. "I saw you building something down the street. What's going on there?"

"Oh, there's a smart one. Enrique asked me to help 'im build a shelter on the roof, cause he sees the house is done for and the traffic north's horrible. He's got it all set up with screens on the windows and insulation. The whole thing. Even built a little outhouse for his generator. He's gonna wait a while and see how things play out. Probably move once the rush is over, before storm season."

"Wow."

"Yeah. It's all illegal, of course, but nobody's checkin' permits anymore."

"So he's stayin' put for now?"

Jim shrugged his bony shoulders while extracting a cigarette from its misshapen pack. He perched the smoke on his bottom lip and let it dangle while he fished out a large silver lighter from his pocket. The lighter's heft in his hand brought back more memories and thoughts than Jim could acknowledge, even to himself. That lighter had seen things. "Can't say, but from the look of their supplies, I'd guess at least a few months."

Carey's mouth watered at the sight of the cigarette. She hadn't smoked or vaped in years, but by some cruel twist of fate, her body suddenly craved tobacco. A fierce craving it was too. She hadn't felt pangs like it before, and she nearly snatched the cigarette from Jim's mouth.

"Hey, Jim, you think I could bum one of those?"

She more than half expected him to say no or to raise an eyebrow at her judgment, given her condition, but not Jim. He shook his head at himself. "Pardon me. I'm ashamed I didn't offer. Didn't realize you smoked."

"I don't," said Carey. "Pregnancy craving, I think? Not a particularly nice one."

He quickly tapped out another cigarette and handed it to her with one of his funny little bows.

Carey took the gift with some embarrassment, but when Jim lit it for her with a smile, and she took her first drag ... good sweet Jesus, that was delicious. She smoked it slowly. Thinking. Some women craved pickles or ice cream or whatever. Her first craving was for something the entire world knew to be poison. Indulging it brought nearly enough guilt to counter her pleasure. Nearly. But pleasure was so hard to come by.

"Jim, could we build one of those additions too? Would our roof hold it?"

"Oh, sure. No problem. We could get you set up nice and tidy."

"I don't know if I could get Ma to live on the roof."

"We could build her stairs."

"You think so?"

"Sure. They'd be rough, but they'd work just fine. All it takes is time and money. Same as everything else."

Smoke curled around Carey. She studied the lit end of the cigarette. If this craving returned, as she suspected it might, she'd have some work to do.

"What's wrong with me, Jim? I'm having a baby, for God's sake. Why don't I wanna leave like everyone else?"

Jim shrugged again and smiled. "Don't know, darlin'." He surveyed the sunken yard. "It's only water."

CHAPTER 7

Sarah lived in a large subdivision about three miles west of Carey. It had once been gated, and that gate had been staffed by a friendly and devoted guard named Eduardo. Eduardo insisted on calling households for permission to open his gate, even if he recognized the visitor, even if he knew them by name, and even if they frequented Flora Bonita more than once a week. He was a man of principles, except when it came to online poker. Then, frankly, he was a man of ruin. In fact, Eduardo had been forced to leave South Florida not because of the rising water, but because of his catastrophic debt. He'd been gone for two months now, and no new guard had been hired. The grounds of Flora Bonita were thus no longer protected, and the gate stood propped open with a cinder block.

The fountains that had once seemed to Carey an odd extravagance were now turned off or broken, and the banks of their swollen ponds were overgrown with weeds and shrubs. A small alligator swam lazily near the entrance road. It didn't seem that long ago that Flora Bonita had been well kept and trimmed, but then, Carey remembered with some guilt, it had been months since she'd last visited with her closest friend. Carey pulled through the open gate and drove over the copious speed bumps along the twisting way to Sarah's house.

Like most other places, Flora Bonita was half abandoned. Several of the identical beige houses with orange tiled roofs were boarded up with plywood. Others were empty and reliant on older iron gratings on the doors and windows. Most cars were missing. Most lawns were wild. Sarah's house still hosted her oversized BMW SUV, but her yard was more lush than typical, and Carey noticed several sheets of plywood leaning against the garage.

The doorbell chimed and Sarah answered. The two women hugged and exchanged compliments. Sarah wore pink lipstick and her black hair slicked back in a pert ponytail, neither of which hid her exhaustion. Carey had never seen her friend so haggard, but she knew better than to say anything. Instead, she said, "Love that lip," as Sarah ushered her into the living room. The white tile floor was miraculously dry. Carey took off her rubber boots and tucked herself into a corner of Sarah's white leather sofa.

Sarah sat at the other end, upright and stiff. She hugged a pale pink throw pillow and chewed her lip. This was a hard meeting for Sarah. She loved her friend Carey. She really did. She admired her and wanted the best for her, and, well, Sarah wasn't proud of the other feelings she felt. It was just that Carey was a bit more free, and a bit careless, and even a bit selfish sometimes, and these personality traits didn't seem to cost her anything. And it felt like maybe they should. Sarah always tried to be careful, and thoughtful, and considerate of how others would feel and respond. But it hadn't made her happy. It had made her anxious and begrudging and often, if she could admit it to herself, lonely.

Sarah tucked a stray wisp of hair behind her ear. "You want something to drink?" she offered.

"No, thanks. I'm good."

"I don't trust the tap water anymore, do you? Joe and I've been drinking nothing but bottled for a month. He's out getting more right now. It's fucking exhausting."

"I hadn't thought of that, but yeah, you're probably right. The taps are bound to be contaminated, aren't they?" Carey absentmindedly rubbed her belly, which at eighteen weeks was just now beginning to show in a way that couldn't be attributed to a large breakfast.

Sarah's bright pink lips arced in a delicate frown. "You should be extra careful, you know. I can't believe you've been drinking tap this whole time."

"Well, yeah, you're right. I've been focused on other problems."

"So, when are you moving?"

It was Carey's turn to frown. "I don't know. We're thinking about it, but so far, we're okay. We have lots of gear, and Jim, our yard guy, is rigging us an emergency shelter on the roof."

"Oh my God, you can't live on the fucking roof, Carey. You're pregnant."

"I know ... I'm pregnant."

Silence padded into the room and sat between them.

Sarah shook her head. This was so like Carey, and it was infuriating. Especially with regards to pregnancy. Here she had the one thing that Sarah most tenderly longed for, and Carey had got it without any trouble. And now she was being careless, reckless even, about it. But that wasn't entirely true, and it wasn't exactly fair. Sarah's shame dropped her gaze to her hands.

Carey waited.

"I'm sorry," said Sarah softly. "It's, you know, hard for me."

"I'm sorry too," said Carey. She reached for Sarah's knee and patted it, unsure how else to comfort her friend. The old strategies of humor and excessive booze weren't easily accessible now.

"There's just so much changing, you know?" Sarah said. "I mean, we blinked and ... how the hell is any of this real? It's the fucking apocalypse."

Okay. So they'd opted for crass analysis of the problem. That was a strategy Carey could get behind. "Yeah," she replied, "for South Florida anyway. So, where are you guys gonna go?"

"I have cousins in New York and an aunty in Oklahoma, of all places. That's where my parents are heading. Joe thinks we should go to Arizona, but that's so far. I can't believe it's like this. I mean, seriously, I'm in shock. And I've been in shock before, but this is totally different." Sarah was beginning to cry now. She reached for a ceramic tissue box on the table behind the couch and pulled several white flags of surrender. She offered one to Carey, but Carey wasn't crying. Carey wasn't feeling much at all.

"You'll figure it out," Carey replied. "It's just life, right? One fucked-up situation after another."

"No. That's not how it's supposed to be."

"Florida has never given a fuck about how things are supposed to be."

Sarah let one laugh escape and blew her nose. "That's true."

"We have fucking alligators in our backyards. How is that part of any plan?"

"Fucking sinkholes ripping up the roads."

"Also not in the plan. I had tadpoles in my bathwater the other week."

"What? Holy shit—not in the plan." Sarah giggled, but then her smile curled south at one edge. "You shouldn't drink that water." She paused. "I just want a baby so bad, you know? I don't even care about moving. I could give a shit if the whole state floats away."

That was the truth, and it helped Sarah to say it. Something loosened ever so slightly in her neck. Sarah knew it was no small thing to have a friend with whom she could share her darkest thoughts. Thoughts that she didn't voice to anyone else. Especially not to Joe.

Carey shifted in her seat. "I know. I know that's what you want. This," she gestured to her belly, "wasn't in my plan."

"Well, you'll name her after me, and then it'll all be okay." Sarah smiled.

"Yep, Sarah Bobby-Jean Shmartzenfartly Marilla. World-famous talent and plan-follower."

Sarah lunged for a hug, and Carey rested against her friend's shoulder. It had been a long time since Carey had hugged anyone but Etta. Sarah smelled like coconut shampoo and makeup, a familiar Sarah-smell that reminded Carey of slumber parties at Sarah's old house, and road trips to Disney World, and gut-busting laughter.

"When are you leaving?" asked Carey, suddenly less aloof.

"I don't know. Soon. Maybe the day after tomorrow? Joe is freaking out."

"So are you."

"Yeah, so am I. So, like, are you really gonna live on your fucking roof?"

"I don't know." It did sound ludicrous.

"You heard about the canals, right? They're digging out Snapper Creek, making it a system. Trying to drain all the water and turn us into some kind of massive Venice. News flash: Canals haven't saved Venice from flooding. They're all deluded, if you ask me."

Carey shook her head. She'd been avoiding the news and its constant oscillations between repair and doom, restoration and destruction.

Sarah continued, "They think they can get things back to normal in like six months. They're so full of shit."

"Yeah, digging up more rock doesn't seem like a good idea right now."

"Right? I mean, think of the sinkholes, for fuck's sake. They don't know what the fuck they're doing."

This was probably an unfair assessment of the hundreds of scientists, engineers, geologists, and oceanographers who were working on the problem, but Carey couldn't bring herself to disagree. Six months would not rebuild the thousands, hundreds of thousands, millions of lives that had already been damaged by the rising water.

"I really wish you'd leave," said Sarah. "I would feel a lot better about going."

"Don't worry, we will. I mean, I don't see how we'll last that long. Especially once the power goes out."

The rest of their conversation roamed over a variety of scenarios to come. Possible escape routes. Potential returns and reunions. Sarah broke down on the topic of pregnancy only once more before the end, and Carey did her best to provide comfort. It was difficult not to resent some part of Sarah's grief. Carey recognized, bitterly, that if she could somehow transfer her pregnancy to Sarah, they would probably both be better off.

At the end of their time together, both women sat drained of worry and words. Carey hugged Sarah again and breathed in that fresh, tropical smell.

"You take care, okay?" said Carey.

"I will. You too. And if you decide that Lil' Sarah needs a different name, I'll work on forgiving you."

Carey began her drive out of Flora Bonita. The sun had set, but the sky still glowed grey and blue. A few blocks later, she hit the brakes for a scrawny kid struggling across the road with a large sheet of plywood. It was Miguel Peraza, her sweet trumpet player. She considered moving on, quickly, as she would for most kids she came across outside of school. They always seemed so flustered at seeing her. But this time she rolled down her window. "Hey, Miguel!" she called cheerfully.

The boy startled and squinted at the car. "Oh, Miss Marilla? Oh, hi!" His smile bloomed bright as jasmine in the gathering darkness.

"Whatcha doin' out there?"

"I'm ... I'm moving a piece of wood." He ran a hand through his hair, baffled by her question, or by his response.

Carey grinned. "Are you boarding something up? You live here?"

"Oh, no, Miss. I'm helping my abuela's friend from church. But yeah, boarding up her house."

"Ah," nodded Carey. "That's so nice of you, Miguel."

The boy nodded at his teacher, unsure how to respond. She nodded back. He waved.

"See you later, Miguel. You take care," Carey said, and waved in response. She rolled up her window, and Miguel watched his teacher's car move away. He immediately wished he hadn't waved. Maybe she thought he was saying goodbye? Or trying to leave? Ugh. So embarrassing. But seeing teachers outside of school felt weird. They didn't seem like people who lived outside school. Maybe not Miss Marilla though. She always felt more real. Like she could be somebody's family.

Carey turned out of Flora Bonita as an evening storm moved in. Its arrival, electric and furious, vibrated even her steering wheel with its roar. Carey cranked Joan Jett and drove slowly through the deluge. Brilliant pink lightning spread like a crown of thorns above West Miami, and Carey's mind strayed to names. She was almost halfway through her pregnancy and hadn't yet let herself seriously consider any names at all. Boy or girl. Sarah was all right, but Joni. Tara. Toni. George. John. Those names were okay. Nice, even. Not inspiring, but then, the students she knew with interesting names generally didn't live up to them. Pleasant, for example, wasn't. And Promise had been caught plagiarizing.

Jett was a good name. She put that one aside—the more androgynous the better. Corey was okay, but then, it was probably too similar to Carey. Maybe something else from music. Harmony? No way. Melody. God, no. How did anyone do this? She probably shouldn't waste her mental energy on names anyway. It was time to schedule another OB appointment, if they were even around anymore. Another flash of electric pink, then a deafening crash of thunder. If any docs were still around, they wouldn't be for long.

The start of May brought Jim pounding on the roof. Carey continued to teach, and children continued to attend class, but even two combined schools couldn't keep her seats filled. Dozens more sinkholes opened across the county and sent even the most reluctant families packing.

There were assistance efforts, plenty of them, underway. The National Guard was brought in to secure and repair infrastructure, assess safety, and provide evacuation support to areas most affected. The Red Cross, as Etta said, were doing their absolute damnedest to help, but they didn't much know what to do with a bunch of holdout stubborn swamp rats and a slow, steady crisis. They were more used to absolute wreckage. Fire and police personnel were depleted, health care was already at a premium, and though the president had long ago declared a national emergency, no one yet felt like that meant anything. After all, there were areas of the country in far worse shape. People could function in South Florida—sort of—and sure, some folks had died, but also the 7-Eleven was still open, so it couldn't be that bad.

Many of the sinkholes were small, opening in areas already abandoned, but a few larger ones made the headlines as they claimed a soul here, a soul there. One collapsed during a church service and took three members of the choir. Carey thought of Gloria Fuentes when she heard the news. Gloria's mother, no doubt, had a spiritual explanation. And yet ... and yet ... that woman's ability to seemingly deny the absurdity of the situation made Carey ever-so-slightly jealous. How pleasant to make any sense of it all. How comforting it must be to have reasons.

On the day that Carey decided to make calls about her next OB appointment, a massive storm brought Miami Beach to its knees. Six bodies were found in the aftermath, face down in the filthy water. It was unclear, officials reported, how they had died, or how long they'd been dead. The storm had perhaps washed them out from somewhere, but little more was said. After all, the casual death of strangers had been a normal, almost expected element of the news for decades. Most Americans were numb and pessimistic after the opioid crisis, the pandemic, rising poverty, failed health care systems, countless mass shootings, and ceaseless climate disasters, not to mention the wars and crises abroad. On and on and on.

A series of recorded messages at her doc's office eventually directed Carey to a hospital still operating in Coconut Grove. Baptist Hospital was also open, as Dr. Paulsen had predicted, but it had closed its obstetrics wing to anyone except high-risk pregnancies. The Coconut Grove facility would accept normal pregnancies, but had no one answering the phone, took no appointments, and was 90 percent reserved strictly for urgent or emergency care. Nevertheless, Carey had been assured by the recordings that they still had a fully functioning maternity ward. She checked and double-checked her calendar and resolved to visit the week of May 13. She remembered her promise to tell Mario about any doctor visits, but she couldn't bring herself to call him. She texted.

u still around?

y what's up?

going to doc on may 17 after work.
might be long line. u can come
if u want

ok

ok u'll come?

y

Unsatisfied, she followed up:

how r u?

fine u?

fine see u soon

Carey reread this thread several times over the next few days, searching for why it made her furious. Probably it was the word "fine." She wasn't fine. She had an alien growing inside her body. There was very little fine about it. Her breasts were sore and swollen, her nipples had begun to darken and enlarge, a thick brown line had appeared running down the center of her belly, and yes, there was now a bump, a definite stretching of her waistband. It wasn't noticeable some of the time, but she needed to undo her jeans' button when she drove or sat for more than a minute. She needed to pee more often. At night, she found she couldn't sleep on her stomach without thoughts of squashing the thing inside her. She started, begrudgingly, to sleep on her back. She dreamt constantly of animals. Mostly scaled creatures, but sometimes those with thick, soft fur that left her weepy and tender when she woke.

Every day, at least three times a day, she craved cigarettes, and though she knew it would be exceedingly bad form to take up smoking while pregnant, she allowed herself a couple puffs on one now and then. Infrequent and careful though this indulgence was, each time the sweet buzz of nicotine gave way to a sickening guilt. She had no business being someone's mother. She couldn't make healthy choices—she couldn't even do pregnancy right.

May 17 arrived, Friday, and Mario suggested by text that they carpool from school. Carey agreed, with the caveat that they pick up Etta on the way.

Mario appeared in her classroom after the last bell, a messenger bag slung over his shoulder and his expression grim. He surveyed Carey's stripped-down classroom but, Carey noticed, did not examine her belly. She clicked on a sump pump in the far corner of the classroom, a new daily ritual made necessary by the rain and a large puddle that grew throughout the day. The majority of the water pumped out at night. Sort of.

"Your room isn't going to last much longer, huh?" said Mario.

"Probably not. Is yours?"

"Mine's on the second floor—it's fine."

"Right, I forgot."

"You ready? What time is your appointment?" He was pacing now.

"I'm ready, but I don't really have an appointment. It could be a long wait, but all the other OB offices I called are already closed."

"Wow. Okay. How many did you call?"

"Four or five."

"Okay, well, if you want, I could try to find another place that still schedules appointments."

Carey shook her head and hefted her bags onto her shoulder. "I doubt it. I'd rather just see if this works."

"Maybe I should take a separate car after all, in case it takes too long?"

"Too long for what?"

Mario frowned, but his gaze caught on her middle, and his feet stopped moving.

"Nothing. It's fine," he said. "Wow. Um, it's, like, growing, huh?"

Carey nodded. They walked in silence to her truck.

On the way to pick up Etta, they made small talk about the flooding, the sinkholes, and the general state of South Florida. Mario made no mention of leaving, so Carey didn't bring it up, but she knew full well it was on both of their minds. They picked up Etta, and in classic Etta style, she pulled no punches.

"Nice to see you again, father of my grandchild," she said, huffing and blowing as she tried to buckle her seatbelt over her substantial girth. It was maybe said in good fun, but Mario, who was now sitting smushed between mother and daughter, didn't find it amusing.

"It's not like I've been hiding," he said.

"Oh, I know, honey. Just giving you grief. You're doing a fine job, as far as I'm concerned. You think you'll stick around?"

"Moooom," Carey groaned.

"Probably not, eh?" continued Etta. "I mean, because of the flood, not the kid. Have you made plans to migrate like the rest of kingdom come?"

Mario shrugged. "Not exactly. We're on a slope. It's not much, but, I mean, they'll probably kick us out at some point."

"A slope?"

"A slope built by bulldozers."

"Sure."

"Can they do that?" asked Carey. "Can they kick us out?"

"Well, they can evacuate people, sure," said Etta. "I don't know if they can force you off your own property. They probably can. It's not like we've ever had any real control. Lord knows they'll have to take me kicking and screaming."

Carey resisted the urge to point out that kicking and screaming weren't likely to result in a better situation.

"So, you're gonna fight to stay?" asked Mario.

"I didn't say that," said Etta. "But I'm not gonna be happy about it if they force us out. That's all. Should be my prerogative. I'd much rather get wet and stay home than end up stuck in some sad apartment somewhere in Georgia."

"You agree with this?" Mario turned to Carey. Her hair, so close to him in the truck cab, caught the afternoon light. It shone soft and brown, and Mario forgot his question before Carey had a chance to answer it.

It should be noted that Mario believed strongly that Carey was a competent adult. He'd known her for a little more than three years, and his opinion of her had never wavered. She was sharp. She was strong. She was not to be crossed. She was well respected among the faculty, and not just because she had good classroom management and comprehensive knowledge of her subject matter. It was something else. Something like his Aunt Fiona, who his mother had never liked. Carey had this way about her that was gentle but sure. Open, but already decided. In short, she was intimidating, but he liked that about her. He just couldn't be sure how to endear himself to her. He didn't want to be creepy or needy; he didn't want to be distant or opaque. He wanted to be, he wanted to be ... less self-conscious around her, that was it. But that seemed impossible, especially now. Mario's brain had a way of running itself in circles, and Carey, it turned out, had a way of being at the center of them.

Carey squeezed the steering wheel. "We haven't discussed it much, but it's on my mind. I'm not happy about leaving either, but we'll do whatever's best for the baby."

"Of course we will," said Etta.

They drove past a series of boarded-up strip malls and gas stations. One drugstore looked like it had been recently looted. Plywood had been torn away from a few of the windows, and packages of food and toys lay scattered around the openings. Nearby, a man wrapped in black trash bags and perched on a stack of palettes nursed a bottle of booze. Carey and her passengers couldn't tell what exactly the bottle was, as he'd hidden it in yet another plastic bag.

It happened to be an expensive tequila. The man had two more of them in his bag. He watched Carey's truck wade past his refuge, its wake fanning slowly behind the rear wheels. He thought of a similar truck his father had driven long ago in Cuba, and the time they'd caught enough fish to cover the whole of the truck's bed. He thought of how his father's smile had always pulled more to one side, the right, and how the texture of his father's hands had changed with age. He drank again. He'd been watching the water rise for a long time now. Like Carey, he wasn't sure what he'd do when it reached him.

Carey and passengers arrived at the hospital and parked in the garage. A skybridge connected them to the adjacent office building, and a neat series of paper signs directed them to reception. Except for the fact that these signs looked temporary, attached as they were with blue tape, it was almost as if the floods hadn't yet reached this building. It was clean, dry, well lit. There were few windows in the hallways. Carey let herself imagine that clever people had engineered some brilliant draining system here for just such an emergency. In fact, the basement and ground floor of the building were closed and deemed hazardous, but no one in their little group discovered that unhappy fact.

The reception area was crammed with people. Most were elderly, some were doubled over with malady or injury, and a few were children whimpering with attendant parents struggling to distract or comfort them.

Carey motioned for Etta and Mario to wait while she met the receptionist. The man behind the counter had pale, sagging skin and looked as if he'd never seen the light of day or consumed a vegetable. His yellowed eyes scanned Carey for the problem and handed her a clipboard.

"Emergency or urgent care?" he asked.

"I need an ultrasound, I think," said Carey. "I'm over twenty weeks pregnant."

"Oh. We don't do that."

"What?"

"If there's no problem, we can't see you."

Carey had expected some kind of hassle or wait. She didn't flinch.

"Isn't this a hospital?"

"Yes, but ..."

"Don't you deliver babies?"

"Yes, it's just ..."

"Then someone can probably do my ultrasound. I can wait."

"Ma'am, you don't understand. I don't make these decisions, and there's a long line ahead of you."

"Of course." Carey smiled at the sallow man and tapped into her most gentle, unthreatening teacher voice. "Your job must be so hard right now. I promise I won't pitch a fit. I'm just hoping someone can have a look and tell me if everything is okay in there. I don't need anything fancy. I can wait as long as you need."

The corners of the man's mouth softened.

Carey sat down on a bench recently abandoned by a grizzled man who now stood talking to himself in the corner. Mario tapped away on his phone. Etta, seated against the far wall, burrowed into one of her crossword books. Carey's sight settled on a young couple fussing over a small bundle in a stroller. Dark half-moons hung under the woman's eyes. The man's face was a startling green. Carey couldn't see the baby, but her mind jumped to various horrors. Maybe the baby was deformed, maybe bleeding. Maybe it had been mauled by a dog or something. Maybe the poor thing was already dead and nothing now but a small grey stone wrapped in blankets, the parents drowning in dark waters of denial ...

Carey pulled her gaze away and shook her head. She'd always had morbid thoughts, but lately, lately she'd begun to wonder if her thoughts were grossly unhealthy.

Another pregnant woman was seated closer to Etta's side of the room. Carey felt an instant kinship, an odd familiarity with the woman simply because they shared a biological status. She wished, earnestly, that she could ask the woman how it was going for her, how she planned to handle the flood. But the other woman's head hung slack to the side with her eyes closed. One hand rested on her giant belly. It was comically huge, almost fake, in appearance. Carey wondered how her skin hadn't split and whether her organs were compromised. It didn't look like she could breathe at all, for God's sake.

Why humans had evolved this way was a complete mystery. Other animals never looked so absurd, did they? But then, everything about humans was ridiculous. Hairless, except for tufts on top and bottom. Upright with bulbous heads. Clothing. Shoes. Electricity. Hair blow-dryers. Q-tips. Carey chuckled. The pregnant woman opened her eyes momentarily, straightening her neck. She closed her eyes again. Maybe, Carey imagined, she was in the early stages of labor. There. That thought wasn't so morbid.

Carey finished her paperwork and returned it to the counter. The receptionist nodded his head but didn't offer any further information. Carey knew better than to ask.

An hour passed, and then another. Carey played games on her phone, listened to music, stood and walked laps around the room, sat again in whatever seat opened. Occasionally she chatted with her mother, Mario, or a stranger. As people were called and disappeared through the double doors, Carey imagined their difficulties, their lives, their homes. She longed, even ached, for her guitar. She made a mental note to stockpile strings before it was too late. On second thought, mental notes weren't reliable these days. She dug a pen from her bag and scrawled "STRINGS" on the back of her left hand.

Nearing the end of hour three, Carey's patience succumbed to hunger.

"Mom, I've got to eat soon; I don't know if I can keep waiting."

"You want me to speak to them?"

"No." If Carey was sometimes rude to service people, Etta was borderline hostile. The last thing they needed was an Etta-style throwdown with the poor guy at the desk.

"I can go get food," Mario offered. "I mean, like, I don't know what's open around here, but I can look."

"That'll take too long," said Carey.

"Here you go." Etta pulled one of her emergency chewy fruit bars out of her purse. "You eat this. Mario needs to stay here in case you get called in. I'll go see about provisions."

"But Ma ..."

"It could be another three hours, honey. No point in arguing." Etta hefted herself up from her seat and made her slow way toward the exit.

Mario scowled. Carey couldn't care less if he felt trapped in the waiting room. She felt trapped and hungry and mad in the goddamn waiting room.

Another hour passed with no action before Etta returned, triumphant and red-faced, hefting a bucket of fried chicken and a two-liter bottle of Sprite. Carey was too cranky and sore to react with any appreciation.

"You forgot napkins," she observed.

Etta, who'd already eaten some on her way over, took it in stride. "Sorry 'bout that. In a rush to get back so I wouldn't miss anything."

"Rushing, what a concept," said Mario, a bit louder than was necessary.

They scarfed down some chicken, gave a piece to a cranky toddler whose mother thanked them like they'd performed a small miracle, and then packed up their garbage. Carey felt her mind grow heavy and her breathing slow with exhaustion.

"Marilla."

Carey snapped awake to a large nurse riffling through some papers while he held the door open with his foot.

"Marilla, Carey," he repeated.

"Here! I'm here!" Carey yanked herself from sleep, stood, dropped her purse, swore, and knocked heads with Mario as she stooped to pick it up. She swore again. Etta, with surprising speed, was already at the door talking to the nurse. He ushered them through the double doors and down a carpeted hallway into a room that used to be a corporate office of some sort. A desk and bookshelves were now tucked in a corner to make room for a portable exam table and a rolling tray of familiar and not-so-familiar instruments.

"Ms. Marilla, how are you feeling tonight?" asked the nurse.

"Fine, but tired," said Carey. She sat on the end of the exam table without being asked and wrestled with the cool fear that she'd probably have to change into a hospital gown in front of Mario.

"I'm glad to hear that," said the nurse. He was busy now on a tablet, ostensibly checking Carey's medical records and not his social media.

Etta and Mario stood to the side in the absence of other seating, an odd couple to be sure. Etta in her rain boots, wide turquoise shorts, bright yellow T-shirt, and red pleather handbag. Her poorly dyed hair and thick silver roots escaped their bobby pins in wisps and curls aplenty. Mario, in his work clothes: grey slacks and a navy button-down. Neat, trim, and slim. Their one similarity was the fish-like downturn of their mouths.

"The ultrasound technician should be here soon, but I need to let you know we can't do a comprehensive exam. She'll just have a quick look."

"Got it." That sounded comprehensive enough to Carey, but Etta's expression soured further.

"What won't you be checking, then?" she asked.

"I should let the technician answer that," said the nurse. He made for the door.

"Wait!" Carey shouted, without meaning to. "No, sorry, I—I just don't see any hospital gown or anything. Am I supposed to get naked?"

The nurse smiled. Mario did not.

"No need, it's not a vaginal ultrasound. You can just unbutton the top of your pants, and we should be fine."

"Oh, okay." Carey's cheeks burned and Etta laughed.

"Sorry, Mario," joked Etta. "No show tonight."

"Mom."

Mario grinned weakly, but shook his head and flushed. There it was. It had been ages since she'd seen it in him, but for a moment, Carey remembered the sweet crush she'd had on him. The flirta- tion. The gentle, shy, even kind person he seemed to be inside. A tenderness brushed lightly through her. Maybe it was her hormones at work, but genuine sympathy stirred her heart. It had to be weird for him, becoming a dad, and so distanced from the process and the mom. It might be disaffecting, even depressing. As if on cue, Mario took out his phone and dove into whatever world he kept there.

They waited. Again.

Eventually, the technician arrived, wheeling a larger cart equipped with a screen and other pieces of tech. Cords dangled off its side. Her name tag read "Diane," and her shock-white hair spread in delicate braids around her head like a labyrinth. Her pronunciation gently suggested her Jamaican background.

"Hi there, Mama. You feeling alright?"

"Yes. I am."

"Good. Okay then, let's see that baby. You lie down and take it easy."

Carey lay back on the table. Etta came and stood near her left shoulder. Mario hung back.

"Are you the proud grandma?" asked Diane cheerfully.

"Yes."

"C'mon, Daddy, you can see this too."

Mario walked slowly around to Carey's right side. Carey reached for his arm and squeezed gently. She could feel his warm muscle beneath the cool fabric.

"This is intense," Carey blurted. "I'm nervous. Are you nervous?" He placed a hand on top of hers.

"Definitely," he said.

A loud, wet farting noise broke the tension as Diane squirted jelly from a tube onto the plastic bag she'd placed over the scanning wand.

"Sorry, but this will be cold," she said.

It was. The jelly slipped and slid across Carey's midriff as the wand searched. The screen on the cart was black and white. Light and dark swirls and masses ghosted here and there with seemingly no order.

Dark thoughts crept again into Carey's mind. This could all be a mistake. The baby might be sick somehow. Maybe she'd never been pregnant at all. Her grip on Mario's arm tightened. Mario rubbed her hand.

Etta gasped.

A bulbous white line and tiny spine flitted on the screen and then off again.

"There we go," said Diane. She typed something on a keyboard, slowed her wand, and went back over the area she'd just covered. Carey felt sure she was pressing too hard. It didn't hurt, but she worried about the baby. Maybe the technician would dislodge something accidentally, or the baby would get suffocated somehow. Could that even happen?

Etta pinched her daughter's shoulder and started to cluck and coo as more white lines emerged on the screen. The profile of a human face appeared.

Carey lifted her head from the table. "Holy shit," she said. "Look at that."

"There's baby, there," said Diane.

Mario's hand pressed harder now.

"Head is there; you see it?"

"Yes," said Carey.

"And there's the spine and the arms. And there are the legs. Looking okay."

"Okay? Just okay?"

"I gotta check more, but so far, so good. Oh fun. Baby's on the move."

The little being on the screen raised an arm and then rolled away. The bright white of its spine slid onto the screen.

"Bit camera-shy," chuckled Diane. She continued to type away on the keyboard and swiftly used the touchscreen to take measurements, snapping screenshots along the way.

"You wanna know the sex now?"

Carey looked at Mario, but he was locked to the screen, unable to look away. "Yeah. I mean, yeah, I guess," she said.

"Okay. Let's see what we got here."

Diane moved the wand on Carey's belly. Two legs arched on the screen. Carey laid her head back on the table.

"Baby girl," said Diane.

Etta whooped. Mario's mouth opened and then shut again without a sound.

"A girl?" asked Carey.

"A girl. See there?"

White, grey, and black shapes moved across the screen, but Carey lost all sense of what they meant. "A girl," she repeated quietly to herself.

The image of a girl child formed in her mind. Dark eyes, dark hair, a quick smile. She ascended a mangrove tree, brown legs dangling, then climbing, then dangling again, strong and limber, wild as the redwing blackbirds she scared from nearby branches.

"Okay, I'm gonna look at her organs now. This is the slow part."

Etta squeezed Carey's shoulder again, and Carey realized she was still gripping Mario's arm, his hand on hers. She relaxed her grip and studied his face. He looked at her.

"A girl," he said.

"Yeah," said Carey. They smiled and released each other.

"I knew it," said Etta. "You've been moody as I was. Had to be a girl." She wiped her streaming face.

"Bullshit, Mom," said Carey. "I'm not moody."

"Ha!" Etta laughed, and Diane chuckled.

"Denial," said Diane. "I like it."

Carey took a breath and watched the screen again. Diane was hard at work.

Several minutes passed in silence, and then Diane said quietly, "Come on now." She typed furiously, frowning and muttering under her breath.

"Is everything okay?" Mario asked eventually. "Does it normally take this long?"

Diane shook her head. "I just need the doc to come take a look at something here. Can't make out what I need to see."

"There's a problem?" asked Mario.

"What's wrong?" asked Etta.

"Just a moment and the doc will have a look. Excuse me." Diane set the wand down on her cart, patted Carey's knee, and exited the room.

Etta shifted into Carey's line of sight.

"What the hell was that supposed to mean?" asked Carey. Her heart stood trembling on the diving board of an unheated pool.

"Could be nothing," said Etta, but she searched the screen, frozen now on some mysterious shape.

"Or could be what?" asked Carey. She jumped, plunging down now into Sarah's cold grief after her miscarriages, the way her friend had hunched over, her shoulders shaking gently at first, then rioting to break free of her body. That drowning despair wasn't Carey's, not yet, even as she swam the cold waters of dread. She pulled herself toward the surface, but found it wasn't there. Maybe the nurse meant there was a problem with the baby, a part missing or malformed. Carey might have brought it on herself. She'd been too ambivalent. She remembered her disappointment and reluctance in the beginning, her resentment even now. If there was a failing, it must be her body's fault. She'd been careless. She flashed to the cigarettes she'd smoked, the beer she'd had, the slamming of the boat up and down as she drove across the waves. Whatever was wrong, whatever came, she knew who she'd blame.

Etta watched her daughter's face. "We're just gonna wait and see. We're not gonna to jump to conclusions."

"I smoked a few cigarettes," said Carey.

"What?" asked Etta.

"I smoked cigarettes a few times. I only puffed, but Jesus, I didn't know ..."

"This has nothing to do with that."

"You don't know that," said Carey.

"I do," said Etta, calmly. "Babies are born every day in the worst conditions you can imagine. You're doing fine. No one is perfect. There's no controlling things like this."

"Things like what?"

"Things like whatever the doc sees in the scan. This is just luck, honey. Dumb luck."

The door opened, and Diane re-entered with an older man with a trim white beard. He had a kind but tired face. His glasses were thick and scratched.

"Hello, Carey, I'm Dr. Leon. Diane would like me to review your scan. May I?"

Carey nodded, unable to speak.

He smiled gently and took up the wand and Diane's seat.

"Right there," said Diane, pointing to the screen. "I stopped there. You see eight?"

"I see. Yes."

The doctor began the scan again and found, swiftly, what Diane had been studying.

"No," he said, "there. You see? There. Six. That's not a problem. No problem at all."

The tension in the room dispersed like so many marbles spilled on the floor. Carey realized she'd been gritting her teeth, and slowly relaxed her jaw.

"He's in great shape," said Dr. Leon.

"She," corrected Diane. "That's wonderful news."

"Ah! She's looking great. Look at that, you see her toes? All ten right there," Dr. Leon offered playfully.

Two tiny footprints appeared on the screen.

"I'm sorry we don't have a good printer for you today. We can email or text you the images. Diane will set that up after she's completed the scan. I've got to run out, several patients waiting, but if you need anything else, Diane will let me know."

"Okay. Thanks. Yeah. Sure. Thanks," said Carey without moving her stunned gaze from the tiny feet on the screen. After waiting so long in relative boredom, she'd been unprepared for the emotional whiplash of the past several minutes. She rubbed the back of her neck.

Etta patted Carey's shoulder, and Carey, for the first time since Diane had raised a concern, dared a look at Mario. He was leaning against the wall now, his right hand gripping a gold necklace she hadn't noticed before. His head was bowed, and his mouth moved as if in silent prayer.

"Okay, we just got to finish up here real quick," said Diane.

She swept the wand again around Carey's belly, asked a few more questions, and texted the photos to their devices. "Now comes the hard part," she said, placing the wand away in the cart and rubbing Carey's knee. "Where are you gonna have this baby? Are you planning to leave Miami?"

Carey found herself nodding. She was staring at the tiny profile on her phone and looked up in a daze. "Yeah," she said, "probably. I mean, if things keep going this way, we'll have to leave."

"Okay, good. Still plenty of doctors just a few hours north."

"Right, that's good to know. I mean, my OB's office is already closed, that's why we're here, so I'm not sure, but we'll probably leave, so ..." Carey's thoughts trailed off.

"We'll be here as long as we can, so you come back if you have any problems. Normally, you're supposed to come in once a month, maybe twice, and then every week when you're close to your due date. Between you and me, it's fine if you don't come that often as long as you're feelin' good and that baby's moving around. You feel her kickin' yet?"

"No."

Diane smiled. "You will soon. Maybe one, maybe two weeks. Like butterfly wings at first."

Etta chuckled. "Ah, I remember that. But you were more of a jackrabbit than a butterfly."

Carey smiled. "Okay, so I'm good to go?"

"Yes, ma'am. But let's do a blood test and a urine test while you're here."

The visit lasted another thirty minutes.

They left the way they'd come, through the makeshift lobby still filled with slumping, leaning figures, heavy eyelids and slack mouths.

They scrunched into the truck, and Carey drove them back to Panther Middle. It was late now, almost ten thirty, and Mario's little black Mazda was the only car left, parked at the edge of the light cast from a single amber streetlight. A perfect reflection of car and lamp rested in the still water that stretched along the length of the lot.

Carey climbed out so Etta could stay put. Mario climbed down and stood next to her, closer than he'd been to her in months.

"Carey, can I say something?" he asked quietly.

She looked up at him and felt something flutter inside her. Not the baby's butterfly wings, something else. Something primal and warm, born of hormones and pheromones and the memory of his body.

"Thank you for doing this," he said. "I didn't think, before, about what it meant."

Carey observed the gentle upward turn of his mouth and the angle of his cheek. The deep brown of his eye color and the late hour meant she couldn't see where his pupils began or ended. They were deep black pools of calm. Instinctively, and almost without knowing she'd done it, she reached for his hands and held them.

He continued, "That was incredible, wasn't it? I think I ... don't know ... I want more than a couple doctor appointments and a conversation, you know? I want to be involved."

A surge of longing swept through Carey's body. Her lips, legs, even her breasts burned with a sudden, overpowering want. She hadn't felt anything like this in months, and now that she did, she was enlivened, even girlish in response. She smiled and squeezed his hand.

He didn't wait but leaned down and kissed her on the mouth, his hands holding hers and then releasing, reaching for her hips and then her back. She kissed him back, gently at first and then more intensely, wanting something she couldn't control or understand. She let her arms hold him.

Their kiss ended soon, but not before Carey's entire being had warmed. She smiled again as their hands came back together.

"That was nice," she said.

"It was," he said. "Can I text you later?"

"Yeah, sure."

Carey climbed back into the truck. She busied herself by undoing her ponytail, redoing it. Checking her phone. Etta said nothing. Carey paused and then put the truck in gear.

"Long night, eh?" asked Etta finally.

"Mom, not a word."

"What? I didn't."

"Just don't."

"He's not so bad."

"Ma."

"Okay, okay." Etta chuckled. "The important thing is that we've got a healthy baby girl on the way, and a healthy mama, and a healthy papa, and a mostly healthy over-the-moon gramma. Could be worse."

They drove home through the drowning city, giddy with their news.

CHAPTER 8

Panther Middle School closed the following week. The official announcement came via text, email, social media, and a robocall. It went something like this:

"We regret to inform you that PMS is closed until further notice. Miami-Dade County Public Schools has suspended all services, in-person and online, district-wide. Because families and staff are largely on the move, it is no longer possible to provide stable support to our students. Principal Villanueva advises all PMS families to stay safe, and looks forward to seeing all students back at school as soon as normal operations resume. Miami-Dade County Public Schools will notify families if there are any updates."

Carey had already removed most of what mattered, but she made one last trip to her classroom to retrieve a few books and personal items. As she drove home that afternoon, sullen with worry about her students, her paychecks, and her career, she stopped in the middle of the intersection of 87th Avenue and Bird Road. A large shape floated in the floodwaters, blocking her turn. Three months ago, there would have been no stopping here. But then, three months ago, there would have been no water. Bird and 87th would have been packed with impatient traffic, horns blaring, drivers threatening Carey's life and limbs.

Carey got out of the truck. The intersection was deserted, except for the black shape and her vehicle. She could have backed up and swerved around it, let it be, but some part of her was sick and tired of obstacles, sick of not having answers, not knowing things, sick of not fully understanding her situation. She waded forward, cursing at herself, and stood over the thing, already regretting her choice.

It was a dead animal. A large one. Probably a Doberman. Its bloated body kept it partially afloat, and its limbs stuck out stiffly like the legs of a morbid coffee table. Its face was submerged, but Carey could make out one white bulging eye, watching her from beneath the surface. The dead eye reminded her of the grouper they'd caught in the Keys. Fish had wide eyes like that, not dogs. She gazed back, unable to pull herself away. A small cloud of minnows swirled around the dog's body and darted behind it, and Carey's mood flipped to curious. The scent of rot kept her from moving closer, but she studied the water at her feet. It was six, maybe seven inches deep, and brown. Sure enough, minnows were investigating her boots, rubbing their noses against the plastic, their bodies whipping in a frenzy of energy.

"I'll be damned," she said aloud. "You're already here."

Something thrashed in the water behind her. She lurched.

"Holy shit!" she shouted, her mind leaping to gator. Giant gator. Giant, starving gator.

But it wasn't a gator. It was an enormous softshell turtle. Its wide, flat shell, at least two feet in length, drove with surprising speed to the far side of the dog's carcass. A snorkel-like snout popped above the water, and bulbous, glittering eyes dared Carey to make a move.

She'd never much liked softshells. They weren't nearly as cute as their more colorful hard-shelled counterparts, and they were infamous for their long, snaking necks and nasty bites. Still, she couldn't deny that she was impressed with this one's size. Probably it had already laid some claim to the dog's carcass and would viciously defend its next meal.

She waded back to the truck and sat for a moment in the cab, thinking about what she'd seen. What it meant. Something about the conquering majesty of nature and the fruitless efforts of human beings to tame the planet. Something about loss and the family that might have loved or left that dog. A grackle screamed and gargled outside. Carey ran her hands along the arc of the steering wheel, rolled her shoulders back, and made an overdue decision. She started the truck.

Back home, Jim was hard at work on the roof. Etta was watching a show at the dining room table, her swollen ankles propped up as usual. Carey busied herself in the kitchen. When she'd finished the dishes and wiped out the sink, she moved to the stove. An hour or so later, the kitchen was spotless, and Etta still hadn't acknowledged her presence.

"Mom," Carey said.

No answer.

"Ma."

No answer.

"Hey, I need to talk to you."

Etta slurped her drink without taking her eyes from the screen. "Go ahead, honey. I've seen this one."

Carey picked up the remote and turned off the TV.

"Hey," Etta protested, "I can listen and watch at the same time."

Carey pulled a chair out and sat down, facing her mother.

Etta sensed her daughter's unease. "Okay. Yeah. Sorry. What's up, sugarplum?"

"I've been thinking." Carey leaned forward.

Etta set her tumbler down on the table. The ice cubes inside it settled.

Carey took a deep breath and continued, "I think maybe we should go."

"They just reopened US 1," said Etta, ready to persuade her daughter that things were improving. "Did you see that? Guess they got their sandbags working."

"No, Mom, listen to me: I'm having a baby, and today, there was this dead dog floating in the road, and I just, I realized it's time. Now that school is closed, there's no real argument for staying. I'll still get paid for a while, they say, so we don't have to rush off, but it's not a good idea to wait for time and money to run out. You know? We can take a week or so to plan and pack, but it just seems really unsafe to stay."

"A week? A week is fast."

"I know. I just think …"

"We should get while the gettin's good."

"Yeah."

Etta took a deep breath and shook her cup of ice. She drank what had melted. "Well, you're probably right. Jim'll be pissed. He did all that work for nothing."

"You want me to tell him?"

"Nah, I'll do it."

"Thanks."

"You betcha."

Carey walked to her room and shut the door. She scanned the piles of clothes and books, the devices and knickknacks that comprised her estate. Her room wasn't as chaotic as it had been when she was a teenager, but it was still a wreck of haphazard crap. Packing would be hell. Jesus. Packing. Maybe they should just leave it all stacked up somewhere high, wrapped in tarps or something, and come back for it later. But how to do that and where to do it were daunting questions. Plus, tarps wouldn't save much in all this wet. And the mold ... Carey shuddered.

She marched back out of her room. "I'm going out."

"Okay."

"We need plastic bins."

"Okay. You need me to do anything?"

"Nope. Just talk to Jim."

"Will do, sure thing."

Carey bought a dozen large bins at the Kendall Walmart, where no doubt some savvy executive had seen an opportunity and devoted an entire corner of the store exclusively to moving supplies. She returned to find Jim back on the roof and her mother watching shows. She set down the first load of bins in the living room and scowled.

"Mom, why is Jim still up there?"

"He doesn't believe me."

"What?"

"I told him we were leaving, and he said well maybe we might not and went back to work."

Carey's scowl deepened. "That's bullshit. We can't keep paying him."

"I know, I said so, but he said he needs something to do and just climbed back up."

"Oh, for Christ's sake."

"Yeah, but maybe it's good to have a backup?"

"No, we're leaving. Look, I got us bins."

"That's great, baby."

"These are yours." Carey gestured to the pile she'd set down next to Etta. "But we can't fit everything in the truck, and I'll bet there isn't a single U-Haul trailer left in all of South Florida. We'll just pile as many as we can in the truck, strap a bunch down in the boat, and leave the rest for now. We'll have to leave the canoe. Maybe Jim can use it. And the furniture is gonna have to stay. It's already half ruined anyway."

Carey went on, thinking out loud, rattling off plans and potential problems. She placed a couple bins in the kitchen and a couple in the living room. Etta didn't move from her spot at the table but watched her daughter quietly, adding only her agreement, and only when prompted. Jim banged away on the roof. Eventually, Carey went back out to get the rest of the bins. She stepped out from under the carport to make eye contact with Jim. He waved at her amicably but didn't stop his work. She couldn't muster the energy to argue with him.

The next few days were spent slowly packing and sorting through the house. Nonessentials were piled in one corner of the living room. Bins of clothing, family heirlooms, tools, and books were beginning to line the already narrow hallway that led to the bedrooms. By the weekend of May 25, Carey was finished with her closet and working on Etta's when heavy rain began to fall.

A text message arrived from Mario. Carey dropped the tangle of wire hangers she'd been working on and checked it.

u around?

yes, u?

can i come by? help u pack?

Mario had taken the news of their departure well. He'd asked, a few times, about their final destination, but Carey wasn't sure yet, and he seemed to take that in stride. He offered a few suggestions but didn't push for any single location. Carey appreciated his patience. Since their kiss, they'd been kinder, sweeter to each other in their communications, but they hadn't been alone together since.

that would b nice

c u soon

Carey navigated through the piles of junk and half-full bins to the bathroom to brush her teeth and remake her ponytail. The mirror reminded her that she was tired, so tired, and gaining weight. She put on a pair of silver hoop earrings, some mascara, and some tinted lip balm. Not much of an improvement, but it was something.

Mario arrived that afternoon as new thunder rolled in. He knocked at the front door, which they hardly ever used, and Carey realized with some embarrassment that he'd never been to her house before. Of course, there was nothing much to see now, just a maze of clutter.

Etta stood up and fussed over Mario, offering him iced tea or coffee, a seat at the table. He politely declined her offers and complimented their progress. Etta thanked him. She sat down again as Jim began to bang on the roof.

"I saw that guy working on your roof," Mario said to Carey. "Should he be up there in this weather?"

"He's not supposed to be up there at all," Carey said. "We told him we're leaving, but Jim does what he wants."

"What's he doing?"

"He's building us a shelter. He insists on doing it. I thought it was a great idea originally, but moving makes more sense." Carey said this with less conviction than she felt. Or, maybe, less than she thought she felt. At her core, she wasn't sure about anything.

Overhead, Jim finished lashing a tarp across the new aluminum roof of the shelter he'd made and surveyed his progress. It wasn't hurricane-proof, not even close, but it was sturdy. The walls were thick plywood on frames of two-by-fours. He covered the outside with cheap plastic house wrap, stapled down. Inside, he'd rolled out slightly used rugs, softening the gravel of the original roof finish. The tarp on the roof was unnecessary, but he wanted to feel a bit better about how waterproof the whole deal was before turning his attention to ventilation and an entrance. A rough door, maybe. They might have something he could use at Home Depot, but he was tempted to rip something off one of the abandoned homes. Supplies were everywhere after all, and just going to rot.

Jim sighed. The shelter, one large rectangular room, was much less interesting than other things he'd crafted, or even that last shelter he'd built with Enrique. He was a little embarrassed by its simplicity, honestly, but he hadn't had much time, and he'd been working mostly alone. (He'd bothered Enrique a few times to help him lift supplies.) The ladies said they weren't gonna need the shelter anyway. They were packing up as he worked, but it didn't feel right not to finish what he'd started. And anyway, plans could change. If life had taught him anything, it was that you never quite end up where you think you will. And even if you don't think at all, you're likely to find yourself redirected from time to time.

He sure as hell hadn't planned on being a yardman in South Florida. Nope. As a boy, he'd wanted to be a pilot, then a soldier, then, in his adolescence, he'd wanted to be rich. And none of that had come to pass. Well, except for the soldier part, but he'd been more sailor than soldier. And he'd never seen battle, thank Jesus. The Navy had been his first step into manhood, but it had been one rude kinda wake-up. So much for dreams of commanding majestic ships of war—turned out he wasn't wired for any of the structure, intensity, or rigor of military life. He was wired for working with his hands, for quiet days, for wide-open schedules, for spending most of his time outside. He hated command structures. He loved people. He hated regulations. He loved projects. The best feeling Jim knew was the one he got when he'd done a job well, helped somebody with a problem, and could knock off early with a beer. That was it. Master of his own time, his own messes, and his own meals.

Sure, this box would do. It would do just fine. He tightened the last knot and slipped down the ladder as lightning popped a mere block away. Thunder followed in a deafening cascade. Jim cursed quietly. Probably better to stop for a bit. Soaked to the bone anyway. Bet Etta would let him dry off inside 'til the worst passed. Stupid to risk injury.

He came around and knocked on the back door. Etta opened it and pulled him in.

"You damn fool," she said and shuffled off to get him a towel.

Jim looked around the house. Shoot, maybe they were gonna move after all.

Carey and Mario entered the living room, each carrying a full bin. Carey was still tired, but Mario's company had improved her mood. He was certainly being a sweetheart, helpful and charming even. She smiled in his direction, but found him standing, startled at the sight of the soaking skeletal man by the back door.

"Jim," said Carey, "good lord, you're a mess! You've got no business out there in this weather."

"Your ma's gettin' me a towel," said Jim grumpily.

"Okay, but seriously, Jim, you've gotta stop working on our roof. We're getting close to leaving, and you're just wasting your time."

"Who's that?" said Jim. He gestured to Mario. Jim looked more like a half-drowned scarecrow than a threat, but he stood up a bit taller and puffed out his chest.

"This is Mario. He's—" Carey paused. "He's the father. Mario, this is Jim. He's basically family."

Mario set down the bin and moved toward Jim. He offered his hand. "Pleased to meet you, Jim. I'm impressed with the work you've done up there."

Carey knew if there was one thing in the world that could endear anyone to Jim, it was good manners. He smiled, baring his few scattered teeth, and nodded.

"Thanks for that. It's rough, but it could keep 'em dry. What's your situation?"

"You mean, where am I living?"

"No, I mean, are you stayin' or goin' or what?"

Carey flushed. "Jim."

"Pardon me. None of my business." Jim hung his head. "Couldn't help myself."

"No, that's okay," said Mario graciously. "I told Carey I'd like to help. I'm hoping to be around, when, um, when I know where they'll be located."

"Sorry," Carey sighed. "I'm trying to figure that out. I am. There's just so much to do, and I need to contact a few friends, and this is just ..."

As Carey searched for how to describe the disappointment, excitement, and flat-out utter absurdity of her situation, a thick pink bolt of lightning struck the local power plant, located two miles away and already partially submerged. Power surged, and then nearly one-third of the Miami-Dade metro area crashed into blackout. Thousands of pupils dilated, thousands of people cursed, and Carey was left, midsentence, in the thick darkness of the storm, with the rumbling of distant thunder and the half-hearted gargling sounds of the dying air conditioner. She laughed, in the distinct way of women who can see clearly, at last, the impossibility of success. "You have got to be fucking kidding me."

"Shit," said Etta.

"Well, that sucks," said Mario.

"Bound to happen, but I thought we might sneak out before it did," said Etta.

"No problem," said Jim cheerfully. "Got the generator hooked up yesterday. Be back in a jiffy."

"Is he for real?" asked Mario.

"God, I hope so," said Carey.

He was for real. Jim had the house running again in an hour or so. It was nearing dusk, but already felt much later due to the storm and outage.

"Best be careful though," he said, once he was back inside. "You'll burn through that fuel quick, and it's pricey now."

He explained, in no uncertain terms, that things like washers, dryers, dishwashers, refrigerators, televisions, and air conditioners would burn the most fuel. Better not to use them at all. The air conditioner could be on its lowest setting for a few hours, maybe, just to take the edge off, but better to use fans. Might be wise to get a small freezer to make ice and then keep everything in coolers.

The evening and the rain plodded on. The carpet in the little pink house was well beyond damp. It squelched and fizzed when stepped on, and the kitchen linoleum stayed slick. Carey dumped salt and sand on the floor for grit and made a kitchen-sink stew of the produce that would go bad quickly. She dished up two extra bowls for Mario and Jim. They hoisted Etta's TV off the dining table to make room for a proper sit-down and ate by candlelight as the rain beat down.

It was a peaceful, if awkward, scene. The candlelight gave each face the glow of health. Jim had turned off the generator for the time being, and now, without the hum and grind of its work, and without the typical sounds of television, and appliances, and traffic, the rain's rhythm on the windows intensified. The earth-rich smells of Carey's stew and its savory warmth in their mouths, combined with the room's rising temperature, relaxed their shoulders. They should have been at ease, but they weren't sure how to make conversation. This was a new kind of quiet in a new kind of gathering.

Etta broke the ice with classic force.

"Good to have some men in this house."

"Ma."

"What?" said Etta. "It is."

CHAPTER 9

By the time Carey Marilla carried the first crate from her house to her truck, South Florida's population had already deflated from millions to hundreds of thousands. The loss of power to a significant portion of Miami-Dade, combined with the lack of sufficient personnel or planning to repair the damage, caused the most significant exodus of people from an American region since the Great Migration. Unlike the Megaquake out west, Florida's floods weren't one and done. People had no option to rebuild. The problem endured, and so the people left. Florida highways were clogged. Gas stations were drained. Trains and planes were stuffed. Even the shoreline was crowded with boats heading north, heavy in the water with the weight of worldly possessions and gallons of slow-draining rainwater.

It had been a bit more than a week since the Marillas and friends began their efforts. Carey, Mario, Jim, and Etta had the truck half packed when they stopped for lunch: more leftover stew. They sat, quiet again and soaked with sweat, in the dark and damp of the house. The single air conditioner they dared to turn on for a few hours a day offered little comfort. It was early June now and close to ninety degrees in the shade. Maybe eighty-five inside. Carey felt all twenty-three weeks of her pregnancy. She used an old Windex spritzer filled with ice water to spray herself down. She aimed it at Etta.

"Go for it," said Etta, her face glowing red and her hair plastered in wet wisps to her head.

Carey sprayed, and Etta groaned with relief.

"You ladies should take it easy," said Mario. "We can finish up without you."

"Sure, but with us, it'll go faster," said Carey. "I need to get the fuck out of here."

Mario nodded. "We're close. Might be ready by nightfall."

"You think?" asked Etta.

"Great," said Carey, unwilling to settle for a different answer. "I say we roll out the second it's done. No point in waiting 'til the morning. Traffic might be better at night anyway."

"Sure," said Mario.

Another silence stretched between them. Yesterday they had decided, against Mario's wishes, that Carey and Etta would travel to Georgia alone. They planned to stop the first place they could grab a motel room and reassess. They'd call Mario then. At that point, they'd choose a place to meet up. True, no one had a sense of what Georgia might look like if it was crammed with environmental refugees, or when they'd even get there, if and when they ran out of gas. So Mario had offered, and pressed, to go with them. Carey resisted, though she lacked good reasons. The best she could come up with was that they'd need to stop often for her bladder or Etta's, and it would be better if Mario went on ahead of them and checked things out. He'd reluctantly agreed.

Jim stretched and sighed. "Y'all are gonna need your patience," he said. "It's gonna take a long time to reach that state line."

"We know," said Etta. "But we gotta try. You should get out too, while you still can."

"Fat lady hasn't sung," said Jim.

"I'm too hot for singing," said Etta.

"I qualify," said Carey, "and I'm taking requests."

Jim laughed. "You ain't fat. You're pregnant."

"You just don't wanna hear me sing."

Jim and Etta both cackled. Mario grinned.

"Sure I do." Jim smiled. "I'm just sayin', there are still other options." He pointed to the roof and winked.

Hard to resist Jim's charms, toothless though they were, but Carey stood up. "Alright, enough yappin'. Back to work."

They worked until sundown, ate dinner, and packed up their trash. Recently, they'd been pitching trash a block down into an overgrown fenced yard. Carey felt vaguely guilty about it, but the property had been abandoned for months now, and run-down before that, and had become the default neighborhood dump long before they started using it.

She locked the doors and checked the windows. Jim and Mario were lashing down the last rope that held the tarps and crates in place on the truck bed. Etta was already in the cab, probably with the air conditioner on full blast. Carey frowned. She'd need to wean Etta off the AC to make their gas stretch as long as possible.

Carey gave awkward hugs to both men.

"Take care," she said. "We'll see you down the line."

Jim blew his nose on a hanky that was no more than a filthy scrap of cloth he kept tucked in his back pocket. Mario gave her a grim nod. Carey had plenty she still wanted to say to him, and more she'd like to hear, but the kindness between them hadn't quite found its way to honesty, and anyway, there was no point in drawing this shit out. She climbed in the cab, slammed the door, revved the engine, threw the truck in reverse, and waited for Jim's signals to back her out. He flagged her in the darkness, lit only by the red of her brake lights. She gently eased the truck back. What with the rain and the load and the dark, she couldn't see a damn thing, but her physical memory of the length of their driveway helped her handle the wheel.

"WHOA!" Jim shouted.

Carey slammed the brakes. Something crashed inside the truck bed.

"What the hell?" Carey rolled down her window to see behind her. Jim was holding up both hands in the unmistakable signal for stop. He was talking to someone behind the truck. Jesus, had she hit Mario?

She shifted to park and stepped out into the rain. Mario and Jim stood on opposite sides of a small figure, bent under the weight of a backpack and a giant duffel bag. Both men were trying to get the figure to move, but it stood perfectly still, face hidden by a sodden hoodie.

"Oh shit," said Carey, recognizing the form. "Yessica? Yessica, is that you? What are you doing here?"

Yessica raised her face in the red light, the line of her mouth set flat and grim. "I came to see you, Miss. I ... need a place to stay."

"What? But where did you come from? How did you get here?"

"I came from home. I walked."

Carey saw that the girl had no rain boots on. She stood in two inches of water in regular tennis shoes.

"Why would you do that? I mean, no. Sorry. No. Yessica, this isn't right. We need to get you home."

"No!" said the girl, loudly at first, and then quieter. "No, Miss, don't send me back."

"But I can't ..." Carey searched Yessica's face. The girl was barely visible in the dark and the shadow cast by her hood, but Carey saw enough. Something was wrong. Very wrong. Carey sighed. "We need to talk about this," she said to the girl. "Let's get you dry."

"Wait, you're taking her with you?" asked Mario.

"No ... Christ, Mario, I can't kidnap her. We'll just postpone. Leave tomorrow or something."

"Mr. Santos?" asked Yessica. "What are you doing here?"

"That's ... a long story," said Mario.

"Not that long," said Jim. "Just human nature."

"Not now, Jim," said Carey.

Yessica turned back to Carey. "You're leaving?"

She shooed Yessica toward the house. "I gotta pull the truck back up and talk to my mom. Can you guys pull some basic provisions out for the night?"

"Sure thing," said Jim.

"Yessica, go wait by the back door, okay?"

"Okay," said Yessica.

Carey shook her head as the girl turned. This was the most emotion and vulnerability Yessica had ever demonstrated, and it was absolutely the worst possible timing.

Etta didn't say a word until they were back in the carport, and Carey turned off the truck. She leaned back, pushed back her hair, and then pulled her hands down the front of her face.

"I take it we're not leaving tonight," said Etta.

"I don't know. One of my students just showed up. She needs shelter. Maybe more than that."

"Okay."

"Okay? That's all you've got?"

"Honey, this is your show. I'll do whatever you need me to do."

"Come on, Mom. I need you to have an opinion about this."

"Okay, I have an opinion. If a little girl needs help, we're gonna give it to her."

"I know."

"Thought so."

They got out of the truck and tramped back inside.

Though they'd been out of the house for less than an hour, the fresh air had woken them up. They'd been free, and now, returning, the interior of the house smelled more poisonous than musty. A burnt electric smell mingled with the putrid scent of mildew. Etta was the first to complain, but Carey felt it too. It wasn't safe. She took a look around and rubbed her growing belly. The little fish inside her was awake and shimmied. Carey couldn't feel those movements yet, but she would very soon.

"Jim, I think you better show us what you've got up there," said Carey. "I don't think I can spend any more time in a rotting cave. We might as well camp out for the night. It's not like we've got a couch to spare. Not a dry one anyway."

Jim, the same Jim who had spent nearly all day packing and loading boxes and supplies. Jim, who was probably in his late sixties or early seventies, and subsisted off little more than coffee and cigarettes—that same Jim—hopped up like a teenager who'd just been offered car keys for the first time. He leapt toward the door.

"You got it, kid!" he said happily. "Just need to get the generator hooked up there. Mario, man, can you help me out?"

Mario, who was significantly younger but unused to manual labor, groaned as he stood. Carey noted, however, that he didn't complain. He just stretched, rubbed his face, and shuffled after the spry old man.

Carey wanted to help, but she knew she didn't have it in her. Instead, she sat stiffly at the dining room table and motioned Yessica to the open chair. Etta already occupied her usual station, feet propped up on a crate of something they'd chosen to leave behind.

Yessica set her duffel bag on the table but kept her backpack on. She sat, coiled and tense, looking at the dark room and the two women across from her. She reminded Carey of an indoor cat just released outside. Ears back, senses alert.

"Are you hungry?" asked Carey.

"Yes," said Yessica without hesitation.

"Okay, well, I've got some leftovers in the truck."

"Thank you." Yessica stood awkwardly.

"I'll get them in a minute."

"Okay." The girl sat back down.

"This is my mom, Etta. Mom, this is Yessica."

Yessica nodded and Etta smiled sadly.

"You've got some trouble at home?" asked Etta.

"Yeah," said Yessica.

"You wanna tell us about it?" Etta continued.

"Not really."

"You live with your dad, right?" asked Carey. "Is he worried about you? We should probably call him and let him know you're here."

"No," said Yessica firmly. "Don't call him, Miss. Please."

"Yessica, I could get in a lot of trouble if—"

"Please, Miss. He's got a bad temper, and lately ..."

"Are you hurt?" Carey asked bluntly. If Yessica had been abused, she'd need to call the police or the Department of Children and Families. She wasn't equipped to handle something like that, least of all now.

"No, Miss, not me," said Yessica. "It's his business, his people. He's got customers that come to the house and, he sells guns and stuff, so ..." She paused. "They aren't good people, Miss. They aren't safe."

The simplicity and innocence of the girl's testimony led Carey to disturbing conclusions. It was possible Yessica's father ran a perfectly legitimate weapons business, but given the state of South Florida, and the girl's obvious fear, it was more likely he ran some kind of black-market operation. Carey's memory flipped back to the men who had chased them in the Keys. The man in the pickup truck with a shotgun. The shark carcasses rotting in the sun. She'd seen it happen over and over again on the news. When society failed, when crisis broke down the existing structures of authority, crime would rise up to take advantage of the gaps. When people grew desperate, some would grow feral. Some would steal and lie and do whatever they could to survive. In a panic, it wasn't unusual for people to brutalize each other to get ahead. Weapons made that sort of scramble lethal.

If Yessica was telling the truth, there was no way in hell Carey could send her back to a potentially dangerous environment.

"It sounds like we should probably call the police," said Carey. Etta's frown concurred.

"No, Miss, please don't. I told him I went with my tía. If he finds out I lied, it'll be so much worse. And he knows the police. I mean, some of them are his customers. Please, please, just let me stay with you. For now."

Carey looked to Etta, but Etta's frown was fixed and offered no advice. Carey's tired mind tumbled through possibilities. The police might still be able to help, but they would likely take Yessica into their custody.

"Where is the tía you're supposed to be with?" asked Carey.

"She already left," replied Yessica. "He doesn't know that. There's no one else. I don't have other family here."

If the girl was lying, the Marillas were inconvenienced, but that seemed like a small price to pay to keep the child from entering the foster care system. A system that Carey knew might bounce her around. A system that was likely more dysfunctional than usual, given the state of things. And that was as far as Carey's mind could take her. She was exhausted. Maybe it was better she wasn't driving for a few hours tonight. Maybe she just needed to lie down.

"You can stay the night," said Carey. "But we'll need to figure something out tomorrow."

She gave Yessica some food. Jim and Mario set up the shelter. They hauled pillows, blankets for padding, sheets, clean water, and food up into the space. Jim had the generator going and two large box fans blowing fresh air in through two makeshift windows. He'd been thoughtful enough to install screens. Carey was the last to hoist herself up the ladder. The shelter smelled of new wood, but that was a welcome, fresh smell after the dank below. It was late, maybe eleven o'clock, when they finally settled into their various sleeping areas. Etta had the only air mattress in a corner to herself. Carey and Mario shared a largish, padded space nearby. Yessica curled into a ball in another padded corner, still wearing her backpack. Jim insisted on sleeping in his van, despite Carey's protests.

"I'm just glad you're dry," he said happily, and closed the door behind him.

It rained hard all night and was still pouring when they woke the next day. The generator had timed out at some point, but there was no sun to speak of, so they didn't desperately need AC. They took turns visiting the bathroom downstairs. The plumbing made new sounds, and the tap water was a faint brown, but the flusher still worked.

Carey and Mario fashioned a kind of kitchen/porch under the edge of the tarps that covered their shelter. It was a small area, but Carey set up her camping stove, which they'd been using frequently since the power cut out. She made coffee. Breakfast was Pop-Tarts from the box, which no one was happy about, except maybe Yessica, who ate them like she'd never seen food before.

Etta eyed the girl over her cup of coffee.

"What's the plan?" asked Mario when they were fed.

Carey bit down. "I don't know yet. I'm figuring it out."

She'd spoken in hushed tones with Yessica early that morning, but the girl was firm: There was no one she trusted to call. There was no one she could stay with. No one at all. And she wouldn't say more about her father's business, except that it was much worse now than it had been before, and her father wouldn't care that she was gone. Carey very much doubted that last part, but she believed Yessica's fear. She knew plenty of fear herself.

Mario studied Carey's face as she moved her fork around her empty plate, scrying some future there. He couldn't read her, but he wanted to. She was so different from him, and so unlike Vanessa, the last girl he'd dated. Vanessa had been cheerful and bubbly and keen to please, probably even conflict-avoidant. Sweet to a fault. Carey was prickly and closed. He couldn't tell if she even liked him being around or if he was in the way. He couldn't tell if her moods were due to circumstance or personality. He couldn't tell if she was stupidly stubborn or brilliantly brave. But he knew she was worth it, somehow. An instinct beyond even their growing biological link told him that Carey Marilla was a force he'd rather have on his side.

Which is probably why he'd stuck around Miami so long. His sisters had both left months ago, taking his mother with them. They were stationed in New Jersey now, living with relatives he hadn't seen in a decade. Maribella, his younger sister by two years, texted him multiple times a day, begging him to join them. He couldn't deny that he wanted to. His family had always been his center, and without them he felt unmoored and disoriented. There was no one to tell him to get a haircut, no one to ask him to drive to Publix for last-minute ingredients for one of Mami's dinners. There was no one to expect him at church, but then, church had been closed for weeks anyway. And now school was shut too. There wasn't much here for him anymore, but there was Carey, and her growing middle, and that shadowy profile on the ultrasound screen. Mario had always felt compelled to do right by the younger and smaller, which is probably why he'd become a teacher and why he understood, in his guts, Carey's impulse to help Yessica.

A knock came on the door. Mario turned toward it. Jim's shaggy head popped inside. "You decent?" he called.

"Yessir," hollered Etta.

The old man came in with two bags of dry goods. "Got a bunch of gas, and water too," he said, his eyebrows arching in triumph.

"Wow. Thank you so much," said Carey. She meant it. She searched for her wallet and passed him several twenties. He seemed reluctant to take them at first but then stuffed the bills in his jeans pocket.

"What's the plan, then?" he asked her.

Carey grimaced. Everyone, except Yessica, stared at her. Why the hell did they keep asking her? She was pregnant, not the goddamned queen of everything.

"I don't know," she repeated. "I guess we'll camp here for a bit, until we can figure out how to make sure Yessica is someplace safe."

Yessica squirmed.

"What do you all think?" Carey asked the room. "I'm not making decisions on my own here."

Mario searched the bottom of his coffee mug, and Etta cleared her throat.

"Truth is, this rain's got the roads near impassable," said Jim. "If you don't go soon, you'll have to float out. Might be wise to get the boats ready anyhow."

"So you're thinking we should go now?" asked Carey. "We can't take Yessica with us."

"Didn't say that," said Jim. "Just saying the roads are bad. Way things look today, you might not have made it even if you left last night."

Carey exhaled audibly. "All our crap won't fit in the boats."

"You'd have to make trips," said Jim.

"To where? We can't make trips back and forth to Georgia."

"Dunno. I guess ..." Jim hesitated, weighing something in his mind. "I guess to wherever you can store things or get a ride."

"We're stuck then," said Carey. "We waited too long."

Jim shook his head. "I don't know," he said. "I'm no expert. It just looks bad out there." He looked again like he had more to say but held it back.

Etta stood and stretched. "Okay, well, we've gotta make this place livable until we can figure out our next move."

This display of energy and decision from Etta was uncharacteristic, and most welcome. Carey's surprise must have shown on her face, because Etta continued, "I mean, we'll be here another night at least, and there ain't no maid service."

Jim's voice burst forth with another idea. "Course there's always my place in the Glades."

Carey smiled at Jim. "That's so generous, Jim, but we're not gonna raid your stash. You've already worked a miracle building this place for us. Thank you. We'll be fine here."

Jim bowed his head, but it was hard to tell if this was a sign of relief or disappointment.

"Can I stay for now?" asked Mario.

His question caught Carey off guard. She faltered. "I mean ..."

"Course you can stay," said Etta, stooping to examine one of the of the bags Jim had set down.

Mario looked to Carey. She nodded. He thanked her with another nod.

So that was that.

"Yessica, can you help me with the boat?" asked Carey.

Yessica jumped up. It was maybe the first time Carey had ever seen the girl without her hood. Her hair was long, dark, and curly, but also oily and slightly matted to her head. It hadn't been washed in a while. None of them had benefited from a hot shower in weeks. Just sporadic scrubbings and rinsings in cold water. Still, it was good to see the entirety of Yessica's face. She was beautiful in the enviable way of the young. No pretense. No effort. Carey thought better than to comment. Best not to make the girl any more self-conscious than she already was.

They shifted several bins and boxes out of the aluminum flat-bottomed boat and then slid it off its trailer and rigged it up. It floated fine in the backyard, which was now at least six inches deep. That wasn't enough water to run the motor safely, so they chained the rig to a fence post. The canoe was blessedly usable. Carey hooked up an electric trolling motor, and adjusted its height so the prop hung just beneath the water's surface. She taught Yessica how to run it up and down 47th Terrace. The girl grinned shyly as she figured out how to turn the boat around, and Carey felt a familiar teacherly pride.

Carey offered several times that day, and in the following days, to talk with Yessica about whatever had happened at home. If there had been a specific incident that caused the girl to run away, Yessica never said. The only thing she would say, repeatedly, was that her dad's business wasn't safe, that the people involved were dangerous, and that she couldn't go back. Carey offered her phone, in case Yessica wanted to call anyone, just to check in, but the girl insisted there was no one to call. Eventually, Yessica began to withdraw and grow quiet at any mention of her home life. In Carey's experience as a teacher, no amount of pressure would get a kid to talk, not in any way that helped, so she eased off, despite the urgency she still felt and the deepening desire to head north.

Meanwhile, everyone was kept busy. Etta and Mario worked on the interior of the shelter while Jim finished a set of crude stairs with a railing. Soon they were easily able to come and go, even with their arms full of supplies. Carey and Yessica developed better systems for the "porch kitchen," including waste disposal in buckets, refrigeration in coolers with ice they made and kept in a small freezer hooked up to the generator, and water filtration. Potable water was their biggest problem. Well, water was. They were surrounded by it, and it fell heavily every afternoon. The hose and house plumbing still worked, barely, but no one trusted it anymore. The heat and lack of air-conditioning meant that they all required more fluids than usual, and Carey drank more than anyone else. Each new hour required more water boiling on the stove or filtering from one bucket to another. They took shifts on water duty and carefully labeled their taps for drinking and washing food versus grey water for laundry and bathing.

To Etta's credit, the interior of their shelter was soon inviting and well organized. She arranged a few lawn chairs around a card table in the center and lit it with storm candles at night. Sleeping areas were kept neat and folded during the day to be easily unrolled when needed. Clothes were kept in duffel bags that perched on top of bedding. Etta fashioned a tote bag of toiletries and personal supplies for each person, which she hung on nails above their respective areas. A few books, decks of cards, and Carey's guitar held places of honor on makeshift hooks and shelves along the wall near the door. A large first aid kit lived atop a stack of spare towels.

Four days after Yessica's arrival, they sat around the card table at the end of supper. Carey leaned back, digesting the mock pot roast Etta had concocted from potatoes, cans of beef stew, and a few yellowing stems of celery. The air was warm, but the fans blew vigorously with the generator still running, and the evening air had already taken the edge off the day's heat. Carey looked at her mother and found her smiling, yapping with Jim about some fishing adventure or another. Mario moved to clear the dishes, but Yessica stopped him.

"It's my night," she said plainly.

"We have nights?" asked Mario, looking to Carey.

Carey shrugged, smiling.

"Everyone else has done dishes except me," said Yessica.

"Okay then," said Mario. "Far be it from me to stop you."

Yessica grinned and piled up the plates.

Carey watched her and wondered, not for the last time, if her baby would be anything like Yessica. Or anything like Mario. Or anything like her. She rubbed her belly and felt a flutter inside. She waited. It came again, a gentle, almost trembling sensation, like a fatigued muscle. But it wasn't a muscle, and Carey knew for the first time, with a jolt of excitement, that her baby was moving.

"Mom," she said quietly. Everyone, instinctively, turned. "I just felt her move."

CHAPTER 10

June in South Florida is an aquatic affair. Each morning is sultry, steaming, and thick with dew. Each evening is storm-ridden. Rain comes heavy and frequent, wearing her bright necklace of lightning and dragging her river-like train across the roads and sidewalks. Typically, to South Floridians, she's an expected and unremarked-upon visitor, despite the glitter and noise. She resents this lack of attention. She loves the limelight. And so, on occasion, she engages in gusting theatrics. She knocks down sheds and garbage cans. She whirls off in a rage. After her most debaucherous nights, Rain sleeps late, hungover and flushed, and the children know it's safe to run out once more into June. Newly released from school, they splash about in front yard puddles and backyard canals, running in flip-flops and skipping in shorts until someone's knee gets skinned. They generate noise and chaos in the unceasing way that children should, thoughtless of Rain's exhaustion. When Rain wakes up, cranky, thirsty, head throbbing from their clamor, she rages again. She pulls on her thunder boots. With her first step outside, the children scramble for shelter. They build blanket forts, raid cabinets for snacks, and play video games until their eyes glaze and their thumbs ache, all to hide from Rain. Normally, Rain ignores them on her way about town. Normally, Rain isn't concerned with the insides of houses. But the summer that Carey Marilla and her mostly adopted family lived on their roof, not much was normal.

The shelter that Jim built held solid through June. Carey had been unable to learn more about Yessica's situation, and so, despite quiet arguments with Mario on the topic, Carey resolved to give the girl more time. It was too late to leave by car or truck anyway, and at least on the roof, they had access to all their own stuff, if not their usual comforts. They could have turned Yessica over to the police, they could have tried to leave by boat, they could have tried to move into one of the shelters set up by the feds, but to Carey, at least, all of these options seemed likely to produce new and unknown problems. She already had problems, but at least these problems were familiar. She knew how to handle them.

Mario and Yessica helped to reinforce and thicken the walls against water and wind with a coating of tarps. Etta kept things surprisingly tidy and spent more time bustling about than she had in years. After all, there was no TV to watch. Carey and Jim took the truck, at first, and then the canoe to stockpile more provisions. Almost every place was closed or empty by now. A single grocery store, two miles away, remained open and provided chiefly canned and nonperishable goods. The store operated out of its second story, its shelves a jumble. It offered the occasional frozen chicken or steak. It seemed to have exactly three employees. This same grocery store, if it could be called that, also sold gasoline, oil, and a variety of tools and fishing supplies. Its all-purpose, small-town chaos reminded Carey of the Keys.

To be clear, it was Carey's fondness for the Keys, and her long history of fishing and exploring the waterways of South Florida, that bolstered her choice to stay. She'd always had a survivalist streak, thin but tough as wire. She didn't hate the idea of living off the land (or water), and if she was completely honest, she held a scrappy sort of love for roughing it. After all, they'd camped in the swamp plenty of times, especially when she was younger and Etta needed a break from the city. Those trips comprised most of her favorite memories, especially when they'd fished for their supper or conquered some unexpected calamity, like a broken motor or raccoons stealing their breakfast. (To be fair, that one wasp-nest encounter was not among her favorites.) Plenty of families from Miami wouldn't know how to fillet a fish, let alone catch one, but Carey knew. Even if the last grocery store closed, she could likely keep them from starving, at least until they found help. And anyway, it was more pleasant to imagine they were on some tropical survival adventure, not hobbling aimlessly through an ecological disaster.

Jim hung around most days, but there were long stretches of time when he vanished, taking his van or borrowing the canoe and forging off west. Carey grew increasingly curious about what exactly Jim had out there in the swamp. Living as they did now, she began to wonder if maybe Jim had been right all along. Better to hoard supplies and buckle down than swarm with the masses of fleeing humans to the north. Hard to know what it was like in North Florida now anyway, or in Georgia or Alabama. Maybe mayhem. At least things were relatively peaceful in Miami. New Miami.

They saw other stay-putters now and then, usually during supply runs—unwashed people with matted hair, long beards, or rough hands. Enrique, the neighbor who had first employed Jim to build a second-story shelter, was still around. He wasn't particularly friendly, but he did offer them a few supplies now and then. Rather, he climbed the stairs and dropped them off unceremoniously at the porch kitchen. A five-gallon bucket. A spare set of boots that didn't fit anyone. Several cans of tomato sauce. It would have been annoying, except that any human interaction outside of the family was welcome these days.

Most folks kept to themselves, but at the store, there might be an occasional chatty exchange with someone who wanted to trade goods or information. Carey didn't like the way people sized her up and shook their heads. She was pregnant, not carrying someone's severed head. But she understood how people might think she was irresponsible. Half the time, she thought that too. Still, there was Yessica to think about, and Etta. Etta didn't want to leave; she'd made that abundantly clear. As for Yessica, Carey's decision to give the girl more time proved fruitless. Yessica seemed happier than ever, and increasingly less inclined to revisit the topic of her home and family.

They lived on the roof for nearly three weeks without significant incident as the water rose around them. Carey watched, and waited, and knew in her bones they'd have to make a move any day. The bottom step of the stairs Jim had built to their shelter was now submerged. The truck's tires were fully two-thirds underwater. They had just finished breakfast and were clearing plates, preparing for another day of pumping water, hand-washing laundry, maybe making a food run, when an engine roared to life outside.

Etta frowned, but Mario opened the door and peered out. A small flat-bottomed boat with an overpowered motor approached the steps. It was occupied by two police officers, wearing wide-brimmed hats and sunglasses. Mario didn't wave or nod to them, but he opened the door wide so that everyone could see.

"Shit," said Etta.

"Mom, it's fine. We haven't done anything wrong," said Carey, making eye contact with Yessica.

"I don't like cops. They never have good news," said Etta. She put an arm around the girl, who sat near her. Yessica shrank into Etta's embrace, her face darkening to a scowl.

Mario backed away from the door as Carey approached it. She guessed this was probably about Yessica, and that would be hard for everyone, but it might also free them up to move at last. And anyway, the girl wasn't here against her will. Carey had done nothing but try and provide for her in difficult conditions. Let them see her belly, Carey thought. Maybe that would buy some goodwill.

The man who wasn't driving tied the boat off on the fence and swung the vessel around as his partner cut the engine. They mounted the stairs without wading in the water and climbed slowly. They were in full gear, bulletproof vests, guns, cuffs. Must be fuckin' hot under all that crap, thought Carey. She backed away from the door as they approached. Everyone inside was seated now, except for her. The first cop stepped onto the top step, still outside the frame of the door, and removed his sunglasses. He was in his fifties, sunburnt, clean-shaven. His presence pierced the atmosphere in the little room.

"Hello there," he said.

"Hello," said Carey.

"This everybody?"

"Yes. Just us."

The man nodded and turned his head slightly toward his partner behind him. "Two adult males, two adult females, one teenage female."

"Can ... we help you with something?" asked Carey.

"No, ma'am. We're on a preliminary visit. There will be a mandatory evacuation shortly."

"Mandatory?"

"Yes, ma'am. This area is unsafe. Everyone will need to leave. Do you have adequate transport?"

"Yes, I think so. When will that be?"

"Soon."

Carey frowned. "Okay. Pardon the question, but what exactly does mandatory mean? Will you arrest us if we don't leave?"

He chuckled as if Carey had said something cute. "Now listen, why wouldn't you leave when we say so? You want that baby to drown?"

Carey clenched her jaw. One careless reference to her unborn infant's death and this man, whoever he was, had pronounced himself the enemy. Every bone in Carey's body confirmed it.

"We're gonna have a look around your setup here," he announced.

"Why?"

"Ma'am, we're just making a safety check."

"Fine," said Carey. "Come in."

They entered the room. Etta stood and offered Carey her seat, but Mario and Jim remained seated. Carey noted that both Jim and Mario were silent, their faces void of any readable emotion. If anyone was in danger, it was them. Police were less likely to find females threatening, especially those who were old, young, or pregnant.

The officers surveyed the room quickly and commented on a few elements.

"Generator for the fans and fridge?"

"Yep," said Carey.

"You still using the toilets in the house?"

"Sometimes."

"Where are you dumping your waste?"

Carey hesitated, then opted for the truth. "Mostly on the roof of an abandoned house, but it was abandoned before the water." She was pretty sure that illegal dumping was still illegal, but hoped they wouldn't fine her, given the circumstances. The man who had entered first, whose badge read "Miller," nodded his consent.

"You have a good setup here. Best one I've seen. Clean and orderly. Almost livable."

"We're doing okay," said Carey.

With one thumb, Miller strummed Carey's guitar hanging on the wall. "Still, it's time to pack it up, folks."

"So the government is ordering us out, as of now?" asked Carey.

"Ma'am, I'm not commenting on the government, I'm telling you to prepare to leave."

"You didn't answer my daughter's other question," said Etta. "Will we be in trouble if we stay?"

Miller chuckled again. "Worse trouble than us."

His partner looked outside again, taking inventory aloud. "Two boats, a truck, a van, a Mazda, and an old Volvo."

"Right," said Miller, "so let's have your names and relations. I assume you're all family?" He took out a small tablet from his front pocket and tapped in a few commands.

"Close enough," mumbled Etta.

Carey and Etta went first, then Mario. "Friend" was the answer he gave for relation. Guilt nipped at Carey's mind. Here was Mario, camping out for weeks on a rooftop, helping out daily, sticking together, simply because of a single night's mistake with a co-worker. He'd earned whatever title he wanted.

Jim went next. Relation: "Employee." Etta corrected him: "Adopted Family." Yessica went last, and Carey nodded to her encouragingly. Maybe this would be the moment Yessica finally shared more of her story. Maybe these policemen would somehow recognize her situation and right it. Even as these possibilities crossed her mind, Carey rejected them. If Yessica ever shared more about her dad's business and her feelings of danger, it wouldn't be with two grown men in uniform, carrying the weapons that terrified her. At least, not these two. Carey attempted to curb these assumptions. The most important thing was Yessica's safety. If she decided to tell the police, that was her decision. Carey waited.

"Relation," prompted Miller. Yessica turned her liquid brown eyes to Carey.

"Niece," said Carey with no hesitation, surprising herself. It was true enough. Plenty of families she knew had "aunts" and "uncles" who weren't related by blood. Yessica grinned her approval. Carey watched Miller key in her response. He probably wouldn't have the time or inclination to cross-check their answers, but he looked up at Yessica again.

"Your parents know you're here?" he asked.

"Yes," Yessica lied, still looking at Carey.

"Alright then," he said. "We're all set here. You got phones and a radio?"

Carey nodded.

"I'd say you've got a week left, tops, so be ready. They'll send out an alert. You'd be wise to start before then." He turned to go.

Carey hesitated but followed them to the door. "How are we supposed to leave if the trucks can't get out? The boats work fine, but we don't know how far they'll take us, or where we should go."

Miller shrugged. "Can't help you there. They might send a convoy of some kind. They might not. There's a shelter over at Coral Heights High School. If you know anybody with a swamp buggy, now's the time to call 'em."

Carey didn't thank him. She re-entered the room with clenched fists. "So much for help."

They listened as the sound of the police boat roared to life. A muffled voice called out a command. The engine noise swelled and then faded slowly in the distance.

Etta fumed. "I don't like them one bit," she said.

Carey didn't answer.

"They came in here and scoped us out and left without offering a single damn thing," Etta continued. "That doesn't feel right."

"They weren't here to help," said Mario. "They were checking things out."

"That's what I mean. It felt like bullshit to me."

"Mom," said Carey, "we don't need help."

"Fair point, but ..."

"She's right," said Jim, rising from his seat. "That safety check business was garbage. They're coming back to steal our stuff. I don't know when, but I'd bet my van on it."

"Comin' back for what?" asked Carey, genuinely confused by the accusation.

Etta gestured to the room, their supplies, inside and out. Jim nodded in agreement. Mario made eye contact with Carey and then looked to Yessica, then back to Carey.

"What? No," Carey protested. "They wouldn't dare." But her mind echoed back to the burnt-out buildings, rotting carcasses, and terrifying boat chase in the Keys, to Yessica's insistence that her father's place was dangerous and that even the police were illegally arming themselves.

Mario stood. "We need to go. We need to get out of here."

"How?" asked Carey. "The trucks won't make it out at this point. We'll just be stranded wherever they stall."

"Then we'll call someone for help."

"How long do you think that'll take?"

"I don't know, but we can't just stay here waiting for trouble."

"No, but we can be ready if it comes," said Etta. She looked to Jim. He nodded. "I'll be back." She went out the door.

"What the hell does that mean?" Carey asked of no one.

Mario walked toward her and reached for her hand. Carey, surprised, looked at him sideways. "What?" she asked.

He opened his mouth, but something in Carey's expression stopped him. He saw she was newly frightened, newly aggressive. "Nothing," he said. He let go of her hand.

"If we're forced to evacuate, you'll have to come with us," she said to Yessica.

"Yeah, I know," said the girl, with a spark of excitement that further irritated Carey.

Carey knew better, but she hissed back, "You're making things very difficult for me."

"Yeah, I know." Yessica's breathing quickened. The girl once again reminded Carey of a cat, this time in position before it attacks, twitching and low and focused with otherworldly intensity. A familiar posture.

Carey sat down at the card table. She leaned her head back and ran her fingers through her hair, damp with sweat. She was tired, and her feet had begun to swell painfully.

Etta re-entered the room with an old purse, a faded black thing adorned with a single sequined and now bedraggled flamingo. She set the bag on the table in front of Carey.

"Yessica, honey, could you excuse us for a minute?"

Yessica's head hung, but she nodded, and without making eye contact with Carey, she stepped outside and closed the door behind her.

Etta slowly unzipped the purse and lowered her voice.

"Now listen, I don't want you to freak out, but I think it's time I showed you this." She lifted a black handgun from the purse.

"What the fuck?" Carey said. "What the hell is that?"

Mario drew closer.

"It's a gun," said Etta.

"No shit."

"I've had it for thirty-some-odd years. I don't even know if it works."

"Jesus, Mom. Put it down! Is it loaded? For Christ's sake." Carey's experience with guns was limited to movies and video games, and that one time in middle school when Jason Markson had shown her his dad's gun case. But Yessica had come to them because she was terrified of her dad's gun business, or something she'd witnessed to do with that business. Who knew how she'd react if she saw this gun here, now? Maybe it was the fear that Yessica would run, or Carey's professional experience with lockdown drills, or maybe it was just that Carey was caught off guard, but the thing might as well have been a live scorpion in her mother's hands.

"No, it's not loaded," said Etta. "Least, I don't think so."

Mario approached the table and lifted the gun. He ejected the clip, pulled the cock back, released it, and then studied both pieces briefly. "It's an LCP," he said, "and it's not loaded. Doesn't look like it's ever been used."

"Of course it hasn't been used," said Etta.

"Are you fuckin' kidding me?" Carey turned on Mario. "You're into guns now too?"

"I'm not into guns," said Mario, frowning. "My dad and older sister were into guns. I learned enough to handle one. That's it." He handed it back to Etta, who flipped it in her hands.

"Okay," Carey chewed her lip. "Okay. This is bad. We can't let Yessica see that."

"Honey," said Etta, "I bought this ages ago, legally, when you were little. It was frightening to be a single mom, and, I don't know, I just needed a sense of security."

"Jesus, Mom. It wasn't locked up?"

"I know," said Etta, shaking her head. "But here we are."

Carey stared at the black metal thing, dormant, seemingly innocuous, and yet. The object in her mother's hand was designed explicitly to kill or intimidate other human beings. It wasn't for hunting or sport. Her mother had owned it all this time—a lethal secret under their roof. Frankly, it freaked Carey out.

Jim broke the silence with the casual declaration, "I've also got a couple shotguns in the van."

"Oh my God," said Carey. "What do you people think we're gonna do? Shoot cops? That's not happening."

"Of course not," said Jim. "But we can let 'em know we're not sittin' ducks, you know, and we ain't gonna lie down and take orders. That's all."

"What does that even mean?" asked Carey. "Hang a sign out that says, 'We've got guns'?"

Jim shrugged. "Something like that."

Carey gaped at him. She gaped at her mom. Etta shrugged too.

"Maybe you didn't watch the same shows I did," said Carey, "but my sense is that the police aren't quick to turn around and ignore people if those people are armed."

Yessica opened the door and re-entered the shelter. Carey moved quickly in front of the table to hide the weapon.

"I could hear everything," said Yessica, defiantly. "I know you have a gun."

"I'm so sorry ..." Carey started.

"I'm not afraid of guns," said Yessica, now meeting Carey's gaze. "I've been around them my whole life. I'm only scared when the wrong people hold them. I just wanted to say, um, my dad's, um, friend ... did this thing where he just kept his old target posters around the yard, like, after they were all used up. You know, on purpose. To scare people away."

Carey thought again of the sharks they'd seen strung up among crude warning signs. The effect was menacing and unsafe. She'd been sure that a closer approach wasn't worth it.

"Okay," she said slowly. "I'm just saying these guys probably won't be scared off that easily ..."

"If they come back for legal reasons, no," said Mario. "But if they show up illegally, it's not a bad idea to let them know we're not going to cooperate."

The boat returned three days later. It came late, around one in the morning, and everyone except Etta was asleep. Etta sat upright and called quietly to the room, "They're back."

Carey struggled into consciousness, Mario leapt to his feet, and Yessica remained asleep, in the blessed way of exhausted children who can rest through nearly anything. Jim wasn't there. He was in his van, parked out front of the house, in what used to be the street but was now just a further stretch of filthy water.

Carey rose and shook Yessica as they heard the motor cut and boots on the bottom of the stairs. She leaned close to the girl's ear to wake her.

"Yessi. Yessica. We need you to flip the switch."

Yessica awoke, registered the news, and lurched out of bed toward the generator. She quickly messed with the wires, yanking and plugging in sequence. Carey grabbed a baseball bat they'd wound with scavenged barbed wire. She stationed herself at the back of the room. Mario held the handgun and crouched behind a chair in the center of the room. Etta, positioned catty-corner, sat in a folding chair at the dining table with her legs wide. She aimed one of Jim's shotguns at the door.

The doorknob rattled, and a fist pounded on the door. The plywood walls shook.

"Open up!"

Mario responded in a voice significantly deeper than his usual tone, "What do you want?"

"It's moving day!" called Miller's voice, unmistakable, but slurred and drunken. Someone laughed behind him, but he shut them up.

"Message received," boomed Mario. "Get off our property!"

"Sir," Miller's voice was falsely sweet, even mocking. "We, um, we still need to do an inspection." More laughter behind him. "Open this door." Miller rattled the doorknob again.

"Go away!" shouted Mario. He was shaking now, the gun visibly trembling in his hands.

"Open this fucking door!" boomed Miller. He kicked at it, but Jim had reinforced it with two-by-four crossbeams.

Carey nodded at Yessica. The girl threw a switch in the corner, and light blazed to life inside and outside the shelter. Music, a deafening carnival of techno beats, blared from two of Carey's old speakers, aimed directly at the door. Yessica handed Carey a megaphone, and Carey shouted into it. "You're on camera, boys! Live feed to the web! We know who you are! Miller. Velazquez. Get the *fuck* off of our property *now*! We're armed!"

A boot slammed into the door, and a volley of curses exploded outside. Carey cranked the music louder. Another slam battered the door, followed by scuffling, cursing, and an engine growling beneath the music.

They waited. A single shot, crisp and silent, ripped through the house near the door and exited through the roof.

No one was hit. Not exactly. No one, that is, except Rain.

Rain had been quietly resting and watching the scuffle below with a vague sort of interest, the way a tired dancer, sitting out a song, might watch another couple argue. She had no cash on this table, no dog in this race. She'd been relaxing, letting her thoughts wander. She'd begun to imagine what damage she might inflict next. And then, she was hit. Smack in her heart. She roared to life, the full force of her electric mind and bass rage rolling off the sea, rumbling toward the little pink cinder block house crowned in plywood, bedecked with floodlights, pulsing with music. If they wanted a fight, she'd give them one.

No one moved inside the shelter. In the aftermath of the shot, they waited, afraid to breathe.

Mario was the first to reset the scene. He lowered his gun. "They're gone," he said.

Etta lowered her shotgun. "Fuck. Been a while since my blood pumped that hard."

A sharp knock came at the door. Mario and Etta raised their guns again.

"Wait!" said Carey. "Wait."

"It's me, goddammit," Jim's voice hollered over the music. "Are you dead?"

Carey waved the guns down and stepped toward the door. It could be a trick. Maybe they had Jim at gunpoint or something.

"You okay, Jim?"

"Fine as frog's fur!"

That was good enough. She unlocked and opened the door, pulled him inside, and peered out into the dark water beyond the house. Nothing. Pink lightning to the east. She closed and bolted the door again. She waved at Yessica to kill the music.

In the silence that came, Etta lit a Coleman lantern. Jim offered Carey a cigarette. She took it and lit up. No one said a word or raised an eyebrow.

"They fucked up the roof, Jim," said Etta. "There. Do you see it?"

"I see it. I'll patch it up."

"What if they come back?" Yessica asked the question everyone was thinking.

"They might," said Etta. "I wouldn't put it past 'em."

Carey took a drag on the cigarette and sat down in a folding chair, adrenaline racing through her system. She looked at Mario, still holding a gun at his side. He was different somehow, shaken and sick. That was understandable. He noticed the gun, too, as her gaze rested on him. He frowned and moved to set it down in the dark corner.

Jim shook his head. "I doubt they'll bother," he said. "There's other camps they can raid without all this fuss."

"Well, that was a brilliant fuss, if I do say so," said Etta. "Must've pissed themselves when the lights and music came on. Wish I coulda seen their faces!" She cackled and slapped her knee.

No one else laughed.

"Miss," said Yessica quietly, "what happens if they come back?"

Carey watched the smoke of her cigarette curling and looping in the dim light. "I don't know."

"Listen," said Jim, "I still got a shotgun in the van. They don't know I'm there. I'll keep watch the rest of the night and let 'em have it if they come back."

Carey nodded but added, "Don't kill anybody."

Jim shrugged.

"You're a saint, Jim," said Carey. "Let's not ruin your record."

"I don't think the law'd agree with you, but sure. What else you folks need?"

Etta yawned, "Nothing. Just sleep."

"How can anyone sleep?" Mario's voice pitched high. His hands shook as he held them out, as if offering a bomb no one would accept. "This is fucked up."

Carey took another drag. "No shit."

"No, this is actually fucked up," he said, still holding the bomb.

"Agreed," said Carey, "but we don't have much choice tonight."

"But we *do* have choices." His voice climbed higher. "We've had them this whole time. What are we still doing here?"

"You know why we're here."

"I don't think I do." His hands flexed and spread. Whatever he'd been holding fell silent and invisible to the floor.

Carey looked at Yessica and frowned. It didn't feel right to have this conversation in front of her, but she could sense Mario wasn't going to back down.

She spoke more slowly, invoking a steadiness and calm in her voice that she usually reserved for students in crisis. "We were all ready to leave, but Yessica showed up and needed our help, so we stayed. We're here because everyone, including Jim, has pitched in and made this place work. We've been okay."

"*That*," Mario pointed at the door, "was not okay. None of that was okay. Yessica, you're old enough to understand what I'm saying. We can't just hang around here anymore. We're messing with guns and police now, and I'm done."

Yessica's face was empty, trance-like. She nodded but didn't speak.

"Don't blame her for this," said Carey.

"You just did," said Mario.

"No, I didn't. I said we stayed. We all stayed."

"I'm done staying." He was flushed, vibrating with rage, or fear, or both. Carey didn't know how to soothe him.

"Okay," she said. "We'll discuss it in the morning."

"Nothing to discuss," he said. "I'm done." He turned his back to her and moved to their bed.

"Okay ..."

Etta had already gone back to bed. She rolled over now. Jim was examining the holes in the roof and wall, or pretending to. Yessica had not moved. Tears streamed down her face.

Carey nodded to her and mouthed, "It's okay." The girl retreated to her bed.

Mario rifled through his belongings, making a show of packing up. Carey sat, smoking her cigarette until it was finished. The baby kicked a few times as if in reminder that she shouldn't be smoking, but Carey's guilt was full up. No more room at the inn.

Out beyond, Rain didn't much care how Carey Marilla felt. Rain was in the business of already too much and more to come. She let down her skirts that night and took position to begin her next and greatest dance.

CHAPTER 11

Mario left the next morning. Jim took him out in the boat and came back alone. Carey didn't ask for details, and avoided conversation with everyone for the rest of the day. She pumped water, cooked meals, played guitar, and sat quietly staring at the garbage floating in the streets and yards nearby. Somehow, the flotsam of a dying city made her feel less of everything.

The water had risen substantially in the last few weeks, and now, in late June, the house beneath them was nearly a foot underwater. Their boots were barely high enough to navigate the drowning space, and the smells of rot and mildew were increasingly hard to ignore. Forty-eight hours after Mario's departure, Carey discovered that the plumbing had finally given up its last ghost, just after she'd used the toilet, of course. Her shit floated there in the bowl, stubborn, vile, going nowhere, and Carey broke down. Mario had been right. This was too much. They had to get out, and now it was too late to tell him. He was already gone.

She could text him or call, maybe. She could apologize and ask him to come back. She could grovel. She should. She should try and repair the damage between them. She climbed back up the stairs and felt, for the first time, the extra weight of her belly as a burden. It was enough to make her pause for breath. All the more reason to move on.

The others agreed without argument. Maybe they sensed that Carey was at the end of her rope, or maybe they just deferred to her because of her pregnancy. Maybe news of the plumbing failure pushed everyone over the edge. Probably the attack of a few nights ago was reason enough. Whatever the case, they packed in silence.

Thus, Carey's third trimester began with a new and bitter hope. Instead of making a run for it in their own vessels, they opted for what, at the time, felt like a more predictable and responsible path. They would head to the local shelter and stay there until they could secure trusted transport to a destination north of the flood. Jim would stay behind, moving to his refuge in the swamp, but he insisted on accompanying them to the shelter and staying with them until they were safely on their way.

They packed the aluminum boat with a few things but moved most of their supplies and belongings inside the rooftop shelter for safekeeping. It was easier now to see how unnecessary the majority of household objects were. Living for a month or so on the roof made baubles and photos and furniture and accessories utterly obsolete. They took with them a few layers of clothing and a few items for hygiene. They brought the water pumps, just in case, and a couple of snack bags. They packed up and stored the generator, fuel, cooking gear, and all nonperishables. Fishing gear was also moved inside the shelter, and they hid Etta's gun well beneath some bedding. Carey gave her spare keys to Jim and insisted that he come and take whatever he needed from the stash any time.

"I'll make sure it's safe," he said. As if she'd asked him to guard it, not to use it.

Carey shook her head, "No, I mean, come and take what you need. If it gets looted, oh well. We'll be fine. Hopefully, we won't need any of this wherever we're headed."

Jim gave a curt nod and spoke to Etta in return. "It won't get looted."

They traveled to the shelter in two waves. Jim took Etta and Yessica first. Carey stayed behind and played her guitar, locked inside their rooftop home, because Etta had insisted. On a folding chair, in the dim light that poured through the window fans, amidst the piles of things that had kept them alive, Carey realized, with some alarm, that it was the first time she'd been truly alone in weeks. Except, she wasn't alone.

The baby inside her was old enough to hear, or so the lone pregnancy book she'd kept had claimed just a few weeks before. She'd given so little thought to the experience of the baby, only to its health and her own discomfort. Now, as she played old songs, she started to wonder if maybe the baby could do more than hear. Could it *enjoy* the music somehow? Could it feel anything like comfort? She began to sing as she played. She hadn't done so, for her own pleasure, since before learning she was pregnant. She remembered playing the piano in her classroom, what seemed like a lifetime ago, but she hadn't sung then. She'd been at work, surrounded by mostly still-dry land, thinking about her problems, or avoiding them.

Now she sang children's songs, thinking of the baby. Then, because she could, she moved on to a few old favorites. Joni Mitchell, Waxahatchee, Fiona Apple. The baby's movements were excited, fluttering, and jumbled inside her. Carey interpreted this as joy. It was a new feeling for her, this connection with the baby, and she surprised herself with tears. She ended with a song she'd made up when she was sixteen. She didn't have lyrics, but she sang the "la la lus" with heart. During this song, the baby calmed, and Carey's blood pressure dropped. So, this was the elusive peace she'd been craving since she discovered tadpoles in her bathtub. Music was still medicine.

She stopped playing when she heard Jim's motor outside, and carefully placed her guitar in its case. Something in her lower back stung as she sat up. She rubbed at it. Jim entered and offered to carry anything else before locking up. Carey asked him to wait. She opened a crate, and then another, until she found what she'd been looking for: several sets of guitar strings and a book of songs. She opened the case again and set them carefully inside.

"More survival supplies," she said.

An hour later, sitting on the prow of the little boat with her belly propped up on her thighs and her guitar case at her feet, Jim at the motor, and the vast new wilderness of West Miami passing slowly by them, Carey was aware, not for the last time, of the bizarre beauty of her life. It was past noon, and the heat of the day lay heavy on her skin like a warm wet towel. It wasn't comforting, exactly, but it was familiar. It was the same summer heat she associated with the Keys, with time off work, with fishing and crabbing trips to the Glades with her mom. She looked out at the yards and streets, now barely definable beneath the water. Fence posts, telephone poles, trees, and traffic signs were now more reliable indicators of where property lines might have been. Trash floated freely and collected in disturbing hazards that Jim deftly avoided. It was all so bleak, except where it wasn't. New crops of cattails and algae grew in and around the abandoned homes. Dragonflies buzzed in the air, and water swirled where mullet and turtles ducked under as the boat approached. Carey looked for alligators and wasn't disappointed. A large one sunned himself on the hood of a mostly submerged ancient Camaro. She caught sight of several smaller gators lazing on hedges. Something about these sights made Carey aware that South Florida would survive. Maybe not with people around, but it would survive.

They arrived at the shelter, and Carey's optimistic mood slipped like a turtle from its log. The shelter was a dismal place. Crowded and loud and dirty and, yes, Carey said it quietly to herself, sickly.

Everyone looked ill, bored, or both. Coughing erupted every other minute from a different source. Sunken eyes and chapped lips surrounded her.

The shelter was located in the second story of Coral Heights High School, a redundant but comforting name in these times. Cleared classrooms were now barracks. Crates of supplies lined the hallways. A kitchen had been set up in one large science lab and a medical facility in another. Toilets were located on the roof of a separate one-story building that could be reached via wide scaffolding. Twenty porta-potties stood there in two neat rows.

It all would have been adequate, even plenty, for the two hundred or so people living there, if there had been janitorial services. But, as far as Carey could tell, there were none. Every surface was darkened by oil and grime. Trash was contained to the appropriate receptacles, but they were all full or nearly full. The smell in the hallways was sour and musty. A lack of comfortable, non-classroom furniture meant that people sprawled on the floor, leaned on boxes, or sagged against doorframes. Most of the cots were half-piled with personal belongings. There was a notable absence of children among the people Carey saw, though there were a few. One five-year-old walked directly up to Carey when he spotted her peeking into a classroom.

"What's your name?" he asked.

"Carey," she said.

"Are you gonna live here too?"

"I think so. For a little while."

"Okay."

"What's your name?"

"Mateo."

"Hi, Mateo. Have you been here a long time?"

"Yeah. This is my room. I share it with those people. And I share my potty too. But I can't share it with you because my old potty got shared too much, and now it's full, and we can't use it anymore."

"Good to know."

"A lot of the potties are too full. You gotta be careful and only use them for number two."

"Right."

"And you gotta wash your hands, but you can't use any soap, you hafta use the lotion, but it makes your hands cold."

"Got it."

"And my mom says it's hot as balls in there, so don't stay too long."

Carey nodded and moved briskly on before Mateo could successfully terrify her further.

They found Etta and Yessica and their bags waiting by a card table labeled, with a sheet of paper and some masking tape, "Registration." The young man who headed the table might have been twenty-two. He had a wholesome, handsome look about him, except that he was sunburnt to all hell.

"Hi there," he greeted them. "Y'all together?"

"We are," said Etta. She didn't much like the sound of this boy's Southern accent. It meant he wasn't from Miami.

"Right. You fill out these papers, and we'll find you a room. I'm supposed to tell everybody that if you got anywhere else to be, we'd appreciate it if you went ahead and got there cuz we're just about outta room here, and there's gonna be a mandatory evacuation soon anyhow."

"If we had somewhere else to be, we'd be there," said Etta.

"Right. You got a wheeled vehicle?"

"No."

"How'd you get here?"

"Boat."

"Yeah?"

"Small boat."

"Alright. That's fine. Y'all have any special needs? Medications, allergies, life-threatening conditions we need to know about?"

Carey was already busy with the paperwork, but she raised her head. "I'm pregnant."

"Sure then." The young man's ears were sunburnt, but their red deepened. Carey had the unsettling impression that he'd never met a pregnant woman before. He frowned and buried himself in the small laptop at his table.

"When is this evacuation happening?" asked Etta.

"And how exactly are you gonna move all these folks?" asked Jim.

"That's unknown as of yet, sir," said the young man. Shifting his focus to Jim, he perked up. He addressed all additional answers to the only man in their group, despite who asked the questions. "We guess it'll be another two weeks or so, but we hear there'll be amphibious transportation."

"Amphibious?" asked Etta.

"That's right. The government has vehicles that can move on land or water."

No one was impressed, a disappointment to their registrar.

They asked more questions about food, water, and toilets. Eventually, another young and imported do-gooder led them to a classroom, gave them locker combinations, and warned them, as Mateo had, about the toilets.

"Just let someone at the desk know if you find one overflowing, and we'll rope it off," she said. "A military truck comes once a week to pump them out, but most of them don't last that long."

"Understood," said Carey.

"Is it a boy or a girl?" asked the worker.

"What?"

"The baby, is it a boy or a girl?"

Carey felt an odd sort of pity for this woman trying to be friendly. "A girl."

"Aw. That's great. I love little girls. You get to dress them up."

Carey shrugged and attempted a smile.

"You got her name yet?"

Carey shrugged again.

"I always liked Amber," said the young woman. "I've got a little cousin called Amber."

Carey wanted to care, she really did. It had been so long since she'd had a real conversation with anyone outside her family. But she couldn't muster a response. The classroom before her had several cots lined up on one side, many already occupied. Desks and chairs were pushed against the far wall under the few high windows. There was enough light but no air-conditioning, of course, and no fans, so the air stood stagnant and thick. There were plenty of ripe, bodily odors, but Carey mainly had grown used to these in the past few weeks.

"If you need anything, let us know," said the young woman, and departed.

"Bit too chipper," observed Etta, plopping down on a cot. "Guess this one's mine. Where you gonna be?" Etta tested the bounce and firmness of the cot. For her part, Etta wasn't that bothered by their new situation. It was cooler in the shelter's large cement building than it had been in their plywood fort. And at least she wouldn't be pumping water through that damn purifier all day and night. That all said, her mind struggled in a net of worries for Carey, the baby, Mario, Yessica, and Jim. She didn't have much worry left for herself, but that was familiar. And anyway, it would be nice, maybe, to have someone outside the family be in charge for a while. Much as she didn't care for officials, generally speaking. At least these cots seemed sufficient.

~~~~~~~

The next few days reminded Carey of that grey feeling she associated with her own adolescent middle school experience—she felt trapped and bored and ever so slightly in constant agitation. She slept poorly. The people around her were miserable too. Jim developed a deep cough to accompany his usual smoker's cough. Etta didn't complain, but Carey noticed that her mother spent nearly all her time away from everyone else, sitting on the roof. Etta had somehow pilfered a lawn chair and a large, broken umbrella. She sat in the shadow of this umbrella or, in the evenings, in the shadow of a giant defunct HVAC unit, with her feet up and a bottle of water resting on a nearby cinder block. She read paperbacks from a tattered collection someone had dumped in one of the hallways, all day, every day. She appeared inside only for meals. Carey questioned her, but Etta's only response was, "It smells like death in there."

Many folks, including Carey, took to wearing medical face masks when inside in an attempt to avoid smells and deter germs. There was no sewing machine, or Carey might have busied herself making cloth masks, as she'd seen her mother do during the early days of her childhood's pandemic. Instead, Carey spent most of her time playing guitar and teaching informal lessons to anyone who needed something to do. Her youngest student was Mateo, who was far too small to hold the guitar properly, but who liked to strum while Carey formed the chords. Her oldest audience was a woman in her eighties, who spoke no English but smiled lovingly and nodded her head whenever Carey played.

On the fourth or fifth day, Yessica came running up in the middle of a lesson with middle-aged Frances. Frances routinely spent more time apologizing than playing, so Carey had been patiently soothing the nervous woman. Yessica was breathless and flushed. Carey instinctively stopped talking and held up her hand to silence the next round of apologies from her student.

"Oh my God! Miss! Oh my God!"

"What is it?"

"Miguel's here."

"What? Miguel who?"

"You know, Miss! Miguel, with the trumpet!"

"Really? Show me."

Carey left the guitar with her student and assured her, several times, it would be okay to continue practicing without supervision. Then Carey followed Yessica down the hall and into the last classroom on the opposite end.

The room was dark and dank, even more than their own, and several of the beds were occupied by reclined figures who coughed or mumbled. Carey hesitated at the door, securing her mask, sure that the level of contagion in the room was high, but Yessica waved her arms near a bed in the corner. Carey moved inside.

Miguel Peraza, the young man whom Carey had so doted on in her classroom, lay ashen in the bed. He had always been thin, but his face, now pocked with what seemed like more than the usual acne, was sunken and angular. He grinned as he recognized Carey, and he tried to sit up, but Yessica laid a soft hand on his shoulder and he reclined again.

"Hello, Miguel," said Carey, with as much cheer as she could muster. She sat carefully on the side of his bed, unsure where his slight body lay under the sheets.

"Hi, Miss," he said, his voice cracking and unfamiliar.

"What's going on here? You're sick, huh?"

"Yeah, me and my abuela have something bad. I should be taking care of her, but I can't do much."

"Of course not," said Carey. "Where is she?"

"Right there," he said, and pointed to the next bed.

A sweet-faced old woman raised her hand in hello and then burst into a frightening coughing fit.

"Oh no," said Carey. "Do you have any medicine? Have you seen the doc?"

"Yeah, I mean, we saw the shelter medic a few days ago. She said it's a bad virus."

"Okay ..." They listened to the room's unsettling sounds, and Carey frowned. "Have you been eating?" she asked.

"I can't really get to the food line that much."

Carey turned to Yessica, but the girl was already on her feet.

Yessica nodded in understanding. "I'll get food." She turned to go.

"Yes, good, anything healthy, but especially soup, or broth, or anything with protein, if there is any," said Carey. "As much as you can carry."

Carey sat with the boy and waited. His breath rattled and crackled. After a few minutes, he slipped into sleep or out of consciousness. Carey gently patted his ankle under the sheets.

Yessica returned with a tray piled high with fruit, bread, and two bowls of noodle soup. They carefully propped up Miguel. Carey held his head with one hand and fed him with the other. On more than one occasion, she wondered if she were endangering the health of her baby by exposing herself to whatever the boy had, but she could see no choice. She wouldn't ignore him in this condition. When she'd finished feeding Miguel, Yessica sat on the side of his bed, while Carey moved on to his grandmother.

The old woman ate far less than the boy, but she ate. By the time Carey had finished feeding her and wiped her mouth gently with a paper napkin, Carey's back was sore, and her arms ached from the awkward posture she'd kept while caring for her patients. The old woman nodded her head in thanks.

"Miss," whispered Yessica a few minutes later, "they're asleep."

"Yes," said Carey. "That's good," she assured her. "They need rest to heal."

"They're going to get better soon, right?"

"I hope so."

"Miss, what about these other people? They need help too."

Carey opened her awareness to the rest of the room. At least four other people looked as ill as Miguel and his grandmother, or worse.

Carey rubbed her sore back. "You're right," she said. "Let's ask what they can do at the front desk."

The strapping young sunburnt man was sympathetic when they described the symptoms and difficulties of the sick people down the hallway, but he shook his head. "We don't have enough staff to nurse all those people, and I don't think we can call an emergency evac unless someone's vitals are really tanking."

"Has anyone checked their vitals recently?" asked Carey.

"I don't know. I mean, the doc can check vitals at the clinic."

"Some of them are too weak to walk to the clinic without help. Some of them can't make it to the food line."

"Jeez," said the young man. He rubbed the back of his neck and frowned. "I mean, sure, I see your point. I'll ask, but I doubt there's much we can do. We're barely keeping the toilets alive." He grimaced at his poor word choice and dove into his laptop to avoid further conversation.

Carey sighed and turned to Yessica. "Go get Jim and my mom. Swing by the clinic for face masks. I'll get more soup."

Over the next few days, they cared for who they could. Yessica paid special attention to Miguel and his grandmother, while Carey, Etta, and Jim ministered to others. Those who they feared needed more than soup and rest, they lifted onto an old book cart and wheeled slowly down to the clinic. There were a few beds set up there, but by the third day, all but one was occupied. The medic, an extremely efficient but equally reserved young woman, expressed heartfelt gratitude when they brought her patients. She provided Carey's team with free Tylenol, fresh face masks, and their own small bottles of hand sanitizer. They asked her directly if she could visit the other rooms with them, but she was adamant that while she could make an emergency visit, when necessary, she could by no means make regular rounds. She had to care for the most severe cases in the clinic, and those required near-constant supervision. She did offer, one day, to check on Carey's baby.

The stethoscope was cool on Carey's skin. Carey focused on the beautiful disk of jade that hung from a simple gold chain around the medic's neck. The color of new leaves, it had delicate lines of darker green running through it, like eelgrass under murky water, or sawgrass in a spring rain.

"Everything sounds good," she said. "The baby sounds healthy. Is it moving a lot?"

Carey nodded and sighed. "Mostly when I try to sleep."

"Yes. Good. Please be careful with all these contagions. We don't want you to get sick. Baby won't like that."

Carey nodded again. This advice was both late and obvious, but she appreciated someone acknowledging her condition nonetheless.

"Is Dad around?" asked the medic.

"What?"

"Is the baby's dad around?"

Carey winced. She hadn't let herself think of Mario in a few days. "No, he ... sort of got fed up with this situation. I can't blame him. I'm feeling that way too. Speaking of which, do you have any insight on our evacuation timeline?"

The medic averted her gaze and shook her head. "No. They don't tell me anything."

"Okay. Thanks. I mean, just for what you're doing here. It's ... needed. Are you from Miami?"

"No. Boston."

"Cool."

They had nothing left to say to each other, so Carey hopped down from the portable exam table and pulled her shirt down. She was big enough now to require a rubber band stretched from buttonhole to button to keep her pants up, but Etta's tops were plenty large enough to cover the rest of Carey's new surface area.

As she walked back to her bunk, Carey let herself wonder where Mario might be by now. In Georgia maybe, or Kentucky, or on the goddamned moon for all she knew. Overall, they'd had little time together, and far less alone, but she acknowledged to herself that she missed him, his quiet and steady presence. In the early morning, sharing a bed, she had sometimes watched him sleep. She could remember the curve under his bottom lip and the gentle curls of dark hair around his ears. She'd allowed herself some tender imaginings, but those felt empty now, or childish.

The shelter provided two charging stations of power strips hooked to a small generator. Carey dutifully kept her phone in operation. She told herself it was so she could call for help if anything happened and she was alone, but now, as she checked the screen, she realized it was really because of Mario. He hadn't yet contacted her. He must be furious.

Other friends had checked in over the weeks. Sarah offered mostly self-absorbed reporting on her own predicament but had, on occasion, continued her insistence, now developed into badgering, that Carey leave South Florida. Maria and Carolina had both landed with family up north for the time being. Carey noted, with bitterness, that Javi, her best friend and lover of several years, never bothered to reach out. Things between them hadn't ended on good terms, exactly, but it was still painful to consider how completely he was gone. He didn't even know she was pregnant. Maybe that was the primary allure of social apps, thought Carey. The ability to know things about people who'd otherwise left your life. The ability to post your status to the universe and imagine someone from your past cared enough to notice. But Carey hadn't had an online presence since becoming a teacher. There wasn't time, and it felt too risky professionally. Plus, if she was honest, she knew Javi engaged heavily with most of the popular social apps, so it was probably best for her mental health to steer clear. And therein lay the truth. She could admit that she both wanted him to know her situation and needed to avoid him.

Arriving at her bunk, she found Jim asleep, Etta nearly there, and Yessica putting on her shoes. It was only two in the afternoon, but from the look of them all, it could have been two in the morning.

"Where are you going?" Carey asked Yessica.

"I wanna check on Miguel and his abuela." Yessica's voice and affect were flat.

"Good, how are they today?"

"Much better. Miguel's walking and stuff. He says I saved his life," Yessica smiled bashfully and shook her head, "but that's not true." The girl and boy had become close friends, and now Carey wondered if there wasn't a deeper affection growing there.

"It's not untrue," said Carey. "You've definitely helped him heal."

Yessi shrugged.

"What are you guys gonna do?"

She shrugged again. "I don't know. Nothing. Just talk and stuff."

Although this response could be interpreted as typical of a tween, Carey knew that in this time and place, it was painfully accurate. There was nothing to do in the shelter. Guitar was fine, playing nurse was necessary, but beyond that, there was only wandering around the hallways, sitting on the roof surfing your phone, or dozing in your bunk. For the first time, it occurred to Carey that they might end up stuck there for weeks, maybe months. She shuddered as she lay down. Stuck. Stuck pregnant. Stuck in Florida or in Georgia or wherever the fuck. Stuck in the muck.

She closed her eyes and listened to her own breathing. Her mind slogged through the mud and the water and the filth. There had to be a way out. A way to a future in which she didn't resent every morning and dread every night. It was past time she grew up and prepared to be someone's mom. She had to find a solution to this unholy mess.

She woke up to Yessica shaking her shoulder.

"Miss. Miss!"

Carey sat up slowly, painfully, dragging herself from murky sleep. "What? What's wrong?"

Yessica vibrated with fear, her voice deep and unnatural. "My uncle's here. He just got here."

"Your uncle?"

"We gotta leave," said the girl.

"Wait, what? Why?"

"My uncle is one of the worst of them, and if he's here, my dad might be here too. If my dad sees me, he's gonna make me go with them. I can't go, Miss. I can't!" Yessica's cheeks were flushed, her aspect feverish.

"But you didn't see your dad, right?"

"No, but ..."

"Would your uncle be willing to contact your dad?"

"What?"

"Yessi, if you want to keep staying with us, if you want to evacuate with us, maybe even to another state, I need someone in your family to give some kind of permission. I've let this go on too long and ..."

"No, Miss." Yessi's voice pitched to a terrified whine. "If you talk to them, I'll be in so much trouble ..."

"I understand that worry, but we could all be in much worse trouble if I don't check in with them."

"No, Miss. Don't talk to him, please. We have to leave."

Yessica's hand gripped Carey's wrist. It hurt. Carey swore and twisted her arm away.

"Yessi, I understand you're upset. I'm not going to send you back to your dad if I can help it."

Yessi bowed her head.

"I promise."

"Okay," said the girl quietly.

"The problem is, I need to know if your family is looking for you. If they've sent the police to find you, anything like that. I could get in a lot of trouble if they are. I should have gone to the police a long time ago."

"No, please," muttered Yessica.

Carey continued. "Listen, it's also possible that your dad has already left the area. He could be long gone. Your uncle might know."

"But what if he's here and he makes me leave?" whispered Yessica, tears streaming down her face.

Carey, still struggling with grogginess from her nap, touched the girl's shoulder gently. There was no doubt in Carey's mind that Yessica's spirit was brighter and healthier now than it had been when the girl lived at home. Carey genuinely had no intention of casually sending the girl back to an environment that she obviously feared. Still, it seemed unethical not to communicate with Yessica's family now that the opportunity had presented itself.

"You're safe," Carey continued. "I want you to stay with us. I really do. You've got me and my mom and Jim all here to back you up. It's just, we're in a very difficult situation." Also known as this unholy mess. "If you're going to stay with us, and come with us wherever we go, it would be better to know that your family is on the same page. That we aren't being hunted by them or the police. I need you to recognize that. I can't go to jail with a baby coming. Can you understand that?"

Yessica nodded but remained silent.

Carey shook her head. "Anyway, we can't hide you from your family members in this shelter. There's no place to go. If your uncle doesn't cooperate, or insists that you go home, we can work to stop that from happening. There are laws that protect children, and there are a lot of responsible adults around here."

Yessica sat down on the floor and pulled her legs up to her chest. She buried her face in her knees and made no further sound. Carey hesitated.

She wanted to help Yessi, she did. There were methods she'd learned as a teacher to reach a kid in distress. She could help her breathe, gently ask questions about other topics, sit and stay with her, be patient. She could make sure Yessica had supervision and a safe place to wait. But Carey didn't do any of these things. She was tired, and sore, and pregnant. She was sick of waiting and comforting.

Later, in the coming hours and weeks, stretching into future years, Carey would blame herself for leaving Yessica's side. She'd badly underestimated Yessica's resolve to never go home. But in that moment, Carey was angry, even furious, that Yessica once again was claiming her limited bandwidth and resources. She couldn't allow that to go on. Enough was enough.

Carey Marilla took a deep breath, wiped the sleep from the corners of her eyes, and rubbed the back of her neck. She pulled herself up off the cot and stood, feeling the weight of her belly on her hips and lower back. Her hopelessness, anxiety, and rage met like three rivers rushing into a new, reckless whitewater.

"Yessi, why don't you go see Miguel?" she nudged. "He'll help distract you. I know he will."

It was early evening now, maybe five o'clock. Etta was reading something. Jim was asleep. It would be dinnertime in a couple hours, and there was nothing else to do but go confront a complete and possibly dangerous stranger about his missing niece. In the middle of a godforsaken shelter, riddled with disease, at the edges of a flooded city. Right. Sure. Nothing to worry about.

CHAPTER 12

~~~~~~~~~

Yessica's uncle wasn't hard to find. Carey asked the Southern boy at registration if anyone with the surname Larges had checked in, and yes, they had, and no, he wasn't sure where they'd gone, but she could try the meal line since they'd asked about it straight away. They. Possibly plural. Usually, Carey wouldn't approach a group of strange men on her own, but given she was in a shelter with plenty of other people around, and given she was in a mood like rushing rapids, she made her way toward the dining area.

In between mealtimes, there wasn't much available, just some coffee, fruit, milk, and a few cartons of cereal. Five youngish men were sitting at a table, hunched over their cereal. Carey pretended to serve herself some coffee and watched them.

They had the swollen, red look of long exposure to the sun. Only one wore a baseball hat, shadowing his face. All were dressed in oversized T-shirts, worse for wear, ragged, and stained. The hair of the man sitting closest to Carey was stiff with dirt or salt. They ate like they hadn't had food in a while, though only one of them was particularly thin. Surely they were just people seeking shelter, like her. Ah, there it was, the frame she needed for the situation. One of these men was the uncle of her student. She switched on her teacher persona and moved toward the table.

The first man to raise his head and notice her was handsome and lean. He took in her face, her boobs, her belly, and his expression changed. He smiled at her and elbowed the man in the baseball cap next to him.

"Mira," was all he said.

Carey nodded her head politely. "Hello," she said, "is there some-one named Larges here? I'm Yessica Larges's teacher."

They were all looking at her now, still chewing, their eyes wan-dering her body. One man, the one wearing the hat, squinted at her.

"I'm her dad," he said. "What do you want?"

Shit. Shit. Shit. Carey steadied her mind and proceeded cautiously.

"I'd like to talk about Yessica, if you have a moment."

"Yeah? Go ahead." He looked down to scoop another bit of cereal, his face disappearing under the brim of his cap.

The lean man nodded suggestively. "What's your name?" he asked.

"I'm Carey," she said, careful not to make eye contact again.

"Carey, that's a nice name. I like that name," he said.

The back of Carey's neck prickled, but she focused on the man who had identified himself as Yessica's father. "If you don't mind, I'd prefer if we spoke privately."

"Aw," said the lean man, "you like Ivan better than me, baby?"

"Shut up, Flaco," said Ivan. He stood and walked around the table. Ivan Larges wasn't tall, but he was thick with muscle. The kind of man, Carey was sure, who could easily overpower any of the others. His walk was heavy and his chin led his gait. She noticed, with some concern, that she couldn't see his belt beneath his untucked T-shirt, or anything that might be strapped there. His face, still shadowed beneath his hat, was cat-like, with high cheekbones and eyebrows that swept aggressive and sharp.

Carey gestured to the next row of tables over, and they sat, not at the same table, but across the aisle from one another. He leaned back on the table behind him, arms crossed, legs wide. Carey sat straight as a pin, official and prim.

"So, what about Yessica?" he asked, as if already bored by the topic.

"I'm wondering if you're aware of your daughter's location."

"What?"

"Yessica. Do you know where she is?"

"Yessi's with her tía. They went to Alabama, or somewhere up there. Schools are closed, you know ..." His tongue sucked on something stuck in between his front teeth.

"Yes. Did Yessi tell you she was with her tía?"

"That's none of your business."

"Okay," said Carey. She took a breath. She'd need to proceed carefully and not reveal that Yessica was here, in the shelter. That could be disastrous. "The truth is that Yessi came to see me when she left home. I tried to convince her to call you and let you know, but she refused, and given the circumstances, I had no other way to reach or find you."

"What?"

"Yessica has been staying with my family, but because school is closed and because Yessica wouldn't share contact information, I had no way to find you until now. She's safe."

"What are you talking about? Where is she now?"

"She's staying with me and my family."

"She's my daughter." His voice rose. "You can't hide her from me." He leaned forward now, elbow on his knees, hands clasped between them, and a vicious calm on this face. Carey felt the bottom drop out of her calm, professional plan. This man was utterly terrifying.

"No. I'm not hiding her at all. That's why I came here, to find a family member when I heard her uncle, or you, might be here. I just wanted to talk about Yessica's safety. We'll be leaving soon, heading north, and I'd like your permission to bring her with us."

"You want to take my daughter with you? Who the hell are you, again?"

"I'm Yessica's music teacher, Carey Marilla."

"You ain't family."

"No, but I care about Yessica. Maybe I could take her to her aunt."

Ivan frowned, but Carey continued. "Her tía, I mean. The one you mentioned."

"My stepsister," said Ivan, but his voice wavered. He wasn't sure. Carey could see he wasn't sure. "Yessi left a note and said she was going with her tía to Alabama."

"Should I contact this tía? Do you have her information?"

"What?" Ivan scowled. His hands squeezed enough to blanch his knuckles. He wasn't a man who many dared to question. "No," he continued slowly, as if speaking to a child, "I don't have her info. I don't need her info. Yessica's old enough to watch out for herself."

"She's thirteen."

"I know she's thirteen." He leaned in closer, and his hands moved to grip his knees. "I don't know what you're after, lady, but you better watch yourself."

Carey met his gaze, steady now. "I'll take care of Yessica."

"Whatever she's telling you is lies."

"I'm sorry?"

"She's a liar. Whatever she told you. She's lying." He was whispering now, but Carey stood. Her instincts, primal and raw, told her with certainty that this man was violent. Not just a gun dealer, or whatever. There was more. He'd hurt people, maybe killed people, and he'd do it again.

"Thank you for your time," she said, and gave a quick nod.

Ivan stood too. "You tell her not to tell no lies."

"I'll do that." Carey turned and walked quickly out of the room, terror rippling through her skin, then her nerves, then her bones. Someone behind her whistled, and someone else laughed.

Fuuuuuuuuck, she thought as her walk turned into a jog, her flesh bristling, her fury amplifying her disgust. She turned toward the reception end of the hall, eager to surround herself with other people, desperate for any familiar face. The Southern boy and the Boston medic were there, thank God, talking and laughing about something on the computer.

Carey sat in a chair along the wall and tried to think. Her blood raced. The baby kicked and rolled. She needed to keep Yessica safe. She needed to think short and long term. She needed to decide whether to alert the authorities that this man, Ivan, was armed and dangerous. But she didn't have any proof, and Yessica clearly didn't want to talk. Worries crowded her mind as she nervously watched the door to the meal area, ready to bolt if the men appeared.

Options, it seemed, were dwindling fast, though there hadn't been many to begin with. Leaving Yessica with her father was out of the question. Carey didn't have any official permission to take the girl with them, but she doubted that Ivan would pursue them. Not if it meant going to the police, and not if he thought Yessica might get him in some sort of trouble. There was no one else to leave her with, no one on the school records that Carey had seen before the closure, no one Yessica would tell her about. This tía Ivan had mentioned sounded like a loose connection at best. That meant Yessica would be with them indefinitely. This thought, though complicated, was of surprising comfort. The girl was moody, but she was also sweet and helpful. She was already a core member of their team.

This all left the questions of where they should go and how soon. The shelter's filth, disease, and crowding worsened every day, but evacuation could still be weeks away. At least people weren't dying. Not yet. Carey bitterly considered that if there were deaths, maybe then the government would be forced to do something. As it was, resources were stretched too thin across multiple national emergencies. One little shelter in South Florida, full of stubborn holdouts, could hardly be a priority when there were actual fires raging elsewhere, and millions of climate refugees scrambling for new homes, jobs, and food.

But now that Ivan had arrived, the shelter had become far more dangerous. Carey couldn't guess if he was staying or just passing through. She needed, at minimum, to make sure that Yessica never saw the man at all. That would be difficult. At least young Miguel was on the mend. Carey could leave the shelter with less worry for his welfare.

Carey wondered again what Jim had set up in the swamp. It might be nothing more than a shack, in which case they'd hardly be better off, but given the structures she'd seen Jim build in such a short time, Carey now suspected he had something a bit more substantial out there. She'd talk to him, see if maybe they could move there for a while. Just until evac was underway. Then they could secure a transport out, maybe contact Mario and figure out where to meet him. In the meantime, her priority would be to keep Yessica hidden and protected. They'd need to move quickly.

She was lost in thought around these plans when someone gripped her shoulder. It was Miguel's abuela, on her feet, frowning and shaking Carey.

"¿Dónde está Miguel?"

"What? I don't know."

"¿Dónde está Miguel? ¿Dónde está la niña?"

Carey made eye contact with the old woman and saw the panic there. "Oh God," she said.

She stood and ran back to the classroom where they bunked.

"Mom!" she shouted at Etta, still reading her paperback.

"What?"

"Where's Yessica?"

"I dunno. She hasn't been in here."

"She was here when I left. How long ago was that?"

"I don't know. Honey, what's wrong?"

"We need to find her, Ma. Now."

"Okay, Jesus. Let me get my shoes on."

Carey didn't wait. She walked briskly down the hall, leaning into every room to check for the kids. She checked the bathrooms. Nothing. The roof. Nothing. She raced to the area where they had first pulled up the boat when they'd arrived at the shelter. A collection of other small boats and Jet Skis bobbed and bumped against each other, but their own boat was gone. It had been locked to the top of a half-submerged chain-link fence near the entrance. The chain, still there, hung slack.

"Damn it," she said aloud.

It was evening now, and clouds piled high and dark to the south and west. It had rained once already and it would pour again soon.

Carey could smell it, fragrant and wicked on the wind. The water stretched, dark and rippling, out across what had probably been a parking lot. It vanished behind the abandoned homes and apartment buildings beyond.

Carey climbed back up the stairs and found Jim and Etta walking toward her down the hall.

"Jim," said Carey. "Did you loan the boat to anyone?"

"Nope."

"Where's the key?"

"You mean for the padlock? It's in my bag in the bunk."

"Can you check?"

They walked at a clip back to the bunk, Carey growing breathless from her efforts.

Jim leaned for his bag and brought it up on his lap. "Oh, hell, is the boat missing?" He rummaged through the bag and came up with a ring of keys. "It ain't on here."

Carey nodded. "Yessi stole the boat. I think she and Miguel are making a run for it because her dad's here and she thought I was gonna send her back."

Etta covered her mouth with both hands. Jim shook his head.

"Lord have mercy," said Jim.

"Let's go," said Carey.

"Go where?" asked Etta. Jim was already pulling on his raincoat and hat.

"We've gotta go find them," said Carey, exasperated. She switched from the sandals she'd been wearing to her own boots.

"We don't have the boat ..."

"I know, Ma!" Carey's voice came hard and bitter. "We're gonna have to borrow somebody else's boat. Let's go."

"Alright, alright."

They dressed as the first thunder sounded in the distance.

"Course it's gotta storm now," said Etta.

"It storms every night, Ma."

"You're right. I'm sorry."

"Don't be sorry, just go borrow a boat."

Etta and Jim went around asking about a boat, while Carey reported the missing kids to the front desk. The fresh-faced Southern lad did not express the level of alarm Carey thought appropriate.

"Aren't you gonna help or anything?" she demanded.

"How long have they been gone?"

"I don't know. Less than an hour."

"That's the thing, see, the police won't help with something like that until it's been twenty-four hours."

Carey's mind lurched with doubt. If she involved the police, then Yessica might be taken away or forced back with Ivan after all. The thought of telling that horrible man what had happened made her nauseous. But if Yessica and Miguel were out there alone, they could be in physical danger. "They're kids," she pleaded, "and they took a boat. There's a storm coming. Can't you call the Coast Guard or something?"

"I mean, the water isn't that deep, and there are loads of places they can pull up or find shelter."

"You've got to be kidding me."

"Look, ma'am, if it makes you feel better, I bet they'll be back in a couple of hours. By morning at the latest. Kids just sneak out sometimes, y'know? Even when conditions aren't the best."

"No, you look, I know this girl, and I know why she left, and she isn't gonna be back in a couple hours."

"Why's that?"

As Carey considered trusting the boy with the truth, Ivan Larges and his crew exited the dining area. With their backs to the registration table, they walked down the hall toward the classrooms at the opposite end, loud and laughing.

"Never mind," said Carey, as another wave of nausea churned in her middle. "You're probably right. She's just on a joyride or something. I'll go, I'll find her myself."

"Right then. Be careful now," said the young man, smiling wide at his victory. "In your condition, you probably shouldn't be out on a manhunt in a thunderstorm."

Carey ground her teeth. She'd like to flip this asshole's table and beat him with his chair, but she nodded politely.

She met Etta and Jim at the end of the hall leading to the makeshift mooring area. They were with a middle-aged man, tall and thick limbed. Carey recognized him as one of the people she'd brought food to a few days before.

"I hear you need to borrow a boat," he said.

"That's right," said Carey.

He nodded. "You got it."

Carey could have kissed him for his lack of questioning. He walked them down, pointed out his aluminum bass boat, and showed them the hatch where the life vests were stowed. He handed them the key. He said he had about a half tank of gas left, and they should use it up cause he didn't plan to run the boat again before evac.

Carey thanked him and climbed down. It took some work, but she fastened one of the larger life vests around her belly and started the motor. Jim was already in the middle seat and working his vest. Etta started to climb down as well, but Carey stopped her.

"You should stay, Ma, in case they come back."

"I don't like this," said Etta. "You stay and I'll go."

"I'm fine. We won't go far. Plus, we'll need room in the boat when we find them."

"How long you gonna be out?"

"Don't know."

"You got your phone?"

"I got it. We're fine."

"Jim." Etta turned the full force of her will on the man. "You be safe."

"Sure thing."

The motor roared. The boat's owner had already unchained it from the fence, and now Etta threw the chain onto the bow. It clanged, and thunder answered, rumbling in the lessening distance. Carey and Jim shoved out to the parking lot lake, and Carey turned them around.

"How you wanna do this?" called Jim over the noise.

"Um. Maybe try the house. If they aren't there, the school? After that, circles, I guess."

"Hit it."

They ran at the highest speed Carey dared go, given the uncertain depths of the water, the rotting obstacles floating and spiking up in their way, the deepening dark, and the approaching storm. It started to rain as they neared the house. They found no sign of the children or the boat and, somewhat surprisingly, no sign of break-in or theft. They ran back toward Carey's school as the rain hardened. Jim used an old bait bucket to bail as they ran. Carey found a switch for a floodlight someone had rigged to the front of the boat, probably for shrimping or frogging.

The school was almost unrecognizable: boarded up, part submerged, all manner of trash and God knows what else floating in and around it.

Carey killed the motor and called out to the kids at the top of her lungs, rainwater falling in her mouth. No answer came. Jim hollered too. They called together. A few pissed-off seagulls emerged from the roof of one of the buildings but quickly resettled, shaking the rain from their feathers and heads.

Carey, her gut heavy with new dread, started the engine again. The city had become a half-sunken labyrinth. If Yessica hadn't come to the house or the school, she could be anywhere. Their chances of finding her in these conditions were terrible at best.

"Damn it," she said aloud and turned back toward the shelter.

They ran in a rough, rectangular spiral around the shelter, until Carey felt sure the motor was running on fumes.

"We've got to head in," she called to Jim through the rain. They were drenched, and Jim had long since stripped off his shirt. In the ambient shine of the floodlight, his skin sagged like a sopping rag off his bones and wiry muscle, though there was more of the latter than you might expect. Carey wondered, not for the last time, exactly how old Jim was, and how he'd come to be such an important part of their lives.

"I can take her out with paddles when this passes," he called back as lightning struck. Another reason they needed to get off the water. "But this don't feel like no normal storm."

"Yeah?"

"She's pissed off, pardon my French."

They made it back and into the shelter without trouble, but also without sign of the kids. As Carey sat on the edge of a plastic chair and peeled her saturated jeans and T-shirt off her body, exhaustion landed heavily on her shoulders and hips. Etta fretted and dried her daughter's hair with a towel, and insisted Carey drink something warm, even though it was still eighty degrees in the shelter. Carey obliged her, and Etta procured a lukewarm chamomile tea and a few sugar packets from the dining area.

"No sign at all?" asked Etta once Carey was dressed again and sipping from her mug.

She shook her head. "I don't know, Mom. Maybe they went to Miguel's house or Yessica's. We ran out of gas, but I'll ask around in the morning, get some fuel, and try and get their addresses. We'll go check again."

"They'll come back," said Etta.

"I don't know. I think Yessi is terrified I was gonna give her up."

"Were you?"

"No. No, I wasn't. And after meeting her dad, it makes a lot more sense why she came to us in the first place. He's a real creep, Ma. If he's still around, we gotta steer clear."

"Well, shit. They're just babies," Etta fretted. "I don't see how they could get that far. Did they take food or anything with 'em?"

"I don't know."

Etta shook her head. "You can't save everyone," she said.

Carey stopped drinking. "What's that supposed to mean?"

"Just what I said: You can't save everyone. You gotta take care of yourself."

Carey set her mug down. Her breath came shallow as a sleeping demon awoke in her voice and posture. Enflamed with guilt, the demon spoke. "You think I don't know that? I'm doing every goddamn thing I can. I don't see you making any grand plans. Jesus Christ, I'm not gonna abandon two children to the fucking elements just because you've suddenly decided it's too hard on me. You're the one who thought this whole apocalypse was just some misunderstanding. You're the one who wanted to stay put while the fucking sky fell down."

Etta didn't say a word. She waited.

"You think I don't want to leave?" Carey's hands shook as she gestured. "You think I want to stay in a fucking filthy high school bunker surrounded by sick strangers and sociopaths? You think I want to have a baby *here*? Maybe you think I'm afraid of heading north and realizing that our whole fucking world is gone and we have to start the fuck over? I'm not afraid of that. It's already happened."

"You done yet?"

"No, I'm not done. Don't tell me who I can save. You wanna do something? Save your own ass."

Etta pursed her lips. She watched her daughter's anger boil over with the steady eyes of decades-long experience. She saw Carey the fifteen-year-old screaming about the injustice of her curfew, she saw Carey the toddler falling apart in a grocery cart because she refused to nap, and she saw Carey the grown woman, pregnant and strung out with worry about children who weren't even hers. She knew her daughter's will, and her rage, and she knew how to handle her. Etta didn't fight back. She shook her head, like those seagulls in the rain, and left Carey alone with her tea and her temper.

CHAPTER 13

Rain didn't let up. She kept at it hard for two whole days, making sure every search for the children met with near-impossible conditions. It wasn't that she wanted them lost—she couldn't care less about two scrawny kids in a boat—it was just that she was sick and tired of containing her power. She would not be subdued. She would cavort with whomever, whenever she wanted. Ocean, Bay, Swamp, Lake, River, Canal. Trees and Grasses. They could all have a turn, a taste, a furious kiss, but none of them would hold her. Not anymore. Not if she could have them all and still spill herself across the sunken wilds.

Carey convinced the staff of the shelter to give her more gas for the boat. Jim and the boat's owner went out, Etta and Carey went out, Carey and Jim went out. Every trip resulted in nothing but less hope. After twenty-four hours, Carey set aside her hesitations and decided it was time to notify the police. There were risks on all sides. The cops might inquire about Yessica's family and figure out that something was amiss. Worse, Ivan, who might be lurking in the shelter somewhere, could find out that Carey had lost track of Yessica and use this against them somehow, even though he'd obviously lost track of her first. And then there was the memory of Miller and his crony, and the corruption that could plague them once the authorities were involved. But Carey's greatest fear was simply that Yessica and Miguel were lost and in danger. This fear surpassed the rest, so she approached registration again. The young man at the desk told her he didn't "imagine the police would be able to do much, swamped as they were. Ha ha. No pun intended ..."

Carey hit the desk with her palm. "You aren't listening to me. I'm not reporting kids skipping class or sneaking off to the mall. I'm reporting two young people who are out in a fucking wasteland, in dangerous weather, in a small boat they barely know how to control. The last time I spoke to cops, it didn't go well, but I need help, so I'm asking you to contact the police, *now*."

The boy's sunburn was now peeling off his forehead. He frowned and scratched at it. "Listen, I'll do what I can. I'll let them know. We're in the business of helping people, in case you hadn't noticed, and we've been notified that evacuations will begin imminently, so I've got lots of extra work."

Carey stood still in front of the boy, taking long slow breaths. Maybe he was tapped out. Maybe he was a control freak who didn't like to be told what to do. Maybe he was part dead inside. Whatever the case, she could see she wouldn't reach him.

Carey returned to her bunk and paced, waiting for the latest search crew to return, anticipating another sleepless night. As she paced, she whispered to Yessica. "Don't do this," she said over and over again. "Just come back now, girl. It's time to come back."

Etta and Jim returned with no news. Carey wept in her cot that night and dreamt of fishing. Fishing in the Keys, and then in the Glades, and then back on the sea and in a storm. Their little boat pitched in the wind, and Carey knew she should head in, but her line was in the water, her line was in the water. Just a few minutes more.

The following morning, they were notified that several amphibious vehicles would be arriving over the next twenty-four hours and begin transporting refugees. People in the shelter were thrilled. There was a cheerful buzz in the hallways and a frenzy of packing.

Everyone felt flush with new energy. Everyone except Carey, Etta, Jim, and Miguel's grandmother.

Later that day, Miguel's abuela collapsed on her way to the toilets, struck down by the shock and stress of her missing grandson. She was emergency evacuated during a pause in the rain. They hooked her up to oxygen and an IV as they wheeled her out of the facility and lifted her onto a police boat.

Carey was relieved to see it wasn't Miller's boat. Or at least, Miller wasn't there. She walked down to the makeshift marina where the boats were tied, and gestured to one of the young cops to step aside. He had the nervous, agitated look of someone who'd seen a lot of violence. He didn't make eye contact and kept one hand on his belt as she spoke to him.

"Did they tell you about her missing grandson? That's why she's so sick."

"No, ma'am." He glanced in Carey's direction.

"She has a grandson, twelve or thirteen years old. He and my niece, the same age, stole a boat the day before yesterday and ran off. We've been looking for them near constantly, but the rain's making it hard. We need help."

"Day before yesterday?" asked the policeman. He looked at Carey and recognized the dread in her face.

"Yes."

"Two kids. Twelve or thirteen years old?"

"Yes."

"Dammit." He pulled a radio off the back of his belt and switched it on. "Dispatch, this is twenty twelve. We need a search team at Shelter Seventeen." He lifted a hand to Carey, mouthed "Stay here," and turned his back to her to continue his report.

Carey allowed herself a single deep breath. Finally, someone to share the burden. Someone in authority who might help. She listened closely to the radio exchange as Miguel's grandmother was buckled onto an orange plastic stretcher in the center of the boat. The old woman's eyes were open but glazed, staring blankly at the sky. For a moment, Carey envied her escape. Wherever she was headed was likely safer than here.

The officer turned back around and produced a small tablet from somewhere else on his belt. "I'm going to need more information," he said. "Descriptions of the children and the boat. Let's find somewhere you can sit down."

An hour or so later, Carey and Etta and Jim had each been interviewed. Carey carefully avoided the topic of Yessica's father. She hadn't seen Ivan Larges or his crew since that first night, which meant they'd probably cleared out. Maybe they hadn't even spent a night there. She hoped to heaven he wouldn't somehow catch wind of Yessica's disappearance. When the police asked about her relation to Yessica, she lied: Aunty. It was a vague enough title. She also lied about the whereabouts of Yessica's parents. They were already up north, she said. She didn't have their contact information. That part was true. And anyway, she wasn't under oath. They could get pissed at her later, but she doubted, again, that anyone had the bandwidth to cross-check family details. Not with the waters still rising and evacuation underway.

The police made no promises and shared very little information about how they would conduct their search. The young cop who had been the first to talk to Carey was the most sympathetic by far, but all Carey could get out of him was a vague assurance that they would do everything they could to find the kids.

Etta reached out for Carey's hand as they watched a police boat return that evening. There were only two figures in the boat, and both were grown men.

"Jesus," said Etta. "Those kids should be back by now."

Carey nodded. "I ran away once, right? When I was that age?"

"Yeah, I remember. You were back eight hours later, though, bitchy as hell and too hungry to put up a fight. I served you ravioli, and that was enough. You decided to move back."

"Why did I run away?"

"I can't remember."

The two women grinned, but with little heart.

"Think I better do one more run with Jim before we lose the light."

"Okay."

Carey didn't move quite yet. "Ma, what if we don't find them?"

Etta squeezed Carey's hand and kissed it. "We'll find 'em."

"I brought her to this hellhole. I brought her here and told her I was gonna go talk to the people that terrify her, whether she liked it or not. What the fuck is wrong with me?"

"This isn't your fault. You can't take that on."

Carey shook her head, unconvinced. She hugged her mother and headed back inside to find Jim.

Jim was already on his way to ask Carey about another search trip. His boots thudded down the hall as he nervously checked his shirt pocket for the cigarettes and lighter that were always there. He hadn't said it out loud yet, but he felt near as guilty as Carey. The kids had stolen his keys. He should have kept them on his belt. This wasn't the first time someone had stolen a vehicle from him.

Although this boat technically wasn't his, he'd lost two cars and a boat before, and in every case, they were never found. It also wasn't Jim's first time searching for a missing person. When he was a kid, an old guy on the next block had gone off into the woods, and when he wasn't home three days later, the police asked everyone to help out. Jim's dad and his mom and a lot of other folks went out, combing two square miles of forest and river looking for the fellow. He'd been pretty well known. Played football for the high school. That type. But they never did find him. All they found was his baseball hat near the railroad tracks. Not a great sign.

Anyway, that was then, and this was now. And there was no good in thinking negative thoughts. Probably those kids were just holed up somewhere, waiting for the rain to stop. Jim hoped they had food, but even if they didn't have much, they'd probably be okay as long as they were found soon. But it wasn't right how Carey was wearing herself down looking for them. Jim wished he had the strength and stamina of a younger man. He'd be out all day and night and never stop 'til those kids were home. Or, you know, back in the temporary home of the shelter. Jim's pace quickened as he spotted Carey down the hall.

Unfortunately, their umpteenth effort at the end of the second full day was unsuccessful. Resignation and panic battled in Carey's mind as she steered and Jim bailed. They had a rhythm now, and Carey knew the waters better, though they continued to change with more rain and more debris floating in and around the buildings and cars. Carey shouted for the kids, and Jim angled the floodlight back and forth when he could. Nothing. No sign. Only the murky water and the mullet jumping and the occasional great blue heron croaking her evening lament as she flew off and away.

Meanwhile, in a small third-story room in the back of St. Francisco's church, Yessica folded a damp cloth and laid it across

Miguel's forehead as darkness thickened around them. The boy had fallen ill again, and the girl was desperate to wake him. His fever raged, and he muttered and shouted as he thrashed among the choir robes they'd piled on the floor to make a bed. He was lost, somewhere between sleep and awake, dreaming of his shining trumpet, and his shining mother, long dead, and his shining abuela, who, unbeknownst to him, was on a stretcher bound for Georgia.

The children had no clean water and had already eaten all the crackers, peanut butter, coffee creamer, and sugar packets they could find in the church kitchen. Yessica knew they were in danger, but she couldn't yet see that this danger was equal to or worse than the danger she felt at home with the thugs and weapons that were her father's world. She'd overheard things she couldn't tell Ms. Marilla. Things about people who'd been hurt, been shot. Things about how to hide evidence, a body. She couldn't bring herself to consider returning to the shelter and the risk of being sent back to all that. No way.

As Miguel settled into deeper sleep, and night consumed the little room, Yessica resolved to take the boat back to Ms. Marilla's house and try to break in. There was food there, and water, and maybe even some medicine or something that could help Miguel. Then, when he was better, they could pack up the boat with more food and stuff and head north, like they'd planned, and find some new people to stay with for a while. Miguel claimed she'd saved his life, so he was gonna help save hers. Period. Just until her dad was gone for good. Then they could find Ms. Marilla again, and Miguel's abuela. Ms. Marilla was a safe person, she just didn't understand.

Thinking of her dad and other threats, like those cops who had scared them all, Yessica chose a large knife from the stash they'd brought up from the kitchen and tucked it carefully into the back of her belt. She climbed out the window and down the rusted fire escape that led to the boat. She was hungry enough that she had to focus on the climb and be extra careful not to let the dizziness in her head make her fall. The boat was well hidden between two church vans that hadn't moved in years. Yessica jumped from the fire escape to the closer van's roof and then climbed down into the boat using the side mirror and door handle as steps. She bailed for half an hour before the boat sat high enough in the water. She was dizzier now, and a throbbing pounded in her temples. Slowly, with effort, she pulled a large flashlight from the dry bag that Ms. Marilla kept in the boat and switched it on. She untied the boat from the vans and used the lines to fasten the flashlight to the prow. Once she'd pushed off into the suburban waters, the motor started easily. They'd only used a little gas, but Yessica wasn't sure how much fuel was left. It better be enough to get her to Ms. Marilla's house and back. She didn't want to have to wade or swim in that dark, nasty water.

While Yessica steered toward the old pink house, large military trucks made their way to the shelter at Coral Heights. There were exactly five of them. Light Medium Tactical Vehicles with high water clearance were in understandably high demand, and these five had started on the west coast of Florida, steadily moving east until arriving in the outskirts of Miami. Each of them could transport about fifteen fully outfitted Marines, which officials hoped would translate to an equivalent number of climate refugees with luggage. They'd been specially outfitted with ladders and railings to aid in the evacuation of civilians, who were generally less fit and agile than Marines. The LMTVs arrived at the shelter at about ten at night, waking everyone who was sleeping with their deafening roars. Carey wasn't asleep anyway, her mind buzzing with worry for the missing children.

In another hour, the evacuation was officially underway. People lined up, holding duffel bags or dragging rolling suitcases, yawning and stretching, but thrilled to be on their way out. It was explained that about eighty people would be evacuated every ten hours or so. It would take that long for the vehicles to load, make their way north, unload, and turn around. They could clear the shelter in approximately thirty-six hours if all went smoothly. The problem was, there were other shelters they needed to empty. So. Whoever missed this thirty-six-hour window (give or take a few hours) could not be guaranteed another opportunity. Whoever stayed behind would be abandoned for the foreseeable future.

Carey, Jim, and Etta discussed their options. The ladies could go ahead, while Jim stayed behind to look for the kids. Carey wouldn't hear of it. Etta could go ahead, while Carey and Jim stayed behind. Etta wouldn't hear of it. Jim wasn't planning on going with the transport, no way, no how. So, they would stay. At least through this first wave of departures. The next would be around ten the next morning. They couldn't head out to look for the kids this late at night, in the pouring rain, but they would leave first thing in the morning and hope to high heaven they found the kids before the third and final transport left the following evening.

They woke the next morning before anyone on staff had stirred, before any of the generators were turned on for the day, and before anyone on site had made any coffee. Carey and Jim pushed out in their borrowed boat. The morning was clear at last. Golden light on the new waters of Miami almost delivered peace, but the grinding of their motor and the warning in Carey's chest prevented any natural relief. Two kids were still missing.

They searched all day, spiraling out from the shelter, out past the store, now shuttered and abandoned, out past the edge of the last neighborhoods east of the Everglades. They refueled back at the shelter midday, as the second transport departed. The shelter was nearly empty now, but Carey found and checked in with the young policeman she'd spoken with before.

"I'm sorry, ma'am, there've been no developments in the search," he said, bowing his head with a shame that seemed sincere enough.

"But you're still looking, right?"

"Oh yes, ma'am. We've dedicated two vessels to the search."

"Two." In the nearly twenty-five hundred square miles of Miami-Dade County, two boats.

The officer nodded solemnly. "I know," he said. "It isn't enough."

"No, it isn't," she said bitterly. This news, like so much other recent and unwelcome information, metabolized in Carey with swift and leaden action. "Guess we better head back out."

"Ma'am, you're aware the last transport from this shelter is leaving tonight?"

"I know," said Carey, walking away. She felt plenty, but she was too damn tired to express it.

"I'll check back here tomorrow," he offered, "if you figure you have to stay."

"I'm not leaving without them," she said with quiet fury.

If he answered, she didn't hear him.

The afternoon's search was fruitless. They saw no other boats and found no signs of the children.

When they returned that night, the last evacuation vehicles were loading. To Carey's horror, she spotted Ivan Larges and his friends in line. She turned to hide but then realized, with a sickening twist in her gut, that he might know something about where Yessica might have headed. Carey knew she had to check. Her body and mind were far beyond exhaustion, but she summoned the steel will of her teaching days to approach him.

"Ivan," she said quietly to his back.

He turned on her with the quick, paranoid movement of someone expecting attack.

"What?" he asked, scowling at Carey as if she were a pile of ripe garbage.

"It's about Yessica … ," said Carey.

"You took her. I got nothing to do with that." He spat into the water and stepped forward in line.

"She ran off," said Carey bluntly. "She took a boat and disappeared and we're looking for her, but—"

Ivan cut in, "She does that, see, she runs away, and she lies. But you said you were gonna watch out for her, so I guess that's your problem now."

Carey's gut twisted again. The baby kicked her lower ribs. "I know. But she's your biological child, so," she continued, "I felt I should inform you that she's missing. In case maybe you know something about where she would go. Or if you wanna help us look …"

Ivan chuckled quietly to himself and shook his head. "Nah, I don't think so. She'll turn up, or she won't."

"You don't understand … ," started Carey, but Ivan took a step toward her. His shoulders were pulled back, but his neck pushed forward and his head tilted wildly to the left.

"No, you don't understand. I'm gonna take this free ride outta here. I have business to get to. That girl is your business now."

Carey stepped back. Ivan moved back in line.

Carey left him there. She turned and walked away from her last link to Yessica's family. That nightmare would soon be swept away in a government boat, but she'd be left here with another. Still here, still searching.

Walking away from evacuation wasn't, it turned out, entirely simple. Carey and Etta spent the next hour arguing with the men in charge about staying. The authorities insisted there would be no other evacuation, not that they could guarantee. They insisted that it was dangerous and irresponsible to remain behind.

Carey explained, in no uncertain terms, that they would not be leaving. She lied easily, insisting they had permission from the police to stay, given the crisis of the missing children. She lied, too, that they had secured other future transport out of the shelter, once the children were found. She assured one older official that she would not be staying in this place, in her condition, unless it was absolutely necessary. This casual reference to her pregnancy, more than any other argument, somehow convinced them.

The last transport departed close to eleven that night. They left no one else besides Carey and company. They did leave a week's supply of food and water, several large fuel canisters, and a comprehensive emergency kit. Carey watched the lights of the last truck disappear into the sinking city and felt a hard knot of fear grow slowly beneath her sternum. That night, the shelter was quiet, the rain let up, and Carey, once again, barely slept at all.

The following morning began much the same as the previous two days. Carey, Etta, and Jim woke early and hardly spoke to one another as they went about the business of basic survival and desperate search. Carey and Jim took the first trip, while Etta remained at the shelter.

They circled the shelter widely once, twice, and then headed north for a while. Carey tried again to imagine what route the kids might have taken. Yessica was bright. She knew that north meant dry land. The question was whether the kids knew their directions well enough to find north and stick to it. Carey doubted they would have used a passage like the turnpike, where they were bound to run into other boats. But maybe.

After roughly an hour north and an hour back along a different route, Carey felt her body call for food. Being pregnant at this stage meant that hunger was familiar, sudden, and violent.

"I need to break," she called to Jim. "But let's run back by the house just in case. We haven't checked there in a while." He nodded.

They pulled up and around the side of the house before they saw it—the little aluminum boat bobbing nearby.

"It's them!" Carey shouted. "Holy shit! It's them!"

She nearly crashed against the other boat as they pulled up. "Yessica!" called Carey. "Yessi, honey, are you here?"

Jim tied off as Carey climbed out of the boat and onto the stairs. The door was still locked. She banged on it. "Yessi! Miguel! It's Ms. Marilla! Are you here?"

No answer came. Carey's throat began to close, no, to fill, like something heavy, something turbid and thick was gathering there. She fought it back. "Jim! You got the keys?"

"Yep. Right here."

Jim came up the stairs behind her and opened the door. Inside was dark, but a broad stream of light poured in from an opening in the far corner. A piece of plywood was broken there, pulled back and splintered. The opening was wide enough for a kid to crawl through. Carey coughed, attempting to dislodge the heaviness in her throat.

As her vision adjusted to the interior light, Carey found boxes opened, food things scattered on the floor, and Yessica, curled in a tight ball under a blanket she'd pulled out of a plastic tub.

Carey knelt near the girl. Yessica's eyes didn't open, but her teeth chattered. Carey held a hand to the girl's cheek and pulled it quickly back.

"She's hot as hell," Carey said to Jim. "We've got to get her medicine. Yessi, where's Miguel?"

The girl didn't answer.

"You're safe, honey. I need you to tell me where Miguel is."

Yessica's body shook, and she curled tighter.

"Yessica, please. Where is Miguel?"

"The church," the girl said quietly. "St. Frank's."

"Let's go."

They carefully moved the girl to the boat. It was still morning, but Rain had already gathered her skirts on the horizon. They sat Yessica on the floor of the boat and leaned her back against Carey's legs. Carey didn't like the girl's color, an olive green, or the way her head hung limply to one side.

"We've got to take her in first, then go back out for Miguel."

Jim gave her a bony thumbs-up and shoved the boat off. He turned his focus toward the water ahead. Better to focus on anything other than that poor little girl. She sure didn't seem right. Needed meds to fix her up quick. Real quick. Best not to think much about the possibilities. Besides, his mind had other problems now: the Marilla house, and how to better secure it, or whether he should just go ahead and start moving things to his place in the Glades. He'd wait until he was sure the ladies were on their way from that shelter.

Carey cranked the motor as much as she dared as they sped back to the high school. She and Jim lifted the girl from the boat as two police officers exited the building. One of them was the young officer who had called for the search. It took him a moment to register their work, but with a shake of his head, he rushed to help.

"You found them," he said.

"Found one of them," said Carey. "She's sick. Burning up. She says the boy is at St. Frank's, the church. That's St. Francisco's. You know where that is?"

The officer nodded.

"My guess is he's the same or worse." Carey's back spasmed with the effort of lifting Yessica, and climbing out of the boat, and carrying a baby. "Ah!" she exclaimed involuntarily, her shoulders rising and stiffening with the pain.

"Sanchez, help me get the girl inside," said the officer to his companion.

Sanchez, who was of larger frame, stooped to gather Yessica's limp frame. He lifted her easily and cradled her in his arms. Jim followed Sanchez inside, gesturing for Carey to stay put and wait.

Carey sat on the steps, out of breath.

"You need to slow down," said the young officer. He squatted near her.

"Got to get the boy first," she said.

"We'll handle that." His radio crackled as he engaged it. "Dispatch, this is twenty twelve. We need assistance in West Kendall."

The radio crackled again. "This is Miller. What do you need? Over."

"Not him," said Carey. She grabbed the officer's elbow.

He looked at her, frowning.

"Not. Him," Carey said again, her tone severe, her grip willing him to understand.

The young man studied her expression and shook his head. "Never mind," he said into the radio. "Adams out."

He waited until Carey let go of his elbow. "You wanna tell me why?"

"He's not a good man," said Carey.

Adams's expression was inscrutable.

Carey's back spasmed again, and she winced.

"Ma'am, I'm gonna suggest you go inside and get some rest. We'll get the boy, and I'll come let you know when he's back."

"You sure you know where St. Francisco's is?"

"Yes, ma'am."

"I think I should come with you."

"Let us do this."

Carey considered the shape of Adams's face. He was young, serious, clean-shaven. He could have been one of her students, grown up a bit.

"Thank you," she said.

Adams nodded again. "I'll see you in." He offered his hands, and Carey took them to stand up. Her back protested as she walked up the stairs with Adams close behind her, monitoring her progress. He slipped around her and opened the heavy door as she arrived at the entrance.

"Thanks," she said one final time.

"You're okay from here?" he asked.

Carey offered a slow, slight smile. "Mostly. Please go."

Sanchez appeared at the end of the hall as Carey made her way inside. She thanked him as he headed to the door Adams still held open.

"Your mother's caring for the girl," said Sanchez.

The door closed shut, and waves of competing emotion rolled through Carey's body. Relief crested first, then exhaustion, then persistent fear. So on and so on, rising and falling. Now that Yessica was found, now that they were on their way to get Miguel, now, finally, Carey felt stress break its bonds and tear through her like a ravenous shark riding those same waves. She made it to the stairs and slowly climbed the flight to the main hallway. Etta and Jim met her there and helped her down the hall and into bed. She lay down on her side, the pressure suddenly and beautifully released from her back and pelvis. The baby, now at nearly thirty weeks, kicked three times and then tumbled to rest.

"We found them," Carey said to Etta, dizzy and delirious.

"I know, baby," said Etta. "You did great."

Carey slept for three and a half hours and woke midday. It was hot, so horribly hot, and she woke with a tongue dry as paper. She reached for the bottle she kept refilled by the head of her cot and drained it. She stood up and stretched, noticing the twinge in her back, less painful than before but still present. She needed a toilet.

She didn't see Etta, Jim, or the kids as she made her way over and outside to the porta-potties. They'd left a few units behind after the evacuation, a cruel kind of mercy.

After exiting and washing her hands with sanitizer, Carey returned to the main hall. The registration area was eerily quiet, empty of people, their things, and their devices. She realized she was hungry, very hungry, and she felt a pang of guilt as she considered if the baby inside her might also feel hunger or something like it. The dining area was desolate, but there were a few crates of food and supplies left behind. She resolved to eat and then go find the kids in the clinic. Maybe she'd bring them both some cookies or something, if she could find any. She ate two bowls of Raisin Bran and drank a glass of orange juice. She was filling cups of apple juice for Yessica and Miguel when Adams and Sanchez appeared in the dining area.

Adams approached. Carey smiled.

"Hello, ma'am," he said.

"Hello, Officer. I feel so much better after a rest. You were right," she added, purposefully flattering the young man who had come to her rescue more than once. She read trouble in his face and set down the juice.

He couldn't rescue her this time.

"I'm sorry, ma'am, but the young man you asked us to find did not survive."

"What?"

"I'm so sorry, but he died, ma'am. We found him outside the church, but he died well before we got there. Maybe last night."

Time slowed, or possibly it sped up. Time didn't move in any familiar way, as Carey felt but could not hear the news.

"I don't understand," she said.

"Please, sit down," said Adams. He gestured to one of the cafeteria tables that came with stools attached, multicolored, plastic and metal. A centipede table. Carey sat and placed one hand on her lap and one hand on the table's smooth, cool surface.

Adams sat near her and gestured to Sanchez. Carey looked again at the shape of Adams's face. It was ruined now. His youth and beauty only called up Miguel's sweet, acned face and then Miguel's sunken, sick face, and then. Carey forgot to exhale.

"What happened?" she asked, her voice trembling.

"We went to the church, and we found a body floating outside. A young male, about thirteen, like you said. It looks like maybe he fell, trying to climb out of the window, and hit his head. I'm so sorry, ma'am."

Carey's grief began in her mouth and traveled behind her eyes, burning. From there, it tunneled back down her spine. By the time it reached her stomach, she was crying fiercely, angrily. It arrived in her guts, slipping gently around her baby, and she bent forward. Officer Adams didn't touch her, but Sanchez came close, sat behind her, and set one warm hand on her back.

Carey's mind played the scene in full color. Miguel climbed out a window. He climbed on a ladder, or a trellis, or a fire escape. He slipped. He fell. His head cracked on cement, or brick, or metal. His body hit dark water. His blood drained into the water, clouding the scene with the treasure of his youth. He floated, face down. That sweet boy. He'd been alive with her.

"Oh fuck," she said, eventually, wiping her face with the neck of her T-shirt. "Jesus Christ." He'd been alive with her. "Does Yessi, does the girl know about this?"

"No, ma'am," said Adams. "The girl's in the clinic area, with your mother and father."

Carey nodded, ignoring Adams's confusion about Jim. "Do they know?"

"No, ma'am ..." Adams hesitated. "I'm sorry, ma'am, but we need someone to ID the body."

"Oh," said Carey. Her breath staggered and sputtered, a failing engine.

"He didn't have any other relatives here at the shelter. Is that correct?"

"No, I mean, no, I don't think so. Just his grandma."

"And she's already been evacuated?"

"Yeah." Carey's mind rested on the tabletop before her. A grey plastic. A slight texture under her fingers. Fingers that could feel and touch.

"Ma'am, when you're ready, would you be willing to ID the body?"

Carey nodded, and cried again, quietly, and this time, Sanchez patted her back.

Adams stood and gathered several paper napkins and a cup of water. He brought them back to her. "I'm sorry about this," he said when she'd calmed down a bit. "Were you close?"

"A little," said Carey. "I mean," she wiped her face with the rough paper, "I was his teacher. His music teacher. He loved ..." She wiped her face again and again as the tears continued to stream, unable to continue. It was a lie. She'd been more than a little close. Miguel had been one of her favorite students, someone she looked forward to seeing every school day, someone who admired her in return. Carey knew, as all loving teachers do, that Miguel was one of *hers*. One of her own. He had been, and would always be, dear to her.

After some time, Carey stood and walked slowly, holding onto Sanchez's arm. Adams led the long way to a separate building, up to the second floor, and down a hall to a small room that must have once been some kind of office. Adams passed out paper face masks and unlocked the door. He turned on the light. They entered one at a time and stood over the body. It was covered with a sheet of white plastic and laid out on an orange stretcher at floor level. Floor level. Damn it. He looked so small down there.

Adams waited until Carey nodded her assent. She took a deep breath through her mask and held it as the young man knelt and uncovered the face.

Miguel's eyes were closed. His skin was the wrong color. Too pale. Too olive. His eyelids and lips too purple and swollen. Otherwise, he was the same. Calm and sweet, as if asleep. Still speckled by his adolescence. His mouth was parted just a bit. His hair was wet.

On the walk over, Carey had imagined horrors, imagined how the water might have misshapen him, how his wound, his death, might have marred his features. But the boy before her was whole and well. But not well at all. He was dead. The boy was dead and gone. This wasn't him.

"It's him," she said.

Adams covered Miguel's face again and stood. He led them out of the room and closed the door behind them.

"Thank you, Ms. Marilla," said Adams, pulling down his mask. It was the first time the young officer had addressed her by name.

She removed her mask. "Okay," she said gently. She didn't thank him back. She couldn't feel grateful.

"Officer Sanchez will escort you safely back to your family. I've got some data to enter."

"Okay."

"Take care, ma'am," he said.

"Okay."

Carey walked back with Sanchez. Mercifully, he didn't talk. When he patted her shoulder goodbye, she hugged him.

He lumbered away, and Carey entered the classroom where she slept. Etta and Jim were not there. Carey climbed back onto her cot and lay there, beyond exhausted but wide awake. On her back, she could feel the baby kick and flutter. Usually, this was a comforting sensation, a sign of health and life. Not today. She rolled to her side and tried to remember the last time she'd heard Miguel play his trumpet. Outside, Rain arrived again, but Rain had never cared much for trumpets, forever favoring the indifferent persistence of drums.

CHAPTER 14

Later that night, Carey told Etta and Jim about Miguel's death. They discussed, quietly, whether to share the news with Yessica when she awoke. Etta convinced them it would be better to wait until the girl recovered her health and strength, but the next day, Carey's resolve wavered as Yessica asked about her friend.

"Why isn't Miguel here?" Yessi asked, her voice dry and small. She kept her eyes closed.

Carey and Etta sat by her bed in the clinic.

"Hmm?" Carey stalled.

"Where's Miguel?"

"Oh, we, uh, we don't know," said Carey.

"But you found him, right?" asked Yessica. She opened her eyes and tried to sit up.

Etta cut in, "Yes, sweetheart, they found him." She patted Yessica on the knee and gently pushed her back down. "He was in bad shape, so he's been evacuated up north. You don't worry about that. You just worry about getting better."

"Was he hurt or something?" Yessica's voice cracked.

"No, honey," said Etta. "He was sick. They'll fix him up. You focus on getting yourself better."

Carey watched her mother lying easily, guiltlessly, and wondered how practiced she must be. Maybe motherhood was all lies, just one long performance of security and optimism, all while knowing better and worse.

Yessica sighed and closed her eyes again. "I should have gone by myself. He shouldn't have come with me."

"He made his own choices, honey." Etta shook her head. "We all do."

Carey noticed, with some shock, that her mother's hair was now fully grey. Neither of them had been to a salon in months, of course, but the gradual change in Etta's hair hadn't registered until now. Etta must have cut her own hair, because only the tips of her shaggy curls were still a faded red.

"His sickness was just a thing of nature," Etta went on. "Same as yours. No one to blame. So that's enough of that. How about a book or something? Want me to read to you? I haven't done that in ages."

Yessica smiled and nodded. Once again, Carey found new awe for Etta's strength. Callous and stubborn as Etta might be, she knew how to survive. She knew how to will those around her to survive.

It was three more touch-and-go days before Yessica's fever broke, and another two before she was strong enough to walk from the clinic back to the bunks. The girl leaned on Etta and paused in doorways for breath. Her cheeks were still flushed, but her eyes were keen. She sometimes peered down hallways warily, even though Carey assured her they hadn't seen any sign of her father or uncle for many days.

"He could still be around, Miss," she said.

"I don't think so," said Carey.

"But you don't know for sure," said Yessica.

"I'm sure," said Carey. "You've been through a lot, so I think it would be good if you tried to relax."

Later that evening, after dinner, Yessica was smiling again and laughing at Jim performing sleight-of-hand tricks with a quarter. But Carey could tell that the girl had a long way to go before she'd be fully well, and something about her—the way her laugh pealed sweetly in the air, her surprise when the quarter appeared behind her ear, her delight when Jim accidentally dropped the coin down his shirt—these things and more made Carey hesitate. No need to open the door for grief just yet.

Yessica's health improved over a few more days. This should have been welcome news, but instead Carey grew more anxious about telling her the truth. Etta finally offered to be the one to speak to Yessica. Carey began to protest, certain she should have that responsibility, but a bitter dread stoppered her voice. She accepted her mother's offer. Miguel's death, along with everything else that had transpired in the past months, had done something to Carey's being. Something inside her wasn't right. She felt like a broken door that could close, but never latch.

After Yessica's talk with Etta, the girl reappeared, red-eyed and quiet. She said nothing to Carey. She asked no questions. No one spoke of Miguel at all after that, and whatever had broken inside Carey remained that way, the door ajar.

Carey resolved to cooperate and evacuate wherever and whenever any new opportunity arose, but not knowing how or when that might happen exhausted her imagination. They'd seen Adams and Sanchez twice more, but the officers could offer no further information about when the trucks might return.

Carey's mind swam with the possibilities of what awaited them beyond the water. She feared they'd be transferred to another shelter somewhere, instead of set loose on actual dry land. But even if they made it to dry land, it could be hard or impossible to find a place to stay. Maybe they'd be taken in by kind strangers. That happened a fair amount during hurricanes, but then, this was all on an unprecedented scale. She guessed that Georgia and Alabama had run out of kind strangers months ago. The government wasn't likely to be able to afford support for much longer. And shelter was one need among many. She'd need a hospital at some point.

And then, after the baby, Carey might not be able to work right away, even if she could find a job. Etta would have to supply child-care, Carey supposed, but it might be too much to ask Etta to watch over both Yessica and a baby. Yessica could help maybe, but she'd need to go to school. And then there was Jim. But he would probably stay behind. That thought didn't give her much comfort.

At dinner one night—more cans, always cans these days—Etta once again expressed her restlessness.

"I'm tellin' you, this is horseshit. They should have come back for us by now. I say we move out."

"How, Mom? How are we gonna do that?"

"Dunno, but I can't stand this place any longer."

"I know, I know."

"How 'bout a day trip?" said Jim. "Get some fresh air, shake yer bones loose."

"What's that mean?" asked Yessica.

"We got boats, and I got a destination. Let's break out for a day. You can skitter right on back here afterward."

"Yes! Please, please, please!" said Yessica, like he'd offered Disney World or a goddamned shopping spree instead of a boat ride through the ruins of a sunken city.

"What's this destination?" asked Carey.

"My swamp palace." Jim winked.

"Oh, it's a palace now, is it?" Etta poked him in the ribs, and he cackled.

"Okay, it ain't no palace, but it's mine. I been dyin' to show it off."

"Please, Miss, please, please, please! If I spend like one more hour here ... I don't know what."

Yessica's young face was hollow with grief and want, while Jim's toothless smile was all delight.

"Well, shit, I guess we've got a plan," said Carey. "We'll need to check the weather though, and make sure we have enough fuel to waste some."

Yessica nodded silently and grinned, but not at Carey. She hadn't smiled at Carey since learning the truth about Miguel.

"Tomorrow," said Jim, slapping the table.

"We're gonna need bug dope," said Etta, standing to clear her tray. "I'll check the loot they left us."

"Mom," said Carey, "pack some food and water too?"

"Course I will."

The following day dawned grey. Storm clouds spread heavy across the sky and piled loosely in the corners like pillows on the bed of an excited dreamer. Jim had been busy. He'd taken the borrowed rig back to the pink house, bailed out the boat Yessica and Miguel had stolen (it was almost completely sunk after being neglected), and then towed it back to the shelter. He'd swapped out Carey's old motor for a newer, lower-horsepower model he said he'd "found" somewhere (Carey guessed correctly that he'd taken it from an abandoned boat). He'd also fueled both vessels.

Etta had indeed packed water and snacks, and even thought to find a couple umbrellas just in case those clouds took a nasty turn.

Carey and her mom rode in their old boat, following Yessica and Jim in the borrowed one. Etta steered, while Carey tried to push visions of Miguel's last boat ride from her mind. They headed due west out of the shelter toward the lingering gloom of the previous night. It could have been a fishing trip from Carey's childhood, except for the abandoned cars and buildings, the tilting telephone poles and hanging wires, the size of her belly and the need to hold it steady as they bounced along, and the constant, dragging weight of her grief. A weight impossible to hold. They left the city's outskirts and veered north as a flock of starlings burst from the roof of what used to be a gas station. The birds swirled, gathered, lost each other, and condensed into a great black ribbon as the two boats turned west once again, gathering speed along a drowned Tamiami Trail.

The River of Grass had outgrown its old nickname. It was a Sea of Grass now, and of water, and of young trees and shrubs that had already taken root on the roofs of long-abandoned tourist shops and airboat companies. Carey had been down this road hundreds of times, and now, like the city behind it, the land was at once familiar and vanished. If there had been patches of high ground in the city—the banks of overpasses, the human-made hills of a golf course, a housing development, or a park—here there was nothing of the sort. The Everglades were flat, comprised of water and grass in all directions, broken only by dark clumps of trees and the steady march of telephone poles that marked where the road had once been. The only difference now: the lack of road. The lack of cars. The absence of all human presence.

They traveled for two hours or so, and Carey had just begun to worry out loud about fuel, when Jim pulled north off the trail. Carey wasn't sure, but she guessed he marked the turn by an osprey nest they'd passed a few poles behind. The path they took through the sawgrass was narrow, less than a boat wide. The grass bent and scraped and whined against the sides of their vessels, but the motors smoked and pushed through.

A family of bright-eyed gallinules scrambled through the reeds. Their long orange legs and bright beaks shone in cheerful contrast to the slick black of their bodies. Carey had always preferred the shy sweetness of their kind to the aggressive snack-crazed ducks that plowed toward any human in the suburbs. She smiled as the anxious parents pipped warnings and counted their delicate fluffs of young.

It was another hour or so before they broke through the reeds and onto a broad expanse of water with no grass or interruptions, a shining dream in the light of day. Jim took them across the silver water and past two thick hammocks of old cypress trees and live oaks, miraculously above the waterline. The grass returned, and the water trail that wound through it was wide enough here to be called a shallow river of its own. It snaked, turquoise and lazy, around a third hammock. Carey saw, with surprise, that the scope and height of this hammock could claim another name: island.

She held her breath. Hidden in the shade of a giant cypress, nestled among its knees, was a large houseboat. She was an old rig, more than fifty years old, but lovingly kept and restored. She was pale yellow, with three white hurricane-shuttered windows across her side, each bearing two dark green stripes running their height. An aluminum door, also green, beckoned from a tiny porch over her stern. Propped upside down on the cypress knees behind her were two canoes, one green, one white. Grasses and plants grew on her flat roof and hung gently past her gutter. Her bow, flat but proud, pointed toward a path that led up onto the island.

Jim killed the motor and floated up. Etta followed suit. They tied off to the cypress knees, and Jim climbed aboard the houseboat, his palace.

"This is it," he said, radiating pride. "The only piece of real estate with my name on it."

"It's beautiful, Jim," said Carey, climbing gently on board.

Yessica climbed out and around to the shoreline. She called back to Jim, "What's up that path? Can I go?"

Jim nodded. "Sure as rain. Just watch out for the wild pigs. They don't like to be surprised."

"Cool!" Yessi bounded up the path.

Carey felt a pang of worry, but reminded herself Yessi couldn't go far. It was an island after all, and a small one. A cool breeze smoothed the fear from her forehead as Yessica's sneakers pattered off and out of sight. It might do the girl some good to have a bit of freedom.

Jim unlocked several locks and cracked the door. He gestured for them to wait and disappeared inside, closing a screen door behind him. Moments later, the hurricane shutters creaked open. One at a time, Jim leaned out to pop their hinges into place and then replaced sturdy screens on each window. When all six had been handled, he reappeared. He took off his hat, once a blue denim, now a filthy brown. He swept it forward in a funny little bow. "My ladies."

Carey and Etta entered the boat. Jim, in his great capacity for care and consistency, had made a palace indeed. A humble one, but the sight of it brought cool relief to Carey. Her shoulders dropped. It was the small details that did her in—a chair with a cushion, a merry little painting of a dancing frog on the wall. It had been so long since she'd been in any space like a real home. Jim's decorating choices were eccentric, to say the least, and the profusion of yellow and orange items was a touch alarming, but there was a cozy woven rug on the floor, surrounded by comfy chairs facing an old-fashioned wood stove. At either end of the rectangular space was a narrow hall. One led into a tiny galley kitchen with a gas stove and oven, the other into a bathroom with a pump toilet and a shower across from a sizable closet. Above the kitchen was a shallow loft with a queen-sized mattress, and above the bathroom was an identical space. The mattresses were bare of sheets and pillows, and there was no sign of Jim's clothes or toiletries. He obviously had not stayed here in quite some time, if ever.

Carey exclaimed her enjoyment of every detail she encountered but eventually felt she had to ask, "But where are your personal things, Jim? Why on earth aren't you living here already?"

"Oh, I plan to," he said. "I just wanted to see where you all ended up first. Didn't seem like the right time." He wriggled uncomfortably.

"I thought you said you had a stash out here," said Etta. "But this isn't a stash, Jim. This is a home."

"Oh, this ain't the stash," said Jim defensively. "That's all in the shed."

"The shed?" asked Carey, incredulous that there could be more. "I can't believe you did all this. I mean, how in hell *did* you do all this?"

Jim wagged his head side to side, too bashful to take the compliments.

"You don't hafta explain nothin'," said Etta. "Come on now, show us the shed!"

Jim hopped up and led them up the path that Yessi had followed into the woods. They passed a small grove of orange trees gone wild and another of bananas. Both crops were green and growing but now tangled in thick vines of kudzu and morning glory. They passed through a place of dense palmettos and finally into a more wooded area, higher than the rest, where a stout shed was tucked in the arms of a low pine. Jim opened three locks and rolled up the door.

"There's no light," he said. "You'll hafta let your eyes adjust."

The interior of the shed was so tightly packed, only one person could enter at a time. A narrow aisle led through the shelves and piles of supplies, forming a loop back to the entrance. Jim wasn't the most organized fellow in the world, but he'd separated his food from his fuel and hardware. On one side of the shed, there were countless cans and boxes of nonperishables, large jars of pickled things, and what looked to be plastic bags of dried meats and fruits. On the other side, hanging on pegboards and leaning in piles, were tools of every shape and size imaginable. Large red cans of gasoline were stacked high in the corner. There was even a small pile of yellowing paperbacks in one corner.

Emerging from the shed, Carey ushered her mom inside and proceeded to lavish Jim with praise and admiration.

"You've worked so hard at this," she said. "I honestly can't believe it. This is amazing."

"Shucks," he said, beaming, "you know I ain't got much else going on. Not like you."

"That doesn't matter. It must have taken you years to get all this stuff up here."

"Well, there were roads before," he said. "At least, part of the way. But yeah, I've been at it for a bit."

"What's this land anyway? Is this state park?"

"No," said Jim. "It was privately owned by an old buddy of mine. Rich fellow used to be in the Navy. Lives up in New York now. He had it fenced once but said I could come and stay whenever I wanted. Then the fences broke down, and now with the floods ... I dunno. Probably illegal one way or another, but I never seen anyone out here. Too many easier places to get to, you know?"

"I do."

And yet, those places might as well be on the moon for all Carey cared to see them. On cue, Yessica bounded up behind her.

"This place is sweet," said Yessica to Jim, out of breath. "Oh my God, it's beautiful." Grief and illness had anchored shadows under her young eyes and in the hollows of her cheeks, but these marks were softened now by her interest and enthusiasm.

Etta emerged from the shed. "Christ, Jim, that's impressive."

"Thank you," said Jim, performing another one of his little bows. Once upright again, he kept his gaze downward and shuffled his feet. "So you like it 'nuff to stay here?"

Etta's eyebrows vaulted, and she looked to Carey and then back to Jim. "We can't do that, Jim."

Jim slung his head in disappointment. "It ain't no real use to me without company."

"But Jim," said Carey, "this is too much to share."

"No," stammered Jim. "It ain't really enough space or nothin', but you said it before, we're like family, so, and that's the gift you keep giving me, so seein' as how I got too much for one man and all ..." He trailed off. "But I understand if you need to move on."

"I want to stay," said Yessica to Jim. She leaned on his shoulder.

"Truth is," he continued with his head bowed, "there's more reason I haven't stayed out here. I'm getting older, and it's tough doing things by myself. Plus, there's safety in numbers. You know how that is, with those wild pigs and pirates and whatnot."

"There's pirates?" asked Yessi.

"He means those dirty cops, honey," said Etta.

Jim turned to lock up the shed. "But I doubt they'd come all the way out here. You think about it," he said. "Offer won't expire."

Carey looked to her mother. Etta smiled and shook her head in sheer disbelief.

"You know what?" said Carey. "You've got a deal. And you've got yourself some live-in ladies for a bit. At least 'til we can sort out the next move."

"Three ladies!" Etta said and chuckled, slapping Jim on the back as he gaped and blushed past pink to nearly lavender.

Yessica squeezed Jim's arm. "Oh my God, this is perfect. Thank you."

Carey's breath came short, but whether from excitement or anxiety, she couldn't tell. Just about any place had to be better than the shelter where they'd been for too long, where Miguel's body had lain. But she couldn't be sure this was the right decision. It was near impossible to be sure of anything. Miguel's death had left her bitterly suspicious of her own judgment, but also desperate to escape the high school.

Above her, the cypress trees nodded and whispered their acknowledgment, as Jim and Etta began discussing which supplies to pull from the shed. Yessica found a tree to climb as a dove cooed.

Carey slowed her breath, and in reward, a red-winged blackbird sailed to a nearby branch. The bird watched Carey with the genuine curiosity of creatures who have no fear of human company and see no reason to defend their lands.

CHAPTER 15

They spent the next few days settling in and transporting more supplies and belongings from the high school shelter and the old pink house. The canoes were loaded and towed by the motorboats to try and cut back on trips and fuel loss. Jim enthusiastically built additional shelves for the shed. He repeated his thanks regularly, as if he weren't the one providing them with all the happy comfort found in new business and purpose.

Carey estimated that their new home was somewhere midway between Tampa and Miami, reachable only by boat, and yes, chock-full of mosquitoes. She supposed bug dope wasn't good for the baby, but contracting some godforsaken disease would be worse, so she used the stuff regularly.

The last time they left the shelter, Carey thought to leave a message for anyone who might come looking for them. She texted the news to Officer Adams. She found some paper and a marker in one of the teachers' desks and left a note on the old registration desk:

> *"We've headed north. Thanks for the shelter.*
> *—Marillas and Co."*

She thought of texting Mario, but he hadn't known they were at the shelter anyway. She hadn't heard from him at all since his departure. Maybe he'd lost his phone or something. It seemed odd, really, that he would completely vanish, but their entire relationship, and all the circumstances around it, were odd at best. Carey couldn't bring herself to be the one who reached out first. He'd done the leaving. He could do the checking in. Still, it might be a long while until they'd reconnect; cell service was spotty at best in the swamp.

They left the pink house that day with a lack of fanfare. Carey had already said goodbye to the place more than once by now. As she locked it shut again, for the final time, she could think only of putting her feet up somewhere, anywhere. All she wanted was rest.

Now the heat of August leaned down on the swamps and Jim's houseboat. Carey's ankles were swollen, horribly so, and the only thing that seemed to help was shoving them deep in the cool mud of the creek or propping them high on Etta's knees or a pile of clothes and towels. Carey's back complained, too, and the skin on her belly itched as it stretched to new limits. She and Yessica shared a bed, as did Etta and Jim. All had agreed this was the arrangement that made the most sense. But Carey could only sleep on her side, and Yessica thrashed as she endured nightmares, sometimes kicking or elbowing Carey in the night. The aches and weight and sleeplessness of it all wore her steadily down. She was less friendly, less patient, and far less tolerant of noise. Not that there was much. Still, the smells and sounds of the boat motors and the generator grated on her heightened senses, and more than once she swore violently when someone turned on the generator just as she was nodding off for a nap.

The only time Carey felt truly at peace was during the afternoon storms. As the skies darkened, each member of the family settled quietly into a corner of the houseboat with a book or a pillow or some small task. The raucous rain and thunder prohibited conversation. Instead, they listened to the sky falling and the wind lashing. The houseboat rocked gently in the tumult. In these moments, Carey imagined holding her infant, and it surprised her to feel some sense of anticipation. Someone soft to hold wouldn't be so bad. Someone new wouldn't be wrong. She hadn't let herself think too much about the person the baby would be, but now, as August began to slink by, she wondered what her daughter would look like. Whether she'd have Mario's eyes. Whether she would love music.

During one particularly uncomfortable night, Carey woke up with sharp leg cramps. The pain, like swords sheathed in her muscle from knee to ankle, made her groan and roll out of bed. She stooped and stretched her calves in the loft. Yessica stirred.

"Are you okay?" asked the girl. She'd spoken so infrequently to Carey lately.

"Yeah. No. Leg cramps."

"Can I get you something?"

"Just need to stretch. Go back to sleep."

Yessica flopped over, and Carey endured. Finally, the pain lessened. With her legs shaking and her breath shallow, Carey climbed back into bed and curled on her side. The baby rolled and kicked, extending Carey's skin so much that she thought she could make out the shape of a heel, or an elbow, or maybe a knee. She massaged the baby gently through her skin, and the baby rolled again and settled out of reach.

Carey slept and dreamt her daughter was born with gills. Bright pink flaps on the newborn's neck, like thickened rose petals, stretched and fell as the baby wailed, then quieted, slowly turning from pink to blue. Carey, terrified, held the baby out over the water around them. She knew, instinctively she knew, that the infant needed to be underwater, but her arms wouldn't obey. They couldn't. She held her daughter, gripping her tighter, refusing to let go, shaking with terror. A calm arrived, at last, another kind of knowing, and she jumped. Mother and daughter plunged into the water, ice-cold at first, and then familiar and warm as a saltwater bath. Carey opened her eyes under the surface.

Her baby, her daughter, stared back, wide-eyed in the water. Alert, alive, and watchful, her gills, pink again, undulating. Bright bubbles caught in her ears and adorned her eyelashes. Carey took a breath, too, but it wouldn't come. She couldn't inhale. Her lungs would not expand.

Carey woke from the dream in a cold sweat, gasping for air. As her consciousness returned, her disorientation gave way to hunger. Specifically, a desperation for greens. It was early, but Jim was awake, and when she quietly reported her craving, he led her directly to a place on the island where he'd planted collards and kale last fall.

Early morning dew hung thick on every leaf. The kale was long past its prime, darkest green and flowering, but the collards were abundant, gone wild in the months between, sparkling with moisture. Carey gathered an armload and fried them up with a small tin of sausages for their morning meal. The greens were bitter and delicious. Carey devoured more than she thought healthy. She couldn't help herself.

"Jim, those were wonderful. What else can we grow out here?"

"Well, your beans, collards, and tomatoes are about all I've managed. But I haven't been around much. I'm guessing most things'll do fine if you keep the critters off 'em."

"We should try eggplant and peppers," said Etta. "My Nan used to grow big, fat eggplants."

Carey nodded. She'd heard plenty about Nan's eggplants. Nan was her great-grandma, Etta's maternal grandmother. She'd lived on a few acres somewhere in Alabama and, as far as Carrie knew, had never forgiven her daughter, Janine, for abandoning Etta. She'd sent letters to Etta monthly, often with no other news than a report on her extensive gardens, until her passing in the pandemic.

"How large is this hammock anyway?" Carey asked.

"No more than a mile around," said Jim. "Not sure who planted some of the fruit trees and things, but like I said, I ain't seen no one out here in years."

"How'd you find it?"

"Fishin' trip, of course, after my buddy told me about the area. Like I said, he told me I was welcome to it. Said he never makes it down here anymore."

The fishing, it should be noted, was excellent in and around their encampment. They caught, with easy regularity, an assortment of large- and smallmouth bass, peacock bass, black-whiskered catfish, butter-bellied cats, bluegills, shellcrackers, and bright-lipped cichlids. Less common but still present were speckled crappies, elusive warmouths, pale tilapia, and shining but bony and tasteless carp. Fish were available for breakfast, lunch, and dinner. Etta declared her disinterest in anything whiskered early on.

"There's only so much mud my gut can handle," she said.

Carey didn't feel the same. Her appetite in her third trimester was insatiable. Though her body harbored less and less room internally, she felt more desire to fill it. Nothing was so delicious to Carey as fried fish, sliced avocado, and canned tomato sprinkled with salt and pepper. Except maybe sautéed fish in a bit of oil, fried collards, and a can of baked beans.

Yessica and Jim ate surprisingly little. The Marilla women had always known Jim to subsist almost entirely on coffee and cigarettes, but in the old days, of course, he'd relished a nice cut of beef. That was impossible to get now. He did, however, have a vast store of jerky in the shed. He chewed on a piece of this nearly all day, every day. Yessica preferred fruit she picked herself on her wanderings around the island. She did, on occasion, eat an entire can of spinach, uncooked and flavored only with a generous dusting of garlic salt. Carey marveled that Yessi's adolescent body, like Carey's pregnant one, must call for what it needed.

A week passed, and then another. What Carey missed most, besides air-conditioning, wasn't what she'd imagined she'd miss. It wasn't fresh eggs or red meat. It wasn't hot showers or a bed of her own. It was milk. They had some canned milk for cooking, but her body yearned increasingly for a cup of ice-cold, whole-fat milk. She mentioned it to Etta one day, who set down the romance novel she'd been reading, lounging in a hammock strung between two cypress trees. Etta pushed her battered reading glasses to the top of her head. Carey sat on a blanket, leaning up against the trunk of another tree, mending a tear in her one pair of maternity pants, which were actually just an old pair of Etta's with a gentle elastic waistband. Needle and thread were items she'd never much appreciated before their current situation. Now, she carefully kept such treasures in a bag tucked by her pillow.

"There's a lot we're gonna need for this baby," said Etta. "Milk is just the beginning."

Guilt settled like a pair of noisy grackles on Carey's shoulders. Dammit. She hadn't even thought of milk for the baby, only her own craving. "I didn't think of that," she admitted, attempting to silence the clamor. She could make milk, hopefully, but what if it wasn't enough? Or what if there was some problem and the baby needed nutrition her body couldn't provide? Maybe she was already calcium deficient.

"We're gonna need diapers and clothes and a whole load of

vitamins and crap. Ointments. Maybe medicine. God, I remember carrying around so much junk with you." Etta stretched in the hammock, unaware of Carey's guilt.

"Right. Yeah." Carey's last few stitches had accidentally involved an extra layer of fabric. She studied it now with the sickening realization she'd probably need to start over.

"We got time," said Etta.

"Not really. A month? Five weeks or something."

"Well, so let's boat up and out. Tampa, or north, or wherever you wanna go. Jim'll loan us the fuel, I'm sure. But he'll probably insist on coming with us. That'd be good if we end up paddling. Or maybe we can find someplace to shop and get everything we need once a month or so. There's gotta be something somewhere. Orlando can't be that far. If it's still there."

Yessica arrived, panting and wild-eyed. She bent over, hands on her knees, trying to catch up with herself.

"There's people!" she whisper-yelled. "On the other side of the island. Just now. Just pulled up. They didn't see me. I ran like hell."

Etta sat up and nearly fell out of the hammock. "What?"

"I saw a boat," continued Yessica, between gasps. "I think there's three people in it. Men, I think. But they had hats on, so I don't know."

"Where?" asked Etta.

"That way," said Yessica, pointing northwest. "Where that big tree is down on the far side."

Etta nodded. "Was it the police?" she asked.

Carey was certain her mother's mind had jumped to the same fear as her own. Maybe it was Miller again, or other dangerous types.

"I don't know," said Yessica. "Are we in trouble?"

"Probably not. Get in the house just in case," said Carey. Yessica nodded and took off, casting a terrified look over her shoulder. Etta waved Carey away with her hand.

"You too," said Etta to Carey. "I'll get Jim and go see about it."

"Maybe they won't know we're here," said Carey. "We could lie low."

"No point," said Etta. "Our tracks are all over the island, and this place isn't big enough to hide anywhere. Besides, if Jim doesn't know they're around, he might bump into them on his own. I think it's better if there's two of us."

"Be careful," said Carey.

"For sure," said Etta.

Carey gathered her sewing things and followed Yessica back to the boat. She closed and locked the windows, but left the main door slightly ajar, in case Etta or Jim needed a fast entrance. Carey rubbed at a small scab on her left hand as she sat by the windows facing inland. She knew where the shotgun was, but not how to use it.

It was quiet in the houseboat. Yessica sat on one of the two chairs with her legs drawn up. Only the top of her head poked up above her knees as she watched Carey and Carey watched the world outside.

Ten minutes passed, then twenty. The houseboat would roast them soon, with the windows closed.

"Do you want me to go check if I can see them?" asked Yessica quietly.

"No," said Carey. "We need to try and be patient ..."

On cue, Jim and Etta became visible through the trees. Three figures followed them, one with a large gun slung on their back. Carey studied Etta's face, but her expression was unreadable. Could be anyone. Could be anything. Carey's breath quickened and her blood raced.

"Hide," she said to Yessica. "Get under something. Behind something."

"What about you?" said Yessica.

"Now!"

Yessica obeyed. She closed the accordion door to the tiny bathroom behind her. The lock clicked into place. Carey grabbed a kitchen knife and sat in the chair Yessica had abandoned. She dangled the knife out of sight, off the side of the chair. Her mind raced through violent scenarios.

The door opened and Etta stepped inside.

"We've got visitors," she said, her voice flat.

Carey nodded, her hand gripping the knife.

"You gonna come out and say hello or what?"

"What?"

"You just gonna sit there?"

"They're safe?"

"How the hell do I know? They seem nice enough."

"Mom, what about Miller?"

"That shithead can rot in hell. These people seem fine. We've got enough to worry about. Come meet your neighbors."

"Neighbors?"

"Of a kind."

Carey stood up and placed the knife on the counter.

"Oh, honey, you got yourself all worked up," said Etta.

The door to the bathroom opened, and Yessica peeked out.

"Yeah, well, of course I did," said Carey.

Etta nodded, her expression thoughtful as she observed her daughter.

"You've been through a lot," she said. "Too much."

Carey didn't answer. She exited the boat.

The neighbors, to Carey's surprise, turned out to be neighborly. She found herself smiling and shaking hands with all three of them.

"This here's Jenn Kelly and Arnie," said the tallest in the group. "I'm Diego. Pleasure to meet you."

Jenn Kelly, Arnie, and Diego were all middle-aged and weather worn. Jenn Kelly stood tall and strong, with blond hair cropped short. She wore a well-kept shotgun slung on her back and a dark pair of sunglasses. Arnie was slighter in build and wiry. He might have been a younger version of Jim, though his hair was long and braided. He wore camouflage head to toe and carried a large knife strapped to his side. Diego was something like a mountain man, thickly bearded and bright-eyed. He wore a fish T-shirt illustrated with a black grouper and a hat from Long Key. He laughed often and deferred to Jenn Kelly when questions were asked. In short time, it became clear that they were also flood refugees. They'd boated up about two months ago and found a small collection of people living on stilted shelters in an area called Fisheating Creek, a swath of swamp west of Lake Okeechobee. There was still a good deal of dry land up that way, but after seeing the water rise so much and so fast, no one wanted to risk being on ground at all. Everything, Jenn Kelly said, was at least ten feet in the air, and built as strong as steel.

"How many folks you got up there?" asked Jim.

"Not many," said Arnie. "Maybe twenty. There's a couple kids too.

And we've got a doc."

"A real doctor?" asked Etta.

All three nodded their agreement.

"Good to know." Etta tilted her head at Carey and made eye contact.

"You got rights to build there?" asked Jim.

"Well, that's left to learn," said Diego. "Not sure what the feds will say about all this new water. Doesn't seem like they'll compensate folks for lost land."

"I'm owed land from the start," said Arnie. "I'm quarter Miccosukee, not that anybody gives a damn. Feds least of all."

"That's the truth," said Jim, and Etta grunted her approval.

"That's a good point though. Not sure who could give permission now, as it's not really land we're talking about," said Diego.

Arnie offered a sad smile. "Oh, they like to claim water territory too. Anyway, don't know where we'd start with permission. Rather ask for forgiveness. This water's got everyone confused. Rain don't care 'bout who owns what."

Diego nodded. The group made sounds of agreement and resignation.

"You got enough supplies here?" asked Jenn Kelly.

Carey hesitated.

"Sorry," said Jenn Kelly right away, eyeing Carey. "Don't mean to pry. That kinda question might make you worry about our intentions, but I promise we got more than enough for ourselves."

"No, it's just—" Carey started.

"Trust me, I get it. We've had a couple folks come through who don't know how to share. I'm only asking if you're safe."

Carey exhaled. "Yeah, we're okay. We've got what we need. That's about it."

"Good," said Jenn Kelly. "We can't offer a lot else, but if you find out you need something you don't have, we should exchange info and things. That way, you can find us if"—she glanced at Carey's belly—"you need new supplies."

Carey nodded. She thought about confessing she had no baby supplies yet, but her shame triumphed.

"This your first?"

"Yeah."

"Is he head down?"

"Not sure."

"None of my business," said Jenn Kelly, "but I've had three babies." She looked to Etta, who nodded eagerly. "Every time was different, but the first was hard. George was sunny-side up, for starters, and contractions didn't get the job done without extra meds. Not saying this to worry you or nothing, but maybe it's a good idea to have some backup in case things get tricky."

"Yeah, of course," said Carey. "I need to figure out how I'm going to ..." She trailed off. There were too many things she needed to figure out.

"You gonna have him here?" Jenn Kelly waved at the houseboat.

"No," said Carey quickly. "No, I don't think so." She didn't know where or how she'd have the baby. She didn't know how they'd get diapers, or ointment, or whatever. The truth, what felt like a horrible, wretched truth, was that Carey hadn't really let herself get that far. She hadn't yet been able to think through the birth and the weeks that would follow. Now she was running out of time. The sharks were circling. Christ, she'd been stupid.

Jenn Kelly seemed to read the rising terror in Carey's face. "Like I said, we got a doc, and we're only a couple hours out. Plus, Tampa's not much farther. Specially if we radio for a chopper or something."

"Thanks," said Carey. "We'll probably be out of here by then."

Jenn Kelly nodded. "Don't wait too long," she said gently, and smiled. "I mean, again, none of my business, but you look about ready to go."

"I've still got a few weeks."

"Right. Like I said, none of my business."

They visited for a while longer, all parties eager to compare knowledge of the area and news of the world beyond. Finally, talk turned to the weather.

"You got a plan if this island gets washed out?" asked Jenn Kelly.

"We float," said Etta, "so I guess we'll just pull anchor."

Jim nodded and scratched at his chin. "You think that water's still rising? It has to stop sometime."

Arnie shook his head. "September rains are coming. I think we'll get another six inches, at least. If I remember right."

"Six inches?" Jim shook his head too. "Damned if there's any Florida left by New Year."

"Damned is right," agreed Arnie. "'Cept there ain't a dam in the world could hold all this." Jim chuckled. Jenn Kelly and Diego groaned. Arnie grinned.

"Alright then, we should be getting back," said Diego. "Let's get our info sorted."

They exchanged phone numbers and coordinates. Jim and Arnie discussed fishing a bit more, then Jim walked the visitors back across the island. Yessica, who had been quietly watching and listening to most of the exchange, scampered off with them and then back, well ahead of Jim. She reported back to Carey.

"They've got a bigger boat," she said. "It's one of those airboats. The ones with the big fans."

"Good for them," said Carey, who was busy reopening and venting the houseboat. Sweat poured down her back, and her feet ached from standing through the conversation. The interior of the house had grown soupy, and the hot air made her gag reflex act up.

"I asked the lady if they had any guys named Mario with them," said Yessica, "but she said no." She made eye contact with Carey, which had been rare for so long that Carey felt genuine surprise. She leaned on the doorframe of the houseboat. Mario's face wavered in her mind as if underwater. "No, I suppose not," she said. Her back spasmed.

"I'm sorry," continued Yessica. She hesitated. "I just thought maybe he'd be there. You know?" In fact, Yessica knew full well that Mario wasn't with the new strangers. She tucked a stray piece of hair behind her ears. The thing was, Yessica had noticed that Ms. Marilla hadn't talked about anything real with her since, well, since that day. Ms. Marilla wouldn't even really look her in the eyes. Maybe she blamed Yessi for everything. For Mario leaving, for Miguel dying. Maybe she hated her now. Maybe Ms. Marilla would never forgive her.

"Oh ... ," said Carey, at a loss for more response.

"Are you mad?" asked Yessica.

But Carey thought she was asking about her query to their neighbors. "What? No. No, it's fine."

"You think he'll come back?" pressed Yessica.

"Who?"

"Mario." The muscles around Yessica's mouth tightened as she attempted to hide her feelings. It was spooky, and it felt like an act, how Ms. Marilla pretended not to think about Mario. Yessica had seen girls lie like that over and over again in school, when it was obvious they were actually obsessed with someone. But it wasn't obvious that Ms. Marilla was obsessed with Mario. It wasn't clear at all why she seemed so disinterested. Except that maybe she didn't trust Yessica anymore. Maybe Yessica had lost her trust forever.

"Oh," said Carey, "I don't know. We've kind of lost touch. I need to text him. It's just complicated." She rubbed at her back and sat down heavily in one of the chairs.

"At least he's still out there," said Yessica, her voice low.

"True," said Carey, her head swimming. The baby stretched and crowded her lungs. Carey's breath came short and she leaned back, rubbing at her middle to persuade the baby to shift and give her some relief. Mario was still out there alright. Not like Miguel. That was the subtext, whether Yessi meant it or not. Carey knew she needed to talk to Yessica about Miguel's death. Of course she did. She had to. It was the right thing to do. She just couldn't bring herself to launch into another traumatic topic. She couldn't bring herself to dredge up the girl's grief, or her own. Yessica had already been through too much. They all had.

Yessica didn't seem okay, not by any stretch, but even though Carey's teacher instincts said she needed to step up and care for the girl, Carey wasn't sure her own body and mind could handle more strain or responsibility.

Maybe sensing Carey's fatigue and discomfort, but likely not her guilt, Yessica left Carey alone in the houseboat. Carey heard her call out across the island for Etta, probably hoping to talk to someone with more energy.

It was quiet and still inside the boat. Light, reflecting off the water outside, moved in slow ripples across the ceiling. Gathering clouds would darken it all too soon. More rain coming. Baby coming. And plenty still missing and gone. It sure would be nice if answers were coming, too, and plans, and any sense of the future. If only such things could be bundled and delivered to her door by a stork, or even better, arrive instantly in a single flash of lightning.

CHAPTER 16

The hormones racing through Carey Marilla's body were only part of her discomfort and agitation over the next week. She slept poorly (the baby tumbling and kicking her awake), she ate poorly (her appetite disrupted by the lessening space in her belly), and she bickered with Etta near constantly (her mind plagued with a vise-like pressure). It was hard to play guitar, hard to put on shoes. It was hard to think straight. It was hard to stand up and sit down. Her incredulity that this was, in fact, how human beings reproduced was mounting. It went beyond impractical. It was unendurable.

"How the hell do women do this more than once?" she asked her mother one evening as rain poured down on the houseboat. Yessica was listening to music, curled in the corner, headphones on, her head bobbing to the rhythm. Jim was already snoring in his bunk. "This is nuts. Evolution should have ironed this shit out by now."

"Some women claim to like it," said Etta.

"Bullshit," said Carey.

Etta smirked. "Well, not everyone chooses to live in a swamp in their third trimester."

Carey hadn't let on how much she'd been bothered by Jenn Kelly's birth plan quiz, but now her defenses rose like the wake behind a heavy ship. "You know what I didn't choose? To have a goddamn flood during my pregnancy."

"Course not," said Etta carefully. "I just mean that some ladies have it easier."

"I'd still be huge and miserable, no matter where the fuck we were."

"Course you would," said Etta.

"Don't patronize me."

Etta raised an eyebrow.

Carey continued, the wave of her anger building strength. "Come on, you can't tell me you liked being pregnant."

"Not all of it."

"So, I'm out of line to whine about it? It's my fault? This is all my doing? The pregnancy, the flood, and the tragedy on every fucking side? That's on me."

"I didn't say that."

Carey dropped her voice to a vicious whisper. "You know, you were the one who didn't want to leave in the first place. And she's the one who showed up out of the blue." Carey's eyes darted toward the girl with headphones and then back to her mother. "And they were the ones who went off and ..."

Etta shook her head in warning.

Carey glanced again at Yessica, but the girl's head still bobbed to the music, and her eyes were closed. Carey's throat clenched. "She's been asking about Mario." Carey attempted to inhale, desperately trying to calm the unstoppable twin waves of terror and rage that built in her mind. "Did she tell you? She asked those people."

"I know," said Etta.

"And what's gonna happen if her family decides they want her back or something? What if they come looking?"

"We'll cross that bridge—"

"Mom." Carey felt the waves crest and crash. "I don't know how to do this."

Etta nodded, stood, and walked to her daughter's chair. This was a moment like thousands of others, a moment when Carey needed her. But every time, and especially if there was hurt of some kind, Etta wished she could fix more than was possible. "We're making it up," she said. And that was true. She ran her fingers through Carey's hair.

Carey didn't cry, though she wanted to. She didn't scream. She didn't curl into her mother's arms and fall asleep for weeks, waking only when the world was right again, and the baby was born and grown and safe and independent. She squeezed her mother's hand and inhaled slowly. "I think I better talk to Jim and go see that doc they have up north. And maybe go stay up in Tampa. If you and Yessi want to come ..."

"Of course we will," said Etta. She kissed the top of her daughter's head. There was nothing more to say for now. She shuffled back to her seat and to the tattered romance she was reading for the third time since their arrival.

Carey leaned her head back and thought about picking up and departing the known, however strange or new that known might be. She thought about leaving places, leaving people, and the people who left. The school, the house, the shelter. Her students, her colleagues, her friends. Sarah, then Mario, then Miguel. And really, there were so many more. Javi, her first love, had left. Her father had. There would always be leavings of one kind or another. There would always be loss.

Carey pulled herself to standing and moved to the door. The rain had stopped in the sudden way of late August storms.

"Where are you going?" asked Etta.

"I just need air," said Carey. She let herself out.

Nighttime in the Everglades is never peaceful. It roars with rain, or buzzes with insects, or, as it did that night after the storm, rings with frog song. Carey waddled off the boat into thick, humid air. She hefted her weight and stepped carefully on the planks that Jim had set as a bridge from the boat to the island's shore. It wasn't named yet, this island, at least not to them. Maybe she was just ignorant of names given by Native tribes that lived in these areas first. Maybe this very island had been important to another family in another age, but she'd probably never know. That bothered her too. She walked several steps inland and then turned west along the water's edge. She walked a trail that had probably been made by Yessica's wanderings, the reeds pushed aside, palmetto branches broken or pulled away. Everything was wet. The ground slopped, sodden around her boots, but the contributing clouds had already run off like startled wild things. Eventually, she came to an opening. A crescent moon, slender and waning, hung low enough to spill glitter on the waters at the edge. The result was a faint beacon, a delicate dusting of light. Carey moved toward it and found a place to sit among the pine needles. It was wet, but so was she, and so, she thought bitterly, there was no point in trying. At other times in her life, Carey would have been afraid to be alone at night, in the deep dark of nature. She might have feared evil men, or reptiles, or the sting of some poisonous spider. But now, in this unfamiliar body, and with the knowledge of the vast waters and wastes that surrounded her, Carey couldn't be afraid of the old things, only of the new ones. If there was anything she longed for in the racket of the night, it wasn't company; she relished her solitude. No, it was clarity she missed. She watched the waters move and listened to the clamor. The frogs, at least, knew what to do. Their volume was approaching absurd.

She found it difficult to be comfortable sitting. Her hips protested if she sat cross-legged, but the small of her back and her arms ached if she straightened her legs and leaned back. Finally, she curled on her side, facing the water. Her pine needle bed was damp but soft, in its way, and she felt she might dose off, though she knew rain or bugs would likely wake her. Neither would be pleasant.

She lowered her lids. The light of the moon on the water blurred and expanded in the filter of her lashes. It could be any light now, the light of cars on a road, the lights on a marquee, the light of candles in someone's room. Something dark moved among the lights, and Carey opened her eyes again, her senses waking.

A juvenile alligator, no more than two years old, walked up out of the water and froze mid-step. The animal wasn't big or heavy enough to pose a serious threat, but Carey felt adrenaline heat her face and quicken her sweat. In all her trips to the Glades, she'd never been this close to a gator in the wild. The ridges of its dark armor glinted, and its yellow eye shone bright as a child's marble. She could swear it saw her. The creature cocked its head and made a noise in its throat like a muffled human shout. Carey didn't move. She waited, slowing her breath, considering the possible danger. As long as this gator was alone, as long as she didn't frighten it, it wouldn't bite. She could, if she relaxed, just enjoy the encounter.

The alligator seemed to agree, flexing its knees to lower itself down on the same pine needles, just a yard or so from Carey. It rested its head on the ground and blinked, the action complex and alien. Carey remembered learning in grade school that alligators have more than one eyelid. She blinked her own eyes to assure herself of her humanity.

Carey watched, patient and still, as the young reptile blinked, breathed, adjusted its body, raised its head to heed some distant sign, and eventually, slowly, gave itself over to sleep. In that time, Carey forgot the flood, her baby, and the long list of decisions and traumas that troubled her. She knew only the soft movements of this delicate scaled child and the sureness that it would grow into a large and powerful adult.

Finally, with reluctance, she noticed that her right arm had gone numb beneath her. Her hip throbbed under the weight of her belly. She needed pillows, a few of them, to approach anything like comfort these days. In one last effort to preserve the peace of the scene, Carey rolled gently onto her back, away from the reptile. She gazed momentarily at the pine tree above her as blood rushed back to her arm. There, in the tangled branches above, she discovered the night wasn't finished with her yet.

On a branch above and to her left, an enormous great horned owl sat watching her with luminous golden orbs. Carey sucked a breath of surprise, and the bird raised her wings in alarm, poised for launch. Her body was mottled brown, but her wings were pale underneath, glowing faintly in the growing dark. A moment later she set them down again, ruffling them into place. She had decided, it seemed, that Carey posed no threat.

Carey followed some ancient instinct and spoke to the bird quietly. "Hello," she said softly. "How are you tonight?"

The owl blinked and swiveled her head away as if bored by the question.

"I don't think I'm what you're after," said Carey, "and that guy seems too big for you."

Carey looked back toward the alligator. It was awake and raised up on its legs in alarm, whether from her voice or the owl, she wasn't sure.

"Spell's broken," said Carey to the gator with some apology. "I'm human."

In one thrashing movement, the gator spun and splashed into the water. The owl raised her wings again, uncertain.

"Some folks just can't relax," said Carey, and shrugged.

The owl laughed. It wasn't a sound of alarm or protest—it was laughter. Simple, shrill, piercing laughter that ricocheted through the trees. Carey, unable to contain herself, cackled with the thrill of it. In response, the bird broke out again in deafening joy. And so, Carey Marilla, nearly nine months pregnant, found herself lying on a cypress island, in the middle of a flooded swamp, laughing hysterically with an owl, at the expense of an alligator.

The laughing jag went on until Carey's back began to spasm and she was forced to sit up. The owl quieted, lifted on her pale wings, and disappeared silently between the cypress trees. Carey rubbed her back and spoke to herself.

"Unreal." Except, of course, it was beautifully real. Carey would remember and dream about that night for years to come.

<hr />

The next morning, Carey found Jim shifting supplies in the shed. She'd lost her breath in reaching him, so she sat on a cooler. Jim continued to work as she laid out the possibility of moving up north for the baby's birth. Her reasons, she felt, were strong: They'd been at the houseboat for nearly a month, it was now September, the baby was due in less than four weeks, and Carey's internal teacher clock insisted that if it wasn't time for back to school, it was at least time for a change. Probably, she admitted to herself, there was also a nesting instinct at work. Never mind the possible need for medical intervention if anything went amiss. Jim, to her surprise, expressed no upset or hurt.

"Thing is, if you'll pardon me sayin' it, I'd feel better if you had a proper doc around. I don't know nothing about, well, 'bout …" He made a circular gesture with his hand in the direction of Carey's belly.

"Birth?" Carey asked with a grin.

"Well, sure. I've only ever seen mine, and I don't remember it, do I?"

Carey chuckled. "Okay then, when do you think we could be ready to load up and head out?"

Jim frowned. "Only trouble is the weather. It's s'posed to storm for the next while. That's why I'm moving these supplies down to the boat. We might be holed up for a bit. Big depression moving through tonight. You know how it is."

"Right." Carey examined the skies. They were calm and blue. No hint of the lashings to come, but she'd lived in Florida long enough to recognize a calm for what it might portend. "Let's plan on heading out once this passes."

"Aye, aye," said Jim.

Carey waddled back to the houseboat to deliver the news to Etta and Yessica.

"But we just got here," Yessi protested.

Etta stood washing dishes in the tiny sink while Carey sat to lift her swollen ankles. Yessi chopped collards for the night's meal.

"Not really," said Carey. "It's been almost a month. And this baby's coming. I'll need a hospital, or at least a doctor or a midwife or something."

"But hospitals are death traps," said Yessica, with surprising authority.

"What?"

"I mean, I heard, you know, that they make you have all this medicine you don't need, and they're full of germs and stuff. It's just what I heard."

"Some of that's true," said Carey, "but hospitals aren't all bad. I'm pretty sure none of us would be here if it weren't for modern medicine."

"I sure as hell wouldn't," said Etta.

"I was born in a hospital, and I'm fine," said Carey.

"Debatable," said Etta.

"Hey!"

Yessi sighed. "I dunno where I was born."

"Well, more likely than not, it was in a hospital," said Carey. "Anyway, I'm late to this decision, but I've made it. We need to go north. Tampa seems like a decent enough first stop, and we know we can get there."

Yessica bit down and nodded. "Yeah, I get it. So we gotta pack up again, I guess?"

"Yes, but Jim says we'll have to wait a few days for the weather. So at least we'll have some time to gather things."

"This storm is s'posed to be a real doozy," said Etta. "I wonder how that'll feel out here."

Packing was a lot less of an ordeal this time around. The number of worldly possessions they owned had dwindled with each subsequent move. Carey found she could fit everything of personal importance in a suitcase and a bin. Etta needed only a suitcase. Yessica, one large duffel bag. The other household items—dishes and tools, towels and pillows—would stay at the houseboat for now. Jim offered to bring them up later if they were needed.

Rain arrived on schedule the following day, shaking her mane in new fury at her latest pursuer, Wind. True to his reputation, Wind was a passionate and unpredictable lover. Unable to catch Rain in his arms, he chose instead to batter the trees, scatter the waters, and send sprawling anything unanchored. Rain was wise to avoid him, but she wouldn't manage it for long. Eventually, she turned to face him, and together they danced their thunderous love across the swamps.

Florida, nearly drowned and dreaming of dry sand, let the drama play out without protest. She couldn't manage much fight anymore. Rain would always win. Wind was just an accomplice.

The little houseboat rocked and creaked in the storm. Each member of the household occupied themselves with some small amusement: Etta read. Jim cleaned and oiled his fishing reels. Carey taught Yessica a few more chords on the guitar.

On the second day of the storm, Jim surprised them with a thousand-piece jigsaw puzzle he'd stashed somewhere on board. The delight this produced was something like Christmas morning.

"I can't promise all the pieces are there," said Jim.

"Perfection's overrated," said Etta, chuckling. "Let's see what shape she's in."

Carey spent a couple hours on the puzzle that morning, but found herself restless and anxious by midday. She turned her attention to the houseboat itself, cleaning and organizing things for Jim, planning to leave it all shipshape and shiny by the time they left.

When a subtle blue dawn revealed the third day of torrential downpour, Carey began to doubt their plans. Maybe they should try and head north now and brave the storm. If they needed to bail, they could probably pull under the cover of trees along the way. It wouldn't be difficult to cover most of their belongings with tarps.

It wasn't like she'd never been out in a boat in bad weather before. Though, she hadn't been so pregnant then. She wondered how it would feel to swim in her condition. Probably blissful to have all this weight lifted and buoyant. But there were the others to think about. Unless she went alone. Course, that was absurd. If anything happened to the boat, it could all turn disastrous.

Carey's mind ached from the back and forth of it all. She bounced her knees and drummed her fingers. There must be something she could do, something to hasten the next phase of whatever this was. Something more productive than another day of canned soup, quiet company, and puzzling.

She beamed her frustration at the puzzle's half-constructed image of a sailboat race. Three boats, one with a bright red hull, sailed merrily forward under a faded blue sky. Damn things had the movement she needed. And the weather.

That night, while Wind stretched for another round and Rain shuddered from exhaustion, Carey slept uneasily. In her dreams, she walked a wooden dock. Deep water moved beneath and around her as warm air caressed her middle. No, it wasn't air. It was Mario, his arms around her waist with surprising ease. She leaned against him, comfortable, hopeful, and he squeezed her again, this time hard enough that she pulled at his arms to free herself. Don't hurt the baby, she thought, but she wasn't pregnant. She wasn't pregnant at all. Without Mario's arms, a second squeeze, and heat filled her body. This is how Carey woke in the early hours and realized she was having contractions.

CHAPTER 17

Carey didn't wake anyone just yet. She still had over three weeks until her due date, so probably, she told herself, this was just a false alarm. Etta had said to expect a few false starts, as she'd remembered having them. Carey adjusted her body so that the baby would move and maybe her muscles would relax. Probably the baby had just triggered some discomfort, and it would all go away.

When the next contraction came, warm and firm, a tightening of her middle, she breathed slowly. She sat up and drank water. She climbed carefully down from the loft and relieved herself in the bathroom. She climbed back up. As she lay back in bed, another contraction spread slow and then tight around her lower back. It had been seven, maybe ten minutes since the last. She relaxed. She relaxed. She breathed. There was still plenty of time. Plus, the sensation was barely there.

But she couldn't fall back asleep. She rested the muscles in her face and made valiant efforts to calm her racing thoughts, but when the next tightening came, clear and firm, Carey sat up. "Mom!" she shouted.

Yessica rolled over and lifted herself from sleep.

"Ma!" Carey shouted again across the houseboat.

"What?" came a coarse voice in the darkness.

"I'm having contractions."

"Oh, shit."

They were up. Jim lit two oil lamps and put on some coffee. Yessica washed her face and tried to enter the day. Carey sat in a chair with her phone on the table, trying not to count minutes between contractions. Etta made instant oatmeal and watched her daughter carefully.

"So, what you wanna do?" asked Etta finally, when Carey had been quiet for an hour. It was not yet dawn.

"I don't know. Can we go?"

"I don't think so," said Etta. The storm still rattled and lashed the little houseboat.

"Now what?" said Carey.

"I don't know. We could call for help."

"You mean the police?" asked Carey.

"Or a helicopter or something."

"Where are they gonna land a helicopter?"

"I don't know. Maybe they'll lift you out or something."

"In the middle of the storm, while I'm having contractions?"

"Okay, not in the storm. Maybe they'll drop somebody down to help."

Carey shook her head. "I don't want the police. How long do you think I have? Maybe the storm'll quit before I'm ready, and we can go."

"That's probably our best bet," said Etta, "but we've got no idea about timing. You took more than thirty hours to be born, but your gramma said I was quick."

"So, somewhere between thirty hours and quick," said Carey.

"Or longer."

"That clears it up."

"Listen, maybe we should just plan on having the baby here," said Etta.

"No."

"Honey, you might not get a choice."

"I'm not having the baby here."

"Okay …"

Jim and Yessica busied themselves in the corners of the tiny space.

"I'm having the baby where there's a doctor or a hospital. Someplace sane."

Etta nodded.

"I can't do this here. I won't do this here. What if something goes wrong?"

"It's going to be okay," said Etta. She squeezed her daughter's hand.

"You don't know that," Carey said, and discovered she was crying. Hormones and exhaustion and fear had cracked the floodgates, but now she consciously opened them. Her baby was coming, they were trapped in a swamp, the weather was relentless, and with soul-shaking terror, she saw fully, for the first time, the real possibility that delivery might kill her or the baby or both. People died. All the time. Miguel had died. That sweet, innocent kid had died. There were no assurances, no guarantees, and there never would be again. She wept and shook, and Etta didn't stop her. No one did.

It was a long time before she calmed again. By then, her contractions were stronger, but not yet as disruptive as the thunder, the wind, the flashes of lightning that lit even the darkest nooks of the houseboat. Carey climbed back up into her bed to rest and breathe through her mounting panic and pain.

The others spent the morning waiting, listening to the storm, checking the weather on their phones, and theorizing escape routes. Yessica and Jim ventured outside to fuel and bail the boats just in case. Etta unpacked and repacked Carey's bag three times.

Four hours or so passed this way, and it was late morning. The storm let up a bit. The wind slowed. Carey moved down from her bed and began pacing, talking loudly about the risks of leaving.

"If the rain doesn't sink us, the wind could cause problems. There might be obstacles in the water, stuff that's stirred up. Visibility will be horrible and—"

"Walking speeds up labor," said Etta. "Why don't you sit down? The rain isn't supposed to stop anytime soon."

"You hear that, though?" asked Carey. "It's the quietest it's been in days. I'm thinking maybe we should make a run for it."

"I don't think so," said Etta, shaking her head. "I don't think that's wise."

"Why not?"

"For all the reasons you just said, but mostly cause it looks like you're in real labor. Things could speed up. Having this baby in a dry room beats having it in a wet boat."

Etta put a kettle on while Jim headed back out to bail the boats again. Just in case.

"This could still be a false start," said Carey. "Could be those Braxton Hicks or something."

"Could be," said Etta, "but from what I can tell, you've been at it pretty steady."

"I guess so, but I'm not due yet."

"Well, you were three weeks early."

"You never told me that. Why the fuck did you never tell me that?"

Etta shook her head. "I forgot."

"Do I even want to know if there were complications and stuff?"

"Probably not. I mean, I don't remember because of all the drugs."

"Great. None of that here."

"Well, no, but we've got whiskey."

"Mom."

"What?"

"I'm not drinking whiskey to give birth."

"Okay, suit yourself. I'll drink for both of us."

"Ma."

"What?"

"Maybe I won't be able to deal with it."

"You will."

"How do you know?"

"That's what motherhood is."

This conversation, or something like it, was repeated two or three more times as Carey's contractions grew in strength. It was two in the afternoon when Jim came in, sopping, and with news, just as Carey bowed her head for her longest and most intense contraction yet.

"We got a problem," he said.

"No shit," said Etta.

"No, we got a bigger problem. The shed's leaking."

"We can't really deal with that now," said Etta, gesturing to Carey.

But Jim shook his head. "I hate to say it, but if we don't deal with it, we're gonna lose a lot. A lotta that stuff ain't waterproofed."

"Shit. What do we do about it?"

"I think we better tarp the roof, but it ain't a one-person job."

"I'll go," said Yessica, pulling on her boots.

"No, you stay," said Carey, standing up. "I'll go."

Everyone in the houseboat froze as if an upright alligator had walked right through the door dressed in a three-piece suit.

"I'm kidding, for Christ's sake," said Carey, chuckling. It felt better than crying. "Ma, I think you better boil some water or something."

"That's not a thing," said Etta.

"No, it's a thing," said Carey, scrolling through her phone. "But not cause of the water, we just hafta sterilize stuff, I think. Where's the first aid kit?"

"You're serious," said Etta. "We're doing this?"

"Oh my God, I don't know." Carey raised her voice. "You said this was real labor. I'm just trying to think, but I can't think. And somebody else should probably be reading this. It's gonna freak me out."

"Right. I'll get some water going first, then I'll read it. You stop and relax. Save your energy." Etta stood and moved toward the stove, all business.

"We still might have to run for it," said Carey. "Stuff could go wrong at any time. Oh God, according to this site, there's gonna be a huge mess."

"Gross," said Yessi.

"You have no idea," said Etta to Yessi, but then she turned back to Carey. "Stop reading that. I mean it."

"Am I gonna see the birth?" asked Yessi, her mouth gaping. "Like, the whole thing?"

"Depends how long it takes you to secure that shed," said Etta.

Carey nodded. Yessi suited up and left with Jim. Another contraction spread, hot and breathtaking, around Carey's middle. According to the site she was scanning, she was probably close to entering active labor now. Her contractions were much stronger and closer, and it was now difficult to speak or think through them. Carey handed her phone to Etta.

The home birth websites she'd been exploring for the past couple hours all said more or less the same thing: Prepare for a mess with clean towels and sheets. Be ready for more than a sweet pink baby. There would be a cord, a placenta, blood, fluid, and probably poop. Be ready with sterile gloves, gauze, string, and scissors for the cord.

There was plenty about what could go wrong, and all the sites said that any emergency birth should be followed by a trip to the hospital, so that mom and baby could be checked out. Carey bitterly scrolled through the warnings. At least she had a small stockpile of antibiotics that the doc at the shelter had provided.

For the next hour or so, Etta prepared the birth space according to Carey's directions, as much as Carey could give between contractions. Pillows and blankets on the floor for padding, a plastic tarp for mess, clean sheets on top of it all for some semblance of normalcy. The sheets Etta chose were printed in a light pink floral pattern that Carey hated. They'd be fine to toss away. A pile of clean towels sat nearby. The sheets and towels probably weren't sterile, but they were clean. A few washcloths and hand towels were sterilized in the soup pot. In the first aid kit, they found latex gloves, rubbing alcohol, sturdy gauze, and a sterilized scalpel blade. Carey's mood shifted from despair to determination, but Etta remained wary. There was no telling how long her daughter's forced optimism might last.

Outside, Rain wore out her dancing shoes. She sat heavily on a dark bench of cloud to rub her heels and bitch about it. Wind, perhaps sensing his chance to make a different kind of move, sat down beside her and listened. Wise man, that Wind. A woman in pain is not a woman to impress.

The quiet that resulted from their pause sent Carey into a new panic. "Okay, maybe we should call for an airlift after all." She panted between contractions. She was sitting on a chair now, leaning forward on the table when contractions began, unable to speak through them and requiring deep mental work to recover. Burning discomfort in her back was partially alleviated by this position. Partially.

"If you want me to call, I'll call," said Etta.

"I don't know," said Carey. "Mom, I don't know." A contraction spread again, and this one wrenched her back muscles, her front, and her pelvis enough to make her moan. Etta moved behind her and pressed her thumbs into the small of Carey's back.

"Oh God," Carey said when it passed. She was pouring sweat. "I'm gonna puke."

Etta lunged for a garbage bag and passed it to Carey. Another contraction arrived a few minutes later, and Carey groaned. Etta pressed again on the small of her back. As the contraction subsided, Carey vomited into the bag.

"Good girl," said Etta, wiping Carey's chin. "Good girl."

"Is there something wrong?" Carey shivered and convulsed as her body settled.

"Nothing's wrong," said Etta. "Puking is normal. Shaking is normal."

"What about terror?" asked Carey.

"Completely normal."

"Jesus Christ."

"Tell me about it. Imagine Mary, eh? She did the whole thing without getting laid."

"Mom."

"What?"

"You can pray if you want."

"Yes, ma'am."

Etta prayed. Carey labored. Out at the shed, Jim and Yessica struggled to strap down the tarp. Rain and Wind launched a new argument, and the tarp escaped its binds once more, lashing the sky and snapping like gunfire. Yessica climbed up and caught hold of her corner, but the plastic billowed, sail-like, and pulled her across the corrugated roof of the shed. Her shin sliced on an edge. Blood ran quick and red. Jim grabbed her, yelling, and pulled her back. He was soaked to the bone, holding the girl with one arm and the tarp with the other. They were at the top of a ladder that had no business in that kind of weather, and he knew it. Yessica climbed down around him, grabbed the cord they needed and passed it up to him. She squatted and held her leg. Her blood mixed with the rain and pooled at her feet. Her hair hung limp and drenched around her face. She didn't cry, but when she sucked air and rain between her teeth, she spat. Jim tied the tarp and tied it again. The storm raged wicked. Jim shook his head. The weather couldn't win, it had taken enough already. This time, the abuse felt personal. He had to bandage that girl, and see to the others, and dammit, he needed to get offa that ladder without breaking his fool neck.

When he finally got the tarp to behave, Jim climbed down, shaky and resolute. They'd barely survived securing the shed, there was no way they'd survive a trip in the boats.

He brought Yessica into the shed and inspected her gash, while rain resumed pounding the newly covered roof. Her cut was deep, but clean. He swabbed it in antiseptic ointment while she chewed on her lip, then he closed the wound carefully with plastic butterfly bandages and covered the whole thing with a jumbo Band-Aid. They'd need to keep a close eye on it and make sure it didn't get infected, which he explained to the girl. At least the roof hadn't rusted—not yet anyway—so he didn't think she'd be in that sort of trouble. He hoped not.

By the time they returned to the houseboat, wounded and exhausted, Carey was only partially aware of their arrival. Etta instructed Yessica on how and where to press on Carey's back.

"Baby's nearly here?" asked Jim, pacing by the door.

"Don't know," said Etta.

"Is he positioned right?"

"No clue."

"What are we gonna do?"

"We're gonna have a baby," said Etta.

"Okay," said Jim, "guess I'll make myself scarce."

"Bullshit," said Etta. "You'll help. Take out this vomit for starters, and then get back in here and scrub up."

Jim looked as if he'd been asked to wrestle a panther, but he did as he was told. Etta discreetly ate a sandwich and made two more for Yessi and Jim.

Carey moaned and swayed and shook. She descended into herself under the influence of a tremendously prolonged and painful contraction. She began to scream and curse.

"I can't do this," she said as a wave of pain subsided, choking on the words. "This is fucking wrong." She shivered and convulsed again in the aftermath.

"You're doing great," said Etta. "You're fucking amazing."

"I can't do this," said Carey.

"Yes, you can," said Etta. "Breathe."

And so it went, for an hour, and another, and another. Exhausted, Carey finally crawled to the ground. Jim helped her down. Etta threw a clean sheet over Carey's bottom half and pulled off her pants and underwear.

"I think things might get graphic now," said Etta.

Yessica, unable to hide her wonder, stood slack-jawed to the side of the action.

It was some time in the next hour that Carey left the room. She was transported to a place of throbbing red and black, with a single slash of teal light in the center. She focused on that light, and named it her pain, and spoke to it silently as it grew and called to her with mesmerizing force. "I will have this baby," she said inside. "You cannot stop me. I will have this baby." The light sharpened to a small glistening point and then burst forward into a nebula of impossible dimension. Carey screamed as a pressure filled her body that threatened to suffocate her and tear her apart.

"The baby's nearly here," called Etta. "Gloves on, everybody." She was positioned beneath Carey now, holding her feet down. Carey arrived back in the room long enough to recognize her reality.

"Get it out!" screamed Carey. "Get it out!"

"You gotta do that, honey," said Etta. "You gotta push her out."

Carey shook her head. "No, no no no."

"Yes," said Etta. "Look at me! Look at me!"

Carey looked at her mom.

"You're gonna summon everything you got, and you're gonna start pushing when the next contraction hits."

"I don't know how to push," said Carey, still shaking her head.

"Like you gotta shit out a watermelon," said Etta.

"Ma, I can't."

"You can. I'm serious," Etta said. "Bear down."

Carey nodded. "Bear down."

"You want whiskey now?"

"Yes."

"Good girl."

Etta nodded, and Jim poured a shot of whiskey down Carey's throat. The next contraction began, and Carey's water broke, fluid gushing from between her legs.

"About time," said Etta as she layered fresh towels.

Etta showed Jim and Yessica how to lift, hold, and apply gentle counter pressure on Carey's legs.

Carey didn't leave the room again. The act of pushing brought her to ground. She knew it was night. She knew it was no longer raining. She heard the quiet around her. She knew the three people in the room, their bodies close to her body, her body transformed, transforming, transitioning. She was aware of the being, small but immense, struggling to emerge from her body into this strange world, this small room floating on water beneath cypress trees, and she knew pressure, inside and everywhere, the incredible pressure to survive. She pushed, she breathed, she focused on the work. There was no choice now.

The baby crowned and Carey roared.

Etta hollered and howled. "Here she comes! Here she comes! You can do this, baby. You're almost there. Bring her home!"

A contraction came and Carey pushed. The baby did not come. A contraction came and Carey pushed and screamed and cried. The baby did not come. Carey could no longer feel any pain. She could no longer feel anything but desperate and total exhaustion.

"Mama," she whispered. "Mama, help me."

Etta's face streamed with tears. "I want that grandbaby," she pleaded. "PUSH."

Carey bore down. She roared the sounds of every grief, every question, every fear she'd ever known. She summoned every strength, every love, every gift she'd given or received. She gave herself entirely. Every muscle of her body and soul raged with the bright fury of birth.

Something tore, and the baby's head burst free, and Carey felt the baby turn and twist, sliding out in one long and fluid motion.

Etta, beaming with joy, lifted the baby so Carey could see her. The infant kicked and grimaced, a mess of red and white and purple and grey, with a long, mottled rope dangling from her body.

She didn't cry.

Carey, panting, reached for the baby. Etta gently placed her on Carey's stomach.

The baby didn't cry. She was ashen now, a pale, light purple, still kicking and grimacing.

Carey studied her, lifted her, pulled her closer, slippery and wet as she was. Carey's instincts, blown open by her battle, keened in alarm. "Something's wrong," she said. "She's not right."

"No, she's fine," said Etta.

"Rub her down," said Jim. "Rub her down like they do with calves."

Carey sat up, alert with terror. She remembered something she'd read about suctioning the baby's nose. She placed her mouth on the baby's nose, sucked gently, and spit. Another contraction spread through her, but she worked through it. She grabbed a towel and gently but firmly wiped the baby's face, torso, and arms. She carefully, trembling, flipped the newborn over and rubbed her back. Pink and red flooded the baby's skin. The infant gurgled, gasped, and screamed.

Carey turned her back over and wrapped her snugly in the towel. The baby screamed in rasping, nasal pulses of rage. For the first time in hours, days, months, it seemed, Carey felt a rush of relief and joy.

Another contraction spread through her, and she leaned back.

"Ma."

"Yup."

"We've gotta clamp her cord," Carey said. "Yessi, pull it up on your phone."

Yessica, flushed and sobbing, pulled out her phone.

"You've gotta take off your gloves, honey," said Carey.

"Right, right. Yes, Miss. That was …" Yessica fumbled and dropped her phone.

"It was," said Carey. "Look up cutting the umbilical cord at home."

The next contraction came, and more fluid, more tissue, slipped from Carey's body.

"How are you?" asked Etta nervously. "That's a lot of blood."

"I don't know," said Carey. "I feel okay. Adrenaline, I guess."

The baby wailed a pitch higher, and Carey laughed. She spoke to her daughter for the first time. "You're okay, little one," she said. "You're alright. We're here."

Yessica read complex directions aloud as Carey marveled at the tiny dark pink ears of her baby. Jim used gauze to tightly bind and clamp off the umbilical cord near the baby, and then again a few inches away. Etta used the scalpel and severed the cord between the two clamps.

As they finished, Carey delivered her placenta. It slipped down into a baking dish Etta had strategically placed to catch the fluids and blood still arriving.

"Holy God howdy," said Jim. "That's a sight right there."

"After everything we just witnessed, you're most impressed by a placenta?" Etta teased. "Men are a mystery."

"But just look at that thing!" said Jim.

"Honey, I think I gotta massage your middle now," said Etta, studying Yessi's phone and then turning back to Carey, "and maybe you should try and feed her soon."

"Massage my middle?"

"It's a uterus thing," said Etta, shaking her head. "I remember hating this part."

"Okay," said Carey.

She groaned and winced as Etta firmly compressed and massaged her tender abdomen.

"Sorry, hon," said Etta. "We gotta make sure it all pulls back together in there."

Carey lay back again and studied her wailing daughter. She wiped the infant down again and rewrapped her. Breastfeeding wasn't something she'd given much thought to. Her boobs were huge and painful, but she hadn't taken any classes or read any online manuals on feeding. She didn't know a damn thing.

"Ma, I don't know how to feed her," Carey confessed.

"I'll look that up too," said Yessica.

"Just shove your nipple in her face," said Etta. "When she opens her mouth, stuff it down in there."

Carey frowned.

"That's all I got," said Etta. "Worth a try."

Carey studied the diagram on Yessica's phone and then, still trembling from her labor, made her first efforts at feeding.

The baby suckled and grunted, but the nipple slipped around and outside her mouth. Carey tried again and again. The baby shook her head, suckled more desperately, and then settled on Carey's breast and quieted.

"Is anything coming out?" asked Carey. "How do I know?"

"Says here it can take a while for milk to come," said Yessica. She read aloud, "'The infant must spend significant time on the mother's breast to stimulate milk production.'"

"Listen to that," said Etta. "We've got a professional here."

Yessica flushed. "Miss," she said quietly. "What's her name?"

All activity paused, except the baby's suckling. Carey studied her daughter. The infant's eyes closed. Her black hair lay in wet swirls and streaks on her head. "Her name's Jet," said Carey. "Jet Michelle Marilla."

CHAPTER 18

Rain and Wind didn't notice the birth of Jet Michelle Marilla. They were wrapped up, as usual, in their own private drama. Eventually, following their ancient pattern of love and heartbreak, they wore themselves out fully. An hour or so after Jet's arrival, they retired to their separate chambers in the East and South. Wind dared a wistful look back as Rain swept away, spent and oblivious, her skirts dragging through the muck they'd made.

Carey's first night as a mother was quiet, though it took a while to get to sleep. Their preparations for bed were long and complicated. She washed slowly, carefully. With Yessica's help, she prepared a dressing of ice and Etta's numbing hemorrhoid ointment for her battered crotch. Carey didn't have much in the way of heavy flow pads, but given the amount of blood still leaving her body, she opted for a homemade diaper fashioned from a towel and safety pins.

Jim and Yessica pulled a mattress and pillows down off the loft for ease of access. They cleared a space on the narrow floor by stacking the dining chairs. When Carey finally lay back in bed, she found she was starving and thirsty. Yessica and Jim prepared her a large meal of canned hearty beef stew and fruit salad. Carey happily cleaned her bowl and asked for seconds.

Etta bathed Jet in a plastic tub of warm water and diapered her in soft, clean, T-shirt material carefully layered and pinned together. She swaddled her granddaughter in a white towel. To say that Etta relished the honor would be, perhaps, too mild. Etta sang and cooed and whistled cheerfully the entire time. It had been the fullest, most terrifying day of her life since the birth of her own child, and this time, this marvelous time, her relief and joy were multiplied as they echoed and rebounded through her daughter and granddaughter's beings. Etta's spirit burst with pride and sang out for witness, for honor, for glory in her beautiful daughter, her spectacular grandbaby, her grandbaby's wonderful mama, her wonderful daughter's perfect daughter. All this life and joy tethered to Etta's own soul by everything good and right.

Jet slept, but when she woke and wriggled and fussed again, Etta dutifully brought her back to Carey for feeding.

Carey, exhausted as she was, fretted about the feeding. "I still don't know if she's getting anything," she mumbled. "What if she's starving?"

"We'll watch her," said Etta, "but milk takes a while sometimes."

Carey laid her head back on her pillows. "What if she needs another diaper change after this? Do we have enough diapers?"

"We'll handle that," assured Etta. "We'll make diapers and launder the used ones. We'll make it work."

"Can I do a diaper change?" asked Yessica. "I haven't held her yet." There was a yearning in the girl's voice, bright and eager.

"Of course," said Carey. "You're her aunty. You get to change all the diapers you want."

"I'm Jet's aunty?" Yessi's lips parted and her eyebrows shot up.

"You bet you are."

The girl didn't answer, but her chin dimpled.

Etta rubbed Yessi's back and nodded.

"Now listen," said Etta, "we're all gonna get less sleep around here for a while, so I suggest we turn in. Tomorrow there'll be time for fighting over diaper changes and cuddle time. The important thing now is to make sure Carey heals up."

Nodding was an effort, so Carey blinked her approval. When Jet had fed on both sides and made no further effort to suckle, Carey passed her to Yessi and Etta, who diligently changed and re-swaddled her, delivering several gentle kisses along the way. Yessi brought the baby back to Carey, who was already asleep on her side. Yessi laid Jet next to her mother and carefully climbed over them both to claim her edge of the bed. Carey woke long enough to wrap a hand gently around her daughter's blanketed toes.

Over the next few days, the little misfit family found new purpose and rhythm. Carey grew to recognize her daughter's signs of hunger or discomfort. They all learned to swaddle, diaper, burp, bathe, and comfort Jet, who could offer little in return except for her tiny hands, her pink mouth, and occasional moments when her dark grey eyes opened in wonder.

On the third day, Carey felt her milk come in, heavy and aching. After that, she knew the odd relief that came each time Jet was able to latch and feed, but breastfeeding was not the miraculous joy that her pregnancy book had described. That night, her right breast developed a painful knot near her nipple. By the following morning, the knot had doubled in size, and a red blotch was visible on the surface of her breast. Carey quickly succumbed to a fever, complete with chills. She consulted the internet and took some antibiotics. It seemed like maybe she'd developed mastitis, an infection in a clogged milk duct. Medical sites claimed the baby was in no significant danger, but on the fourth day, Carey's other breast developed a similar painful lump, and she despaired.

The following afternoon, Carey found she could finally walk again, with only mild discomfort down below. Her usual maxi pads were now enough to control her flow. Her breasts, however, were in no better shape, though her fever had settled with medication. It hadn't rained for a few days, and Carey's mind turned toward the world they had forsaken. Jet had no birth certificate and no vaccines. No doctor or professional had checked on either of them, and though Carey felt, in her gut, that both she and Jet were mostly healthy, the prick of doubt was impossible to deny. Miguel had died because he lacked the medical help he needed, and because he'd exerted himself in ignorance. What if there was some invisible thing Jet needed that Carey didn't know? What if her own body, though it seemed to be healing in some ways, had been damaged by birth in ways she couldn't yet recognize? What if the infection in her breasts worsened, or spread to vital organs, or somehow transferred to Jet? And what would happen if they were—no, *when* they were—eventually discovered by authorities and asked about the baby? Would Jet be in danger or taken away if Carey couldn't prove immediately that she was her own flesh and blood? Carey slowly grew sick with her mounting doubts and worries. If Jet made a new sound, if she slept longer than thirty minutes or less than thirty minutes, if she didn't seem interested in feeding when she fussed, at any of these moments and dozens like them, Carey's anxiety spiked. Etta's assurances that babies were unpredictable and naturally fussy held less and less sway.

During a particularly vicious spiral, Carey's phone buzzed. It hadn't done so in weeks. She fished it out of her raincoat and found a text from Mario.

> How r u? Ur due date is
> approaching. Can we be in touch?

Carey winced. Guilt tromped into her mind like a local bully, scattering the worries of a moment before like a flock of startled birds. She should've called Mario when Jet was born. She should've sent him pictures. She'd been distracted, to say the least, but she'd thought of him. Of course she had. She'd just been so afraid. So bound up in her own body and mind. He could have been there. He should have been there. It was possible he'd never forgive her.

She texted him back.

> Our daughter, Jet Michelle Marilla, was born at 8:07pm on September 5. Healthy & beautiful. We r both ok. I'm so sorry I didn't tell u. She was early. I've been healing and worried and working thru it. Have an infection. Little sleep.

She attached a picture of the baby.

The reply was slow, but it came:

Thank u. She is perfect.

> Do u want to see her? Where r u?

Tampa. Was hoping to find u before she came.

Carey didn't respond. Unsure if he was angry or hurt or both. He texted a few moments later.

I'm sorry
I'm sorry I wasn't there

> I'm sorry too

Where r u? U are sick?

> We r in the swamp at Jim's place. But there's a pop-up village southeast of Tampa. I think we're gonna head that way, then Tampa. They have a doc.

New Stiltsville?

Dunno the name

Been on the news. First new
settlement of South FL refugees.

Maybe. Yeah.
Just a bunch of houses on stilts.

You have one?

N

But r u ok? Infections can be bad.

Mostly. I know. Y

Can I come there?

Now?

Y please. I want to see u both.

Jet fussed and squirmed in Carey's lap. It would be time to feed her again soon. The thought of seeing Mario was frightening and comforting at the same time. Carey would need more practice in holding such contradictory feelings together, but for the first time she could remember, she welcomed that complexity. She pulled her mind back to her baby. Jet deserved more than the rumor of a father.

We r in the middle of nowhere.
Only accessible by boat. Not easy

Are E, J, & Y with u?

Y

Ok, can u make it to Tampa soon?
Lots of docs here. I have a place u

all can crash. Will be crowded,
but we can make it work.

Y. We can do that, I think.

Can't wait. Thank u. Or I can
come meet u. Lmk

Will text when we make plans

Carey exhaled and looked up from her phone. Etta and Yessica
were watching her intently.

"What?" asked Carey.

"Who was that?" asked Etta.

Carey took a deep breath and nodded. "It was Mario."

Etta clapped her hands once, and Yessica stifled a cry of joy.

"He's in Tampa," continued Carey, "and wants to meet Jet. He
invited us to visit."

"Oh my God, Miss, that's awesome!" squealed Yessi.

"It's good," said Carey, partly to convince herself. "It's good." It
was just that the cloud of worries, momentarily dispelled by Mario's
texts, had already begun to regather. It swarmed and billowed in her
mind, a murmuration of starving birds.

On the morning of the sixth day after Jet's birthday, Carey broke
down when Jet wouldn't eat. The baby screamed. Carey's breasts
ached. They were splotched with red now, and hot to the touch.
Tears blurred her vision. As she moved to lift the baby to her shoulder, she knocked her water glass to the ground. Etta swooped in.

"What's wrong? What's wrong with her?" Carey begged.

"There's nothing wrong, honey. She just isn't hungry."

"She should be," said Carey, snuffling and bouncing Jet on her
shoulder nervously. "She usually eats now."

"Babies are unpredict—"

"But what if there's something wrong? She's never been checked out."

"She's fine. Look at her," said Etta.

"But if something happens to her ..." Carey couldn't finish the thought. She choked on a new wave of love and terror.

Etta reached to stroke her daughter's hair. Carey pulled away defensively.

"Okay, honey," said Etta. "What do you need? How can I convince you she's alright?"

"I don't know," mumbled Carey, but she did. "I think we should take her to see a doctor. Get her checked out. Get her registered and vaccinated and all that stuff. And I think, I think, I might need better medication. I don't feel right. Maybe it's just hormones, I don't know."

Etta nodded. "Right. We can do that. I'll go see about getting the boats ready."

"We don't need both boats ..."

"If you're going anywhere with that baby, we're all coming with you. That's not up for debate."

Carey's smile broke weakly through her exhaustion.

And so it was, on Jet's one-week birthday, the day dawned clear and calm. After breakfast, they loaded the boats with plans to visit the northern encampment first, to seek out information about how best to approach the Tampa metropolitan area. Carey planned to text Mario once they reached the village.

She climbed aboard their aluminum boat and sat up front. Once she was safely seated, Etta passed Jet over, freshly changed and bundled. It was difficult for Carey to hold her. Carey's breasts pressed, tender and swollen, against her life vest. Usually, she wouldn't feel the need for a flotation device, but given her new role and healing body, she'd buckled the vest on without suggestion. She tucked Jet tightly against her lap.

They headed north, motors roaring, first through winding rivers and shallows among the cypress trees, then out onto open water where there had not been open water the year before. Sawgrass still waved above the flats in vast patches, but many areas were more sunken, resulting in a stubbled, unfamiliar version of the Everglades. September breeze blew warm on Carey's face. Jet snuggled deeply in her blanket, her eyelashes fluttering briefly in her sleep against the rush of air.

It felt like an age since Carey had inhabited the world beyond their odd little post in the wilderness. Horizons spread green and strange around her. She hummed under the grind of the engines. They startled a great blue heron, and the bird took off in the loping, long way of its kind.

It was late morning when the swamp thickened, and the ground rose again to wooded hammocks and pine forests. Many large trees had fallen in the recent summer storms. It became difficult to navigate safely at speed, so their convoy slowed. Carey used the opportunity to remove her life vest and feed Jet. The baby latched easily this time, but the feeding was exceptionally painful for Carey. Each gentle tug at her breast resulted in a sensation like barbed needles raking through inflamed tissue. Carey bit down and focused on her breathing. She had endured birth; she could endure this.

As they passed another massive cypress half drowned on its side, Carey's confidence in their plan began to flag. They were hours away from home, and there was no sign of human habitation yet. If the weather turned, if an engine failed, if anything at all went wrong, they didn't have supplies enough to last more than a day. They'd brought extra fuel, but would it be enough?

A hot prickling crept up Carey's neck and shortened her breath. Jet was finished eating. Carey gripped her baby tightly and looked up to the wide, indifferent skies. She didn't believe in God—not in the Christian God anyway. She knew of no forces that could grant or deny her survival. Still, she felt in her deepest self that her will to live had been immeasurably strengthened by her daughter's birth. She had to survive this moment, this ride, this era, for Jet's sake. If ever their lives were threatened, as they were now, Carey knew she'd do everything she could, everything possible, to secure Jet's health and safety. Carey's own life mattered, and now, beyond her, Jet's life called like a song, a melody of deep connection and influence.

They rounded the fallen cypress and found, to everyone's surprise, the village on stilts. Dozens of small structures sprouted here and there, sturdy legs in the water, peaked aluminum roofs gleaming in the sun. From a few of these homes, thin pipes emitted smoke or vapor. From others, generators whined. Most had at least two solar panels strategically hung to maximize exposure. Boats of all shapes and sizes were lashed to the stilts or tied to buoys in the water nearby. Two people banged away on a new construction in the distance. Etta and Jim slowed the boats and approached quietly. A man hung laundry on a line outside his window. The line, equipped with a pulley system, stretched to a grove of cypress and oak on a nearby hammock. He called to them and waved. Carey recognized Diego, the bearded visitor they'd met back on their island.

They ran their boats up to Diego's house and tied off. A small floating platform at the base of the house provided a place to disembark. Carey and Etta tied Jet carefully to Carey's aching chest in a wide swath of cloth, and Carey slowly climbed the ladder up to the house's front door. Diego greeted them with wide arms and delight in Jet. For Carey, who had never known much in the way of extended family, it felt strangely like Diego was a long-lost uncle, or someone who'd been lovingly waiting for them all this time. The interior of his cottage was cluttered with fishing gear, cooking implements, and laundry, but it was otherwise clean and welcoming.

"You made it!" he boomed. "You had the baby! Look at that little angel! How was the trip? What can I get you? You need food? You need coffee? I've gotta run and get Jenn Kelly and Arnie, or they'll never forgive me. But let's feed you first."

Carey laughed. "You're so kind, Diego. I just need to use your bathroom, if that's alright, and probably change the baby."

"Course, of course," Diego gestured to an accordion door for Carey and turned his attentions to the rest of his guests.

When everyone was settled and fed and watered, Diego and Jim set out with promises to bring back Jenn Kelly, Arnie, and the village doctor, a woman by the name of Karina Gomez.

"Karina," Diego had said, "is a miracle worker." He went on to report that she made regular trips to Tampa for supplies and also served as the town pharmacist.

Carey stood at one of Diego's windows and watched the crooked and leggy town outside. Someone passed behind a window in one of the nearby homes. Another figure climbed down a ladder in the distance. A boat puttered between two cabins several yards to the west. Carey hadn't realized how much she'd missed the comfort of proximity to others, of safety in numbers. She turned back to say as much to Etta and Yessica, and found them both laughing at Diego's table.

Carey couldn't tell the source of their chuckling, but she saw, quite plainly and suddenly, that the past months had transformed both women. They were worse for wear in terms of hygiene and laundry. Their clothes were wrinkled and fraying. Their hair was long and wild, braided tightly to keep up and out of the way. But Yessica was older, taller, and more energetic than she'd been as a slinking student. She chatted happily with Etta. She'd been especially alert and attentive ever since Jet's arrival. Plus, Carey thought warmly, she'd seen the girl hold her own when she wanted something. Yessi showed few signs of the anxiety she'd carried before, though there was a heaviness, a gravity behind her eyes.

As for Etta, it looked like she'd aged backwards, despite the silver of her hair. She'd been active, especially since the baby arrived, forced to move and carry and climb. It showed. She didn't groan every time she sat down or stood up. She didn't tune out with her TV for hours every day. The sun and wind and weather had cleared the cobwebs from Etta's joints and spirit. She was more alive, present, and positive than Carey had seen her in years. She smiled near constantly at Jet. It was embarrassing, really, how delighted Etta was by Jet's every burble and fart.

Carey took out her phone and texted Mario:

> Hi. We're at the stilts village. Just got here. Gonna see doc here and then come to Tampa. Do u still have room?

The response came immediately:

> Which house?

> What?

> Which house r u in?

Carey's mind raced.

> Diego's house? Nice guy we met.

Wait, why?

Hold on a min

Carey must have expressed her surprise out loud because Etta questioned her. "What's goin' on over there?"

Carey smiled. "It's Mario."

Etta nodded again and slapped her hands on the table. "Can't wait for him to see that baby. Tampa's our next stop, huh? Though I gotta say, it's a shame to rush off. I was hoping to have a look around this place some more before we go. I like the feel of it."

"Me too," said Carey, looking out the window again. "I wonder what it costs to get a place out here."

"My guess is this isn't all that popular a choice," said Etta. "We'd still be roughin' it. But if any insurance money ever kicks in, it might be doable. Somewhere between our boat in the swamp and regular city life. Could be nice."

Outside Carey's window, in the hammock closest to Diego's house, two children climbed nimbly up a cypress tree to a low platform someone had built for them out over the water. They dangled their legs off the side and threw out a fishing line. One of them, the smaller, had long black hair.

Carey imagined Jet climbing the tree, catching fish, running through the hammock. Maybe Jet would like it here too.

The older child nudged the younger so she would scoot over. The little one punched the older kid in the shoulder in return, but she laughed, unfazed by the attack. Something about their exchange struck a chord.

Carey turned back to Etta and Yessica.

"Ma, can you take Jet for a minute? I need to talk to Yessi."

"Of course."

Carey unwrapped Jet and passed her to Etta, who cooed and shushed, even though Jet was still sound asleep, a sweet little sack of potatoes.

Carey gestured for Yessica to follow her outside onto Diego's porch. They leaned on the rails and watched the kids fishing.

"I've wanted to talk to you for a while now," said Carey.

Yessica nodded, silent. A warm breeze moved through the trees and across the water. In the distance, a boat motor buzzed.

Carey inhaled, then exhaled. "I'm sorry I haven't talked to you about Miguel."

"You were angry at me," said Yessica quietly.

Carey leaned back in shock. "No, no, that's not it. That's not it at all."

"It was my fault," said Yessica.

"No, it wasn't. Absolutely not," said Carey.

"But it was ..." Yessica's voice cracked.

"No," said Carey firmly, turning her whole body toward Yessica. "He was sick, very sick, and he fell. There was nothing anyone could do. That is not your fault."

"But I'm the one who made him leave the shelter," said the girl. "And I thought you were mad at me, and you probably want me to go back to my family now that you have a baby, and—"

"No," said Carey again. "No, no, no. I'm not mad at you at all, and you're not leaving us. We're your family now." Carey paused. "What I mean is, I want to be your family. Is that okay with you?"

Yessica nodded, then curled forward and placed her head on her arms on the rail. She made no sound, but her back shuddered with the grief she'd been holding.

Carey continued, "None of this was your fault, but I know how terrible guilt feels. I blame myself too. If I'd listened to you, if I'd understood how scared you were, you wouldn't have run away, and I'm just so sorry, Yessi. I'm so sorry it took me this long to be able to talk to you. You're important to me, to all of us, and I want you to know that. I'm here now, and I'm not leaving."

Carey set one hand on Yessica's shoulder and pressed gently.

Yessica pulled up again with staggering breath and turned to Carey.

"I can't believe Miguel's gone," she cried. "I still just ... nothing feels real. And why? You know? He was so nice, Miss."

"He was wonderful," said Carey, wiping her own tears away. "He died because he was sick and we all had terrible luck. There's no other reason."

"But that's not fair," said Yessica, her voice rising.

"It's not," said Carey. She wished she could offer Yessica some worldly wisdom on how to handle the cold indifference of the world, but no words came. She could only occupy this space with the girl. She could only hold her hand. Yessica gripped hers in return.

"What do we do if things get worse?" asked Yessica.

Carey looked out across the rising water, the village of stubborn homes, the trees, the children in the trees. She'd been asking herself that question, or avoiding it, for the better part of a year. Now, countless rains later, she was a mom. She had not one, but two beautiful daughters, and no more clarity than she'd had at the start. What she did have was experience. She had family. She had instincts and strength. She had new reasons to cultivate that strength.

"We make choices," she said. "We stay together and hold on."

Yessica squeezed Carey's hand and leaned on her shoulder. Carey encircled the girl with her arm as the day and its sounds flooded back. Jet woke and fussed. Etta cooed and sang. A seagull circled. Somewhere a hammer worked as a boat approached them, slung low in the bright water.

ACKNOWLEDGMENTS

Breakwater would not exist without the kindness, care, and generosity of every good person in my life.

I'll start with my beloved Michael, and our wonderful kids, Calvin and Wesley. There's nothing as important to me as your love. Sharing life, adventures, and stories with you is simply the best.

To my brother, Christopher, thank you for your understanding and constant inspiration.

Thanks to my mother who taught me to love stories and poetry, and whose motherly love is at the heart of this story. To my father who showed me Florida's natural wonders and taught me good ol' rock n'roll. Thank you to my broader family for cheering me on.

Wolves, you know how important you are, but let me say it out loud: Thank you Darian Lindle, Lola Lindle, Tiffany Trent, and Ysabeau Wilce for your sisterhood in the long years of crafting *Breakwater*. I'm an author because of you.

Thank you to Jennifer Adam and Kelly Jones for your constant professional support and friendship through the many highs and lows of my path to this point.

To my wonderful teacher friends and former students from Art School, your support and love matter to me tremendously. You have my heart.

Thank you to everyone who read early drafts and offered criticism, encouragement, and feedback. Meridian moms, you rock.

Erica Goldsmith and Kate Dunlop, you nurture my spirit, and I love you for it. Justin Krebs, your steady enthusiasm and fellowship are treasured.

Martha Reynolds, your care and guidance made this story, and my health, possible.

Thanks also to Mike Allen, C.G. Aubrey, Susan Bagrationoff, Monica Beletsky, Lindsey Buller, Francesca Forrest, Artemis Grey, Suzi Gruber, Feather Hilger, Joy Kim, Ellen Kushner, Bri Little, Tina Myers, Nia Pineiro-Hall, Delia Sherman, Mik Stahlke, Tegan Tigani, Ana Torres, Mary Wesolowicz, Terri Windling, and all my beloved Sirens sisters who have brightened my life immeasurably. Shout out to my Book Club.

Thanks also to the superb professional guidance of Lisa Abellera, Kyra Freestar, and Robin Maxwell.

Thanks to Kodie Buford for a rad logo and to Molly Pearce for her beautiful cover art and illustrations.

To friends and teachers from my childhood in South Florida, I hope you can feel the love here. To friends, colleagues, mentors, and kindred spirits from college and beyond, if you find this note, please know that I'm grateful for you too.

Last, but not least, to my darling Phoebe and to all who ever loved her with me, sparkles for you.

AUTHOR BIO

Vivian Wilderbridge lives in a bright blue house surrounded by trees in Seattle, Washington. She frequently walks the rainy beach nearby and searches for broken things and living creatures. She occasionally spots orcas from the shore, but more commonly visits with sea lions. Viv grew up in South Florida where she swam in warmer waters and climbed high in sun-drenched trees. These days, she writes novels, poetry, and songs, often at her dining room table or at a desk heavily cluttered with sea glass and seashells. She adores science fiction, fantasy, seafood, and old-fashioned mail.